Tattooed

Hearts

Book One of the Tattooed Duet

A Forever Inked Novel

Sabrina Wagner

Stay Connected!

**Want to be the first to learn book news, updates and more?
Sign up for my Newsletter.**

https://www.subscribepage.com/sabrinawagnernewsletter

**Want to know about my new releases and upcoming sales?
Stay connected on:**

Facebook~Instagram~Twitter~TikTok
Goodreads~BookBub~Amazon

**I'd love to hear from you.
Visit my website to connect with me.**

www.sabrinawagnerauthor.com

Books by Sabrina Wagner

Hearts Trilogy
Hearts on Fire
Shattered Hearts
Reviving my Heart

Wild Hearts Trilogy
Wild Hearts
Secrets of the Heart
Eternal Hearts

Forever Inked Novels
Tattooed Hearts: Tattooed Duet #1
Tattooed Souls: Tattooed Duet #2
Smoke and Mirrors
Regret and Redemption
Sin and Salvation

Vegas Love Series
What Happens in Vegas (Hot Vegas Nights)
Billionaire Bachelor in Vegas

Table of Contents

Prologue

*"Not everything is supposed to become
something beautiful and long-lasting.
Sometimes people come into your life to show
you what is right and what is wrong, to show
you who you can be, to teach you to love
yourself, to make you feel better for a little
while, or just to be someone to walk with at
night and spill your life to. Not everyone is
going to stay forever, and we still have to keep
on going and thank them for what they've
given us."*

~Emery Allen

Chapter 1
Zack

I zipped up the garment bag that contained my only suit. I used to own several suits in a variety of colors-- black, gray, dark brown. I left them behind with the life I turned my back on. Now I only needed one. It was designated for weddings and funerals.

I'd cancelled all my appointments for the next week. I wouldn't be gone longer than that. Much less if I had my way about it. When my mom called, I knew I had to go, if only to say good-bye. He deserved that much from me.

I picked up my suitcase and my garment bag and headed down the back stairs. Setting my bags by the door, I walked to the front of my shop. Forever Inked was my baby. I'd started this tattoo shop with determination and a dream.

"You all set to go?" Layla asked.

I ran my hand through my short, spiked hair. "Yeah. I shouldn't be gone too long. You sure you guys can handle everything? I feel bad ditching you."

Layla put her hands on her hips. "Zack, Chase and I have got this. Stop worrying. Go do what you need to do. We promise not to burn the place down."

I laughed. "I'm not worried about that. Thanks for coming in early."

"For you, anything." Layla wrapped me in a big hug, and I squeezed her back. "I love ya. Be safe."

"I will. I'll see you in a week." I made my way to the back door and out to the garage where my '69 Chevelle sat next to my Harley. It was my pride and joy. She had been a piece of junk when I bought her, but I'd had her completely rebuilt from top to bottom, painted cherry red with black racing stripes.

I popped the trunk and placed my bags inside. Once settled in the car, I turned up the radio and set out for the long drive from Utica, Michigan to Forest Hills, New York. I'd only been back a handful of times and I was dreading the ten-hour drive.

I drove straight across I-80, only stopping once to get gas, grab something to eat and take a piss. It was almost seven by the time I got to the hotel. I valeted my car and headed to the front desk. To say I looked out of place in this neighborhood was an understatement. The desk clerk gave me a disgusted look as he took in my tattoos and piercings. It didn't bother me one bit, I'd received worse from my father. "Can I help you?"

"I'm checking in. Reservation is under Kincaid," I said as I handed over my black Amex card.

The desk clerk stared at the card. "Of course, Mr. Kincaid. We have you in the Presidential Suite for the week. Is there anything we can get you to make your stay more comfortable?"

I took my card back. "No thanks. It's been a long day. All I need is a shower and room service."

I made my way to the gold elevators, muttering under my breath, "pretentious asshole." I was ready to put this day behind me, even though I knew tomorrow would be worse.

As I entered the suite, I took in my posh and luxurious surroundings. Every time I returned to Forest Hills I stayed in this same room for two reasons. One, it reminded me of home. The place I grew up and the privileged life I had. Two, it solidified I had made the right choice by leaving and never returning to it. Pretentious was the word that came to mind. Just like the thirty-something desk clerk who had given me a once-over, like I was a piece of trash, before he knew who I was. Kincaid. That name was sacred in this city.

My father was a business mogul. He was the CEO of the company that bore our name, Kincaid Industries. My great-grandfather had built the business from the bottom up. He came to America as a Scottish immigrant when he was just a boy. Determined not to sink into the gutters of New York, he hustled the streets. He was the kid who could slink about unseen and run errands for those who mattered. By the time he reached his twenties he'd found his niche as a bootlegger during Prohibition. It was lucrative, to say the least.

My great-grandfather, Alistair Kincaid, used that money to start Kincaid Industries. A company that preyed on weak businesses that were in dire straits. He provided the financial relief they desperately needed when the banks turned them down. When the lowly business owners couldn't pay their debt, Alistair swooped in and took over. He was ruthless and unforgiving.

Kincaid Industries was a conglomerate that owned many subsidiaries. It was a force to be reckoned with and a name that had become synonymous with power and wealth.

It was a story I knew well. I'd been educated on the source of our wealth, as a lesson in determination and hard work. I appreciated that part of the history lesson and took it to heart, but I never missed where our family started. Poor. We were no better than anyone else. We came from lowly beginnings, and the tactics used to gain our wealth were unscrupulous at best.

When my grandfather took over Kincaid Industries, he used a kinder touch. He exuded empathy. Gregor Kincaid was a good man. He was my hero.

My father, Malcolm Kincaid, was an exact replica of Alistair. I was much more like Gregor. Hence, the reason we didn't get along.

It was my destiny to someday take over for my father and become the CEO of Kincaid Industries. It was a future I never wanted, but I wanted to please my father, so I played the good son and went to Yale to major in business my first year of college. I hated it.

I couldn't stand the entitled attitude that ran rampant through the campus. Who was better than who and who knew who? Who had the most money? Old money was always superior to new money, and everyone knew which category you fell into.

Worse than that, I couldn't stand the box I felt I was put in. Going to prep school had felt like chains shackled to my ankles. College was more of the same. I didn't give two shits about business and the classes I was taking. I was more interested in art and music. I felt trapped.

I dropped out after my first year and joined the Marines. My father was pissed, but at least the Marines was a respectable option. It was the first time in my life I didn't feel suffocated. I got to see other parts of the world and lived with honorable men, most of who came from much humbler beginnings than myself. I learned about real-life and real people outside the bubble of privilege I was raised in. It was in the Marines I got my first tattoo.

I learned the art of tattooing from one of the guys in my unit. He was the master, and I was his apprentice. I spent all my free time watching and studying him, learning the tricks of the trade and I was fucking good at it. I loved it. I was finally doing something I liked, even if it was only for the other guys in my unit. After three years in the Marines and two tours in the Middle East, I returned home.

My father viewed my stint in the Marines as a folly. He figured if nothing else it would knock some sense into me and teach me discipline. He was right on both accounts, but his ideas of those things were very different than mine. Malcolm Kincaid expected me to return to Yale to finish my degree; to fulfill my destiny. I had other plans.

It was a source of contention between the two of us. My father pulled strings and used his influence to get me back into Yale. The first week of classes, I didn't show. Nor the next week or the week after that.

I moved in with my grandfather and worked at a tattoo shop in Brooklyn. Occasionally, I'd take my guitar and perform at an open mic night at a local bar. My father cut off all financial support. I was fucking happy.

One day my grandfather, who always supported me, asked me what I wanted to do with my life. I told him my dream was to start my own business. To be my own boss. I wanted to open a tattoo shop. He sat back in his leather chair and steepled his fingers, contemplating my idea. He finally looked at me and said, "It's not what I would have chosen, but it has potential. Let's come up with a business plan."

That night, my grandfather and I worked tirelessly to come up with a solid plan. Part of that plan included me moving from New York. We both knew the ruthless nature of my father. Malcolm would sabotage anything I attempted that veered away from Kincaid Industries. My father was powerful and influential. He'd make it impossible for me to succeed.

I blindly threw a dart at a map, and it landed near Detroit. A week later I told my parents I was leaving.

My mother sobbed. She was already upset with the discord between my father and me. Catherine Kincaid was the sweetest, most kind-hearted person you could ever meet. How she ended up with my father, I'd never know. She must have seen some redeeming qualities that I didn't. My mother was the one who encouraged my art and music as a child. She was the reason I took guitar lessons. My father said they were a ridiculous waste of time and money but permitted it for my mother's sake. She was the only one who could convince Malcolm of anything. She was his only weak spot. The only thing he outwardly loved beyond power and wealth.

I have no doubt he loved his three children in his own fucked up way. I was the oldest and a disappointment. The one who wasted his potential. The one who abandoned his responsibilities. It didn't make a difference to him that at twenty-seven, I was a successful business owner who built something out of nothing. He would never forgive me for choosing myself over the family legacy.

My sister, Veronica, was twenty-five. Two years younger than me. She became the son I should have been. My sister finished her degree at Yale and had been working for our father ever since. She worked eighty hours a week. Veronica was a beautiful woman, but if she continued this path, she'd be single forever. The pressure she was under was incredible. Had I not left five years ago, she might be happily married with a family of her own. Instead, she stepped up and took my place. The future of Kincaid Industries rested on her shoulders.

My brother, Wesley, was four years younger than me. He was a free spirit. He never had any ambition to work for our father. Wes followed my footsteps, took his guitar and moved to Brooklyn. My father didn't have many expectations for my brother. It was clear from the time he was a child, that my father couldn't mold him. Wesley was wild and reckless. His music always meant more to him than school, and he was damn talented. That boy could pick up any instrument and play the hell out of it. My mother encouraged it. My father tolerated it. Malcolm Kincaid never passed up the opportunity to let me know I had set a bad example for my brother. That my brother looked up to me and I had led him down the wrong path. I believed Wes had chosen his own path a long time ago.

I remember my father's parting sentiment when I left. "Good luck with that. Don't starve." Maybe it was his own way of telling me he cared. I have no doubt he was hoping I would fail and come crawling back. I never did, and it pissed him off.

My grandfather made sure I wouldn't fail. The day I left, he handed me a check for a million dollars. I didn't want to take it, but he insisted. I'll never forget his words. "You're smart and I know you'll invest it wisely, Zackary. I have faith in you. You're a Kincaid, and Kincaids can do anything they set their mind to. Make me proud."

I was determined to do just that. I settled in Utica, Michigan, a small city thirty minutes north of Detroit. I loved the tiny historic district that housed several old buildings. I bought one for my shop and lived in the apartment above it. Over the next six months, I worked like a dog to renovate the lower part of the building into a trendy tattoo parlor that boasted state-of-the-art equipment and professionalism. Six months later, Forever Inked was so successful I had to hire two more artists to keep up with business.

My grandfather came out to pay me a visit and inspect his investment. I walked him through every part of the shop, showing him all the hard work I had done. He looked over the books and scrutinized my finances. Several nods and a few "Mmmhmms" later, he smiled and patted me on the shoulder. "I'm proud of you, Zackary. You've done well."

Nothing meant more to me than his approval. I didn't want to disappoint Gregor Kincaid. He'd supported my dream, even if he didn't understand it.

I only saw him a few times after that. Two years after I left New York, my grandfather died. He left each one of his three grandchildren an exorbitant inheritance. His will specified that we should all follow our dreams, whatever they may be. None of us would ever have to be concerned with money as long as we lived. It was like a big "fuck you" to my father. It pissed off Malcolm to no end. He liked knowing his children would be dependent upon him, and now we weren't. It made my father surlier and even less tolerable.

I was dreading tomorrow. Although I couldn't wait to see my mother and my sister, my father would make it damn miserable. But at twenty-seven, I wasn't a boy anymore. He didn't hold the power over me he used to. I wished our relationship could be better, that he could respect me as a man, and put our differences aside for once. But the chances of that happening, were slim to none.

Tomorrow I'd walk in wearing my black Armani suit. I'd look exactly like the wealthy Kincaid I was. I'd summon up all the etiquette and manners I was taught as a child. I'd be respectful to my father, even if it killed me. Tomorrow wasn't about me.

It was about Wesley.

Chapter 2
Rissa

I wasn't prepared for this. My only plan was to get through the next two days. I wasn't sure how I was going to do it, but I didn't have a choice.

Step one was to get out of bed. That would be good.

My body stayed tucked under the sheets. I couldn't get the nightmare I'd walked in on three nights ago out of my head. I was devastated, and I was angry. How could he do this to me?

I was a bartender at The Hot Spot, just a couple of blocks from our flat in Brooklyn. I was also an aspiring musician and bar boasted live music. It was a win-win for me. Three nights ago, I was scheduled to go on stage at nine. Wes promised me he would come. I watched for him during my entire set, but he never showed. I was upset because we were going to do a duet and it wasn't like Wes to break a promise. I called his phone, and it went right to voicemail. Two more calls and I started to freak out.

I was supposed to finish my bartending shift after my performance, but something nagged at me to get home. Tina, the owner of The Hot Spot, saw the worry etched across my face. She assured me she had me covered. I grabbed my guitar and left the bar in a rush. I practically sprinted the two plus blocks to our home. Not patient enough for the elevator, I raced up the three flights of stairs.

I hoped to God he'd had too much to drink and had fallen asleep. I couldn't have been more wrong.

When I entered our flat, my worst fears came true. He was slumped back against the couch. His head hung to the side and the color was drained from his face. *Please tell me I'm wrong*, I prayed. I tentatively approached his lifeless body and felt for a pulse. His skin was cold and there was no pulse.

I couldn't call 911. He was a Kincaid and cocaine covered the coffee table in front of him. It was too late for EMS anyway.

10

I called the only person I could. I picked up Wes's phone from the table, my missed calls showing on the screen, and called Catherine. Wes's mother was a kind woman, who loved her children. No one was prouder than Catherine of the success Wes had found. Wesley Kincaid was a local music star in the process of signing his first recording contract. Guys loved him for his talent. Women loved him for his devastatingly sexy good looks and his voice that sounded like smooth dark chocolate. I loved him for all the things people didn't see.

I liked Catherine. She treated me with respect. Wes had gotten his kind heart and soft soul from his mother. His determination he got from his father. I wasn't fond of Malcolm. He was a cold-hearted business man, with little tolerance. He looked at me like I was trash.

He wasn't wrong.

I was born Clarissa Lynne Black. I grew up in what some would call a shack, in the Dust Bowl of Oklahoma. My mama worked as a waitress in a small diner. My daddy worked as a ranch hand. We were poor, but we were happy. That was until my mama got brain cancer. We didn't have money for doctors, so there's no telling how long she had it before the debilitating headaches started coming. The tumor was inoperable, a literal death sentence. She refused to bankrupt our family and so she denied any treatment.

At sixteen, I dropped out of school and picked up her shifts at the diner to make ends meet. For a year I watched my mother slowly dying. My only refuge was my music. I'd sit on the back porch and play my guitar just like my daddy taught me. I learned how to play the piano from my mama. We had an old second-hand Kimball that was slightly out of tune. I didn't care about that, I just loved making music. I'd sing for hours, sometimes making up my own words. Whatever I was feeling inside, came out in a song.

When I was seventeen, she called me to her bedroom for a talk. I sat cross-legged on her bed and she held my hand in her frail one. She looked me in the eyes and said, "Clarissa Lynne, you've got the voice of an angel. Get yourself out of this town. Take your dreams and make something of yourself. There ain't nothin' left for you here."

11

She died that night, my daddy holding one hand, me holding the other. We didn't have money for a proper funeral and so the town scraped up enough money to give her a simple burial. She was buried in the back of the cemetery with no headstone, just a wooden cross my daddy had carved her name on.

My daddy loved my mama, and without her he was lost. He started drinking. Drowning all his sorrows with booze. I worked at the diner during the day and took care of daddy at night. I had to carry him to bed more nights than I cared to remember.

He made it to work most days, but the bills started piling up. Just after my eighteenth birthday, my daddy called me into our tiny kitchen. He handed me a Mason jar full of money and the keys to his truck. I'll never forget his words. "Clarissa Lynne you're better than this. This ain't the life your mama wanted for you. There's a few thousand bucks in there. I been saving it for you. Take my truck and go to New York. Use your music and make a life for yourself."

I couldn't leave him. He needed me too much. I loved him. "I won't leave you, daddy," I said as tears streamed down my cheeks.

"Baby girl, we both know I already been gone a long time. I loved your mama and I love you too much to put you through this. Don't you worry about me." He kissed me on the forehead and then helped me pack. He practically pushed me out the door. I turned and waved to him over my shoulder with tears in my eyes and then he was gone. I hadn't even made it to his old Ford pick-up before I heard the shotgun blast.

I dropped to my knees and covered my head with my hands. Sobs racked my chest. I didn't want it to be true, but I knew it was. It all made sense now. My daddy sacrificed his life for mine. That's why he let the bills pile up. He was saving that money to get me out of here.

I wouldn't let him die in vain. I wiped my eyes and drove, following the route my daddy had mapped out for me. I didn't want to waste the money daddy gave me, so I slept in truck stops along the way. After three days, I arrived in New York and found myself a cheap, sleazy motel. It was the best sleep I'd gotten in two years. The next day, I set out to make a life for myself.

I went by Rissa Black now. I tried to erase the Oklahoma twang from my voice, but when I got nervous or excited it occasionally slipped out. Malcolm Kincaid made me nervous. His mere presence reminded me no matter how far I'd come, I was still nothin' but poor white trash.

It was his belief I was leeching off his son and was only with him for his money. That wasn't true at all. Yes, he treated me well, but I fell in love with Wesley Kincaid way before I knew he was wealthy. I wasn't rich when I met him, but I had been in New York a year and was making it on my own. It was the music that connected us. It bonded our souls and wove through our hearts.

When Catherine arrived, she came alone. For that I was thankful. I had waited outside the door for her, so I could prepare her for what had happened. The tears started falling down her face before we even made it inside.

She had no choice but to call Malcolm. While we waited, we cleaned the coffee table flushing whatever was left down the toilet. By the time Malcolm arrived there was no trace of cocaine left in the apartment. Malcolm coldly made some calls, and everything was handled very quietly.

The newspaper and media cited his death a result of cardiac arrest due to a birth defect in his heart. It wasn't a lie. Wesley did have a defective heart and he was diligent about getting it checked at least twice a year. There was no mention of cocaine or any other drugs in the article. My bet was Malcolm paid off the coroner. No Kincaid would ever be associated with cocaine.

Wesley and I had been together for two years. To my knowledge, Wesley hadn't used cocaine until a month ago when he went to meet with a record executive in Los Angeles. When he came home, he was different… high strung and not sleeping. I chalked it up to his excitement and nervousness about signing his first contract, until I found the baggie of white powder tucked into his underwear drawer.

It was the first real fight we'd ever had. Wesley admitted to trying it in LA but promised me he wouldn't do it anymore. He assured me he didn't have a problem, that it was just to take the edge off. I watched him flush it all. I thought it was over.

And now… it was over. He left me alone. The life we had planned was gone. My heart was broken. I didn't know how to pick myself up and move on without him.

I wiped the tears from my eyes and headed to the shower. I let the water run hot and I stood under the spray. It scalded my skin, but I barely felt it. Sobs racked my chest. I pounded my fists against the hard tile. "How could you do this to me?" I screamed. "I love you and you left me! Fuck you, Wesley! Fuck you!" I slid down the wall.

After my breakdown, I put on a simple black dress and smoothed down the front, thankful I wasn't showing yet. I secured the diamond earrings Wes bought me and clasped the matching pendant around my neck. I didn't want to look like the simple girl I was in front of the Kincaids. I kept my make-up light and pulled my naturally wavy hair off my face in a fancy clip. I slipped on my shoes, grabbed my clutch, and headed down to the parking garage.

I rarely drove Wes's Hummer, but I didn't think he would care today. I walked to our parking spot, only to find it empty. Attached to the wall was a letter. I snatched it off the wall. "Property seized by the Estate of Wesley Alexander Kincaid by order of Malcolm Kincaid."

"Fucking fantastic," I muttered to myself. Now what? I couldn't take a cab to the funeral home, so I pulled out my phone and called for an Uber to take me to Forest Hills.

Chapter 3
Zack

I was dressed to impress. I'd taken my piercings out and left them on the hotel dresser. My tattoos were covered by my shirt and suit. I'd always made sure my tattoos could be covered, there were none too high on my neck and nothing went past my wrists. It was a decision I'd made for occasions like this. I was, after all, a Kincaid. There were certain expectations of the way you presented yourself.

I walked apprehensively towards the entrance of the funeral home. This was the last place I thought I'd be today. When I'd talked to Wes last week, he was so damn excited about his pending record deal. I never thought it would end like this.

Sitting outside the funeral home on one of the benches was a young woman. I knew her. Not well, but I recognized her immediately.

"Rissa?"

She lifted her head, her eyes full of tears. "Hey, Zack."

I reached down and gave her a tight hug. "What are you doing out here? Why aren't you inside?"

She wiped at her eyes. "Apparently, I'm not on the *approved guest list*," she finger-quoted.

"Excuse me?" I didn't think there was such a thing at funerals. This had my father written all over it.

"Malcolm's security team escorted me out. I'm not allowed inside." Another tear fell down Rissa's cheek and she wiped it away. "How could he do this to me? Wes is my fiancé. Who does that?"

My father was an asshole. I pulled Rissa to her feet and wiped the mascara that had run under her eye. "You're coming in," I assured her. I kissed her on the forehead and wrapped my arm around her waist.

"Are you sure? I don't want to cause a problem," she said quietly.

"I'm positive." I opened the door for her, and she slipped inside. I followed behind and then sidled up next to her. We were stopped by security almost immediately.

"Excuse me, sir. Your name?"

"Zackary Kincaid."

He nodded at me. I took Rissa's hand and started to lead her in.

"She can't go in, Mr. Kincaid. She's not on the list," he called after me.

I kept moving us forward. "The hell she can't. Miss Black is with me." One of the big guys started talking into his mic. "Don't worry about Malcolm. I'll handle him." I glared. I strode sure-footed toward my family. There was no way my mother would have ever allowed this.

I stood in the open doorway. Another security guard watched me as I scanned the room for my mom. Our eyes met and although they were red from crying, she smiled at me and started my way. My mom was a beautiful woman. Always classy, never pompous. She was as sweet as she appeared. There was nothing fake about her.

I met her halfway, still holding tight to Rissa's hand. I let go to hug my mom. She kissed me on the cheek. "Zack, I'm so glad you came home. I've missed you so much."

"I've missed you too, mom."

Then my mom enveloped Rissa in a tight hug. "How are you holding up, sweetheart?"

"I'm doing okay. I can't believe we're here. I just…" Rissa tried to keep it together, but she couldn't stop the tears.

My mom's eyes well up. "I know, sweetheart."

I knew this wasn't the time or the place, but something had to be said. I wouldn't let him get away with this. "I found Rissa outside. Did you know father had her banned from the funeral?"

My mom's hand came up to cover her mouth. "No. I'm so sorry, Rissa. I'll talk to Malcolm. I'm sure it wasn't intentional."

"I'm sure it wasn't. I understand him wanting to keep out Wes's fans and the media. I'm sure I just slipped his mind," Rissa defended my father. I internally rolled my eyes. We both knew that wasn't the truth. My father was evil, plain and simple.

Speak of the devil, my father approached our little group, arrogance emanating from him. His hands stayed tucked into his pants pockets. "Zackary, glad you could make time for us." He gave me an appraising look. I'd made sure there would be nothing for him to criticize.

"Wesley is my brother. Did you really think I wouldn't come?" There was nothing pleasant in my tone. I hated this man.

My father scowled and turned his attention to Wes's fiancé. "Rissa," he said curtly.

"Hello, Malcolm," she said with a tight smile.

"Rissa wasn't on *the list*," I said harshly. "I corrected that issue."

My father raised his eyebrow at me. "Hmmm. Must have been an oversight. We can't let just anyone in."

"She's not just anyone. Rissa is Wes's fiancé."

"Was. And I know exactly who she is." My father turned his back and walked away.

Rissa's face paled. "I should leave," she whispered.

"You'll do no such thing. Right, mom?" I asked, seeking her support.

"You're staying," my mother agreed. "You'll have to ignore Malcolm. This is a tough time for all of us."

Rissa nodded. She looked lost. This wasn't her world. It wasn't mine either, but I grew up in it. I knew how to adapt.

My mom excused herself to greet someone at the door, leaving us alone. "You gonna be okay?" I asked her.

"Yeah. I feel out of place. I don't know any of these people. None of our friends are here."

It was a sad truth, but I'd bet their friends didn't make *the list* either. "Stick with me. I don't know anyone here either, except my family." I gave her a reassuring smile.

"Are you sure?" she asked tentatively.

"Yes, Rissa. I'm sure." I felt bad for her. My father had made an awful situation, even worse. A feat only my father would be capable of achieving. I saw my sister across the room. "Come on," I said.

I snuck up behind my sister and tapped her on the shoulder. She turned her head and started crying. I wrapped her in a big bear hug and lifted her off the floor.

17

"Zack, I'm so glad you're here." She hugged me tightly. "How's my big brother?"

"Better now that I've seen you, Ronni." I smiled down at her. At six-three, I dwarfed her small stature.

"You know dad hates it when you call me that," she said pursing her lips.

"Why do you think I call you Ronni? I know it irritates him, but you've always been Ronni to me. Veronica is way too formal."

She rolled her eyes. "My whole life is formal." Then she turned to Rissa and hugged her too. "Rissa, I'm so sorry. You must be devastated."

"I'm still in shock," Rissa said.

"We all are. My brother loved you very much. Don't ever doubt that."

"I know. I loved him too." Rissa looked towards the casket where my brother's body laid. "If you'll excuse me, I need to…"

"Of course," Ronni answered.

We watched as Rissa made her way to the casket. She was so sad.

"I feel bad for her," Ronni said. "I don't think she has any family. Wes said both of her parents died. At least we have each other to lean on. She has no one. Her whole world just came crashing down."

A lump caught in my throat. "No one?"

Ronni shook her head. "I mean, I'm sure she has friends, but she and Wes were pretty inseparable."

I watched as Rissa wiped at her face, her lips moving quietly. I hardly knew her. We'd only seen each other a few times over the past two years. I had come to visit a handful of times and once she and Wes had made it to Michigan. She was young, if I remembered correctly. Wes had proposed to Rissa on her twenty-first birthday.

I saw her pull a note from her purse and slip it into the pocket of Wes's pants. Then she kissed her hand and placed her fingers to his lips. It stirred emotions deep inside me that threatened to bubble to the surface. I took a breath and pushed it back down.

None of this made any sense. Wes had always been hyperattentive to his heart condition. I knew he had regular check-ups. As a matter of fact, the last time I talked to him, he'd just had one. Maybe his condition had gotten worse, and he didn't tell me. I'd have to ask about that later. Maybe my mom or Rissa could tell me more.

I leaned over and spoke to Ronnie. "Keep an eye on her, will ya? Malcolm tried to have her banned from the funeral. I don't trust him."

Ronnie narrowed her eyes. "You've got to be fucking kidding me?"

I shook my head. "Not kidding."

"I've got her," Ronnie huffed. "Go say your good-byes."

I wandered over to the place Rissa had just left and looked down on my brother, hands in my pockets. "What the fuck happened, Wes? You weren't supposed to leave us like this. I thought we had years left together. Everything was falling into place for you. Pretty fiancé. Record deal." I shook my head at him.

"I don't know if I ever told you how much I admired you. You were so goddamn talented. You always followed your heart, never let Malcolm sway you. You chose your own path because you knew exactly who you were. It took me a hell of a lot longer."

"I'm going to miss the hell out of you, you know that? I love you, baby brother." A tear dripped from my eye, and I quickly wiped it away. "My life is going to be empty without you calling me every other day. Why did you have to go and die on us? It's so fucking unfair." I looked up at the ceiling and tried to compose myself. He was never supposed to die before me. I was older. I was the reckless one. Wes had always been the one with a kind and gentle soul. I took the silver ring from my pocket and placed it in his, next to Rissa's note.

Wes and I had matching silver skull rings. It was our bond of brotherhood. His wasn't on his hand, so I'd have to ask Rissa about it. That ring was the only thing I wanted of my brother's. I had given him mine and I wanted his. "Good-bye, Wes. I hope you know how much I fucking loved you. Brothers forever. Don't ever forget. 'Cuz you'll always have a place right here." I pounded my fist against my heart.

The night lingered on, and I spoke to the few people I knew, old neighbors and such. I always kept one eye open for Rissa. She seemed to be holding her own. She was one of those people that others couldn't help but love. Everyone, but my father. She had this aura around her, that sucked you in. I understood what Wes had seen in her. Why he had fallen in love with Rissa Black.

When the night ended, I put my hand on her shoulder. "Come on. I'll walk you to your car."

Her cheeks flushed, and she looked at the ground. "You can go without me."

That was bullshit. "I'm not letting you walk out into a dark parking lot by yourself."

"I umm… I have to call for an Uber. It could be a while." She pulled out her phone.

I stuck my hands back in my pockets. "Why didn't you drive Wes's Hummer? You know how to drive, right?"

"Zack, I've been driving since I was fourteen. Malcolm had it towed this morning." She let out a sigh. "I sold my pick-up a year ago. I didn't have a choice but to take an Uber or a taxi. I thought an Uber would be less conspicuous."

My jaw clenched. "Fucking A. I'll drive you home. Come on."

"It's out of the way, Zack. Really, I'm fine taking an Uber," she insisted.

"It's not fine. I'm driving you home. Let's go." My father never failed to amaze me.

We walked out to my Chevelle, and I opened the door for Rissa. She slipped inside, and I went to the driver's side. My father was a Grade A asshole. He couldn't even wait until Wes was in the ground before being a prick.

Rissa looked quietly out the window as I made my way to their apartment. I had questions and they were eating at me. Now was the perfect opportunity to get some answers. "Rissa, what happened to my brother?"

She turned her head. "What do you know?"

That didn't sound good. "My mom said he went into cardiac arrest."

She nodded. "That's true."

"But?" I questioned. There had to be more to the story.

Her eyes turned cold as she stared at me. "You want the truth?"

"Yeah. I want the truth."

20

"It was cocaine. I walked into our apartment and found him dead, with a table full of cocaine in front of him. I'm fucking pissed at him."

She was lying. I was sure of it. "My brother didn't do drugs," I said adamantly.

"You're right," she said. "He didn't until he went to LA to meet that damn record executive. I don't know what happened, but he came home different. He promised me he would quit, but he didn't. I guess the high was more important than me." She crossed her arms over her chest and looked back out the side window.

I couldn't believe what she was telling me, but she had no reason to lie. "He loved you, Rissa."

"What difference does that make now? I don't know what to do without him. He was everything to me." She wiped at her face again.

I patted her knee. "You're going to be okay."

"I always am," she said, as I pulled up in front of their building. "Thanks for the ride and everything else. I'll see you tomorrow."

She started to open her door. "Do you want me to walk you up?" I asked.

"No, I'm good. Thanks again."

"I'll pick you up at ten. Apartment 3C, right?"

Rissa looked at the door to their building and then back at me. "You don't have to. I'll figure it out."

"You can't take an Uber to a funeral, Rissa. I'll be here at ten."

She nodded her head. "Thank you. I'll see you in the morning."

I watched to make sure she made it inside, then pulled away from the curb. "Cocaine?" I slammed my hand into the steering wheel. "What the fuck, Wes?"

Chapter 4
Rissa

I dragged myself up the stairs and to our apartment. Thank God, Zack had recognized me. Otherwise, I could have been stuck outside all night. I'd have to thank him again tomorrow. I felt bad he was driving from Forest Hills to Brooklyn to get me, but it was way better than my other options.

I stripped out of my dress and put on my pajamas. I could have really used a drink, but that wasn't an option. Wesley had left more than me when he decided to snort cocaine. It wasn't like he didn't know. He knew. For two weeks, he knew. I couldn't stop being mad at him. I needed to find a way to forgive him. I didn't think he intended to kill himself, but the result was the same.

I laid awake until 3am. When my alarm went off a few hours later, I felt like I hadn't slept at all. I got dressed and made myself a cup of coffee. I knew it was bad for me, but I needed it. I just had to get through today and then I would come up with a plan. I needed to go to the bank and take some money out of our account. The rent would be due soon.

I wouldn't be able to afford this luxury apartment much longer, but I could buy myself some time. Time to find something more affordable. Time to pack. Time to heal my heart.

At 9:45, a knock sounded at my door. If this was Zack, he was early. I rushed to the door to answer. I opened it and Zack stood there looking so handsome in his black suit. I felt guilty for thinking it, but he and Wes looked a lot alike.

Zack held up an envelope. "This was taped to your door."

I took it from his hand. "Thanks. You didn't have to come up. I would have come down."

"I was early, so I figured I might as well," he said.

I opened the envelope and read the letter inside. "Fuck."

"What is it?" Zack asked.

"Nothing," I dismissed him. "I can't deal with it now. It'll have to wait. Do you want some coffee?"

"Sure. I'll take a cup."

I motioned for him to follow me to the kitchen and placed the letter on the table. I grabbed a mug from the cupboard and poured his coffee. "All I have is French vanilla creamer and sugar. I hope that's okay."

"I take it black," he said.

I nodded and handed him the mug. "Zack, I really appreciate you picking me up. You're a life saver."

"It's not a problem," he assured me. "Wes would have wanted it this way."

"That's true," I said. "But that doesn't mean I appreciate it any less."

"Rissa?"

"Yeah."

"I know this may not be the time, but do you know what happened to Wes's ring?" he asked.

I knew exactly what he was talking about. "Yeah. I took it off before your mom got here. I was afraid it would disappear."

Zack looked at the floor and then back at me. "I hate to ask you this, but can I have it? It was our brother bond. I took mine off and left it with him at the funeral home yesterday."

I was a little shocked that Zack was already asking for something from Wes, but it made sense. I knew how much that ring meant to Wes. "Sure. I'll go get it." I set my coffee mug on the counter and went to our bedroom. I opened my jewelry box and pulled out the ring. I held it up and kissed it good-bye. One more piece of Wes I had to let go of.

I returned to the kitchen and Zack was reading the letter I had set on the table. I wished he wasn't. I ignored his reading and held out the ring. "Here you go. Wes would want you to have this."

Zack held up the letter. "Three days?"

"I guess so," I answered.

"Where will you go?" he asked.

I shook my head. "I don't know. I can't worry about it today." Malcolm had given me three days to vacate the apartment. It was leased

23

under Wes's name and considered a part of his assets. It shouldn't have surprised me, considering he had the Hummer towed yesterday. But three days? That was hardly any time at all. I would probably have to stay in a motel for a while. There was no way I would be able to find another apartment in three days. "Do you think we can stop by the bank on the way?" I needed to take some money out. It would only be a matter of time before Malcolm froze our bank account.

"Sure. Are you ready to go?"

I set my mug next to the sink. "Yeah. It's just down the street. I'll be really quick. I promise."

We walked down to Zack's car. He drove me to the bank, and I hurried inside. I walked up to the teller. "I need to make a withdrawal," I said. I gave her the account number and waited impatiently.

The teller typed into her computer. "I'm sorry. That account has been closed." She cocked her head to the side. "Is there anything else I can do for you?"

I let out a sigh of frustration. "No. Thank you." What the hell was I going to do? I left the bank feeling even worse than I did when I woke up. I hurried back out to Zack's car and slipped inside.

"Did you get what you needed?" he asked.

This wasn't his problem, but I couldn't lie. "No. The account was closed."

"Asshole," Zack muttered.

"I'll figure it out. It's not a big deal," I lied.

Zack nodded to me, and we were on our way to the church. That was our first stop. I sat between Veronica and Zack. Malcolm sat two down from me. I couldn't not see the scathing looks he sent my way. I tried to disregard them, but it was damn hard. I knew Zack hadn't missed any of it.

After the service, it was time for the funeral procession. Malcolm faced Zack with a hard stare. "Zackary, we'll wait in the limo for you. My driver can bring you back to get your car."

Zack looked at Malcolm with an equally hard stare. "I prefer my own car. We'll meet you there."

"Who's we?" Malcolm asked harshly.

"Rissa and me." He turned to his sister. "Ronni?"

24

"I'm going with mom and dad. We'll see you there," Veronica answered, with a tight smile. I sensed that she was torn between her parents and her brother. It was an awful situation to be put in at a funeral.

Zack nodded, then he took me by the hand and led me out of the church. "You could have gone with them," I said.

"I don't want to spend any more time with my father than I have to," he said. "It's fine."

Zack pulled his car behind Malcolm's limo. "Thank you," I said. "You didn't have to do this for me."

"I'm not," he answered in a clipped tone. "I'm doing it for me. I wouldn't have driven with him regardless."

"Oh, okay," I said. I decided to sit back and shut up. He was in a foul mood. It made me wonder what the history was there. I was thankful for Zack's decision, no matter what his motives were.

We arrived at the cemetery, just outside Forest Hills Gardens, where his parents lived. It was an exclusive neighborhood I'd only been to a handful of times. Zack parked behind the limo and put his hand on my knee. "Hey, I didn't mean to snap at you. I didn't mean to take my frustration with my father out on you."

I patted his hand. "It's fine. I understand." I motioned to the others getting out of their cars. "We should go."

Zack nodded. We exited the car and headed to the burial site. I hid my eyes behind dark sunglasses and stood next to Zack. I listened to the minister talk about Wes. He talked about how talented Wes was. What a caring brother and son he was. How much his family loved him. How much his family would miss him. What a loss it was to the Kincaids.

I was never mentioned once. Our relationship wasn't acknowledged or the fact that we were engaged. It was as if I didn't exist at all. I felt more alone than ever.

At the end of the service, the family was invited forward to say their last goodbyes. I followed behind Zack. When it was my turn, Malcolm grabbed me by the arm. "You're not family," he said coldly.

I'd had enough. Enough of his callousness. Enough of his cruelty. Enough of his obvious hate for me.

I ripped my arm from his grip and mustered up all my courage. I glared at him through my sunglasses. "Excuse *you*. I may not be your family, but he was mine. You've taken enough from me. You're not taking *this* away from me too." I continued toward the casket and pulled a red rose from one of the flower arrangements.

This was all that was left. An expensive box that held the man I loved. I placed the rose on his casket. Then I kissed the tips of my fingers and laid my hand next to the rose. I talked to him for the very last time. "I love you, Wesley Kincaid. Thank you for giving me the very best part of you. I'll never forget you. You'll forever be in my heart. Goodbye, my love."

Without looking at anyone, I turned and stormed off. I headed back toward Zack's car, my heels sinking into the wet grass. When I got to the road, I bypassed the car and kept walking. I needed to go home. I needed to be alone. I would call for an Uber when I got to the entrance. I didn't want to talk to anyone, not even Zack.

I had almost made it to the entrance when the red Chevelle pulled up next to me. I just kept walking. I wasn't pissed at Zack. I was just pissed in general at how my entire day had gone. I had so much to do in a very short amount of time.

The window rolled down as Zack kept pace with me. "Where are you going, Rissa?"

I kept my forward march. "Home, while I still have one."

"Let me take you," he said.

"I don't need your help," I barked at him. He didn't deserve it, but he was an easy target for my anger.

"You can't do this alone, Rissa."

I stopped in my tracks and faced him. "I've been doing shit alone for a long, long time. Being with your brother was just a pleasant interlude. I appreciate everything you've done for me, but I've got it from here."

"Why won't you let me help you?" he asked.

I stepped forward and leaned on the open window. "Why do you even want to help me? I'm not your responsibility. I'm not a charity case."

Zack ran his hand over his short hair. "I don't think you're a charity case. That's not what I was implying. You obviously meant a lot to my brother. He would want me to help you. Now get in the fucking car."

"Excuse me?"

"I said, get in the fucking car, Rissa," he reiterated.

"Who the fuck do ya think yer talkin' to?" I asked. My blood was boiling. I took deep breaths, trying to calm myself.

"A stubborn ass woman who's too goddamn proud to take help when it's offered."

He was right about that. Letting Zack take me home would save me money. And right now... I needed every penny I had. "Fine!" I wrenched open the door and plopped into the passenger seat. "Happy?"

"Very," he said smugly.

I wanted to smack that cute smile right off his gorgeous face. I squinted my eyes at him and let out a sigh of frustration. "You won, now drive."

He cautiously drove the car out of the cemetery and onto the road, headed back to the apartment I wouldn't live in much longer. I glared at him with a side-eye, and he had a shit-eating grin on his face. "What?" I barked at him.

"You've got a little twang when you get pissed, you know that? Where are you from anyway?" he asked.

I rolled my eyes. "Not here."

"Really? I could've sworn everyone in Brooklyn said words like *ya* and *yer*," he said imitating my accent humorously.

"I don't sound like that," I answered, careful to keep the twang from my voice.

"Yeah, you do, sweetheart. So where are you from?" he persisted.

I relaxed back into the seat and sighed. "Oklahoma. Three years ago."

"Huh. So, how'd you end up in New York?"

I guessed we were having small talk now. What difference did it matter if he knew? Chances were I'd probably never see him again anyways. "Got in my daddy's old Ford pick-up and drove three days across the country with my guitar and not much else."

He scrunched up his face. "How old were you?"

"Eighteen."

He shook his head. "That's young. Why'd you leave?"

27

I leaned against the door. "Why are you so interested in my life?" Then I thought about what he was implying. "I wasn't looking for a sugar daddy. I wasn't with Wes for his money. I didn't even know he had any when we met or for a long time after that," I stated.

Zack held up his hand toward me, "Whoa! I didn't say you were. I'm curious that's all. I'm just wondering how an eighteen-year-old decides to up and leave her family to come to New York."

I instantly felt bad for assuming the worst. I had been conditioned to accept judgement from Malcolm. I needed to remember that Zack wasn't his father. He'd been nothing but nice to me since he'd arrived.

I decided to be truthful. I didn't worry about the twang in my voice, I just told the short version of my story. "I didn't have any family. My mama died of brain cancer and my daddy was lost without her. He turned to booze. One day he pushed me outta the house and told me to come to New York to try to make sumthin' of myself with my music. Shot himself before I even got to the truck. There was nuthin' left for me there." I looked out the window remembering my mama and daddy.

Zack reached over the console and took my hand. It felt good to have some physical interaction with someone. "I'm so sorry, Rissa. So, you don't have any family?"

"Nope. It's just me. Wes was all I had."

He sat quietly taking in everything I had told him. He pulled up next to the curb in front of my building and I detached his hand from mine. Before I left, I gave him one more truth. "My name's not even Rissa. It's Clarissa Lynne. I was never meant to live this life. Your daddy was right about me. I'm nuthin' but poor white trash." I gave him a sad smile. "Thanks for being nice to me when ya had no reason to be. You're a good guy, Zack. Maybe sometime in the future, I'll see ya around." I gave him a wink, opened my door and left him at the curb.

Chapter 5
Zack

I watched her walk inside. My heart felt like it had sunk to the bottom of my chest. I don't know that I had ever met a stronger person in my life. I had a profound appreciation for Clarissa Lynne Black. She was a fighter, is what she was. She was a lot like me.

What my father was doing to her was wrong. There was no way any person could be expected to bounce back in three days, let alone someone whose resources had been stripped from them.

I heard her little rant to my father at the cemetery. Not many people had the guts to stand up to him. But she did. Rissa Black was a feisty thing. I would bet anything, that was one of the qualities that drew my brother to her.

Wes. He would be pissed if he knew what my father was doing. I needed to set Malcolm straight about the way he was treating her. If not for Rissa, then for Wes. I needed to try to make things right.

I drove from Brooklyn to Forest Hills Garden. When I pulled through the gated entrance memories flashed back at me. This used to be my life. I left five years ago and never looked back.

I wasn't ever meant for this life either, but it had been handed to me on a silver platter. I walked away willingly. I had my business, my friends, my own success. Rissa had nothing but a firm determination to not succumb to her circumstances. And again, I hated everything that was my father.

I pulled into the cobblestone drive and stared up at the house I had grown up in. I took a deep breath and made my way up the walkway. The brass knocker that adorned the front door stared back at me. A symbol of wealth and power. I grabbed ahold of it and made my presence known.

My mom answered the door with shock. I hadn't walked back into this house in five years. "Zack." She looked over her shoulder. "What are you doing here?"

When I came into town, I always met my mom and sister at a restaurant or some other neutral territory. I hugged my mom tightly. "I came to see Malcolm."

"Your father is in his office. He's not in the best of moods," she said.

"That's okay, because neither am I." I pushed past her and strode toward his office. I thrust open the heavy wooden doors. My father was seated behind his expensive desk, talking on the phone like he was a king. Nothing ruffled this man.

"Jonathan, I'll have to call you back," he said. "I have an unexpected visitor." He ended his call and glared at me. "So, the prodigal son returns. Are you crawling back or are you here to gloat?"

"I'm not crawling back," I said definitively. "I don't need anything from you."

My father stood from his desk and walked to the side table. He dropped a couple of ice cubes in a glass and filled it with Scotch. He took a long drink, licking his lips. "You must want something, or you wouldn't be here."

His arrogance made my pulse quicken and my muscles constrict. "I want you to act like a goddamn human being."

He took another sip. "You'll have to be a little more specific."

"Rissa," I said. "You froze her bank accounts and gave her three days to get out of the apartment."

"Pfft. That's what this is about? I thought it was something important," he answered nonchalantly.

"It is important," I said. "How could you be so cold?"

"Jesus Christ, Zack. She's nothing but trash. Pretty trash. But trash none the less."

I clenched my fists. "She's not trash. She's a woman who has lost the man she loved and you're making it worse."

My father rolled his eyes. "Oh, for Christ's sake, please tell me you're not being sucked in by a pretty face. I thought you were smarter than your brother."

"Fuck you! Wes loved her. Have some goddamn compassion for once in your life. You gave her three days."

"And I'm pretty sure it took less than that for her to convince your brother to take her in. She's like a damn stray puppy. Cute, but with fleas and in need of serious training. She's not one of us."

"She's not a dog! She's a woman."

My father grabbed another glass and filled it with Scotch, offering it to me. "Think with your brain, Zack. Don't let your cock make decisions for you. Let it go. Jesus, I'm surprised you've made it this long without me."

I took the glass from him, poured it on a potted plant and slammed it back on the desk. "I'm not thinking with my cock. I'm thinking with my heart. I should have known you wouldn't understand. You don't have a goddamn heart."

He laughed at me. "My heart tells me to protect this family. That's what I'm doing. You want to take in a stray? By all means, have at it. Take her with you when you leave. It'll be one less thing for me to deal with."

I was fuming. "Shame on me for thinking there was one last bit of human decency left in you. You're nothing but a selfish bastard!"

"If by selfish, you mean practical, then you're right. I'm not going to let some two-bit, money-grubbing whore ruin this family or its reputation."

"Reputation? Do you know what your reputation is?" I asked.

He took a sip of his Scotch with a smug smile. "Enlighten me."

"Malcolm Kincaid," I started. "Ruthless, unforgiving, hard-ass, cold, pompous prick. Shall I go on?"

"You forgot good-looking, successful, wealthy, and generous. I've given more money to charity than you'll make in a lifetime at your little tattoo shop where you draw pictures," he said condescendingly.

"Yeah. You're probably right, but I'm not afraid to get my hands dirty. You'll give money to a charity as long as you don't have to interact with the people it supports. Right? It's hypocritical."

"Are we back to Rissa Black again? Forget about her. She's not family. She's nothing!"

I clenched my fists at my sides and my blood boiled. "She's not nothing! Fuck you!" I turned on my heel and stormed from his office.

Before I made it to the front door his voice boomed once more, "You're falling for her, aren't you? Stop thinking with your dick, Zack! Don't be an idiot like your brother!"

31

That was it! He'd finally pushed me too far. I turned and charged him. I pushed his body against the wall and wrapped my hand around his neck. We were the same size, but I was younger and faster. "Don't you dare talk about Wes like that! My brother was a good man. He was better than you'll ever be!" His face reddened, and his eyes bulged.

"Zack!" my mom yelled. "Please! Stop!"

My mom's voice cut through my rage, and I released my hand from my father's throat. A look of relief passed over his face as he took a deep breath. "We're done!"

I took a step back and faced my mom. "I'm sorry. I can't be around him. I don't know why you stay; you deserve so much better. I love you, but this is the last time I'll ever set foot in this house." I hugged my mom like it was the last time I'd see her. It wasn't, but things would never be the same. "Call if you need me. I'm only a phone call away. Maybe we can have lunch tomorrow."

She nodded her head with tears in her eyes. It wasn't a secret that my father and I didn't get along, but I'd never laid a hand on him before. I'd just passed over an invisible boundary. Any hope she'd had for us repairing our relationship was gone.

I left my parents' house and went back to the hotel. I stripped out of my suit and threw on a black t-shirt and jeans. I grabbed a beer and sat back on the couch. This day had sucked, and it had only gotten worse.

I flipped on the TV to the news. A story about Wes's death played on the screen. My brother wasn't just a Kincaid, he was a local music star. A picture of me holding Rissa's hand as we exited the church had been captured on film. I leaned forward with my arms on my knees and stared at the screen.

Rissa Black. My father was wrong. I wasn't falling for Rissa, but I had to see her before I left town. Maybe there was something I could do. Some way I could help. I had the resources, but I doubted she would take any money from me. I had to try. There was no way I could leave without at least trying.

Thirty minutes later, I stood outside her door, unannounced and uninvited. I lifted my hand hesitantly and knocked softly. I stuffed my hands deep in my pockets and waited patiently.

The door inched open, and Rissa stared at me through the crack. "Zack? What are you doing here?"

I lifted my head to her. "Can I come in?"

"Of course." She opened the door wider to let me through. Her naturally curly, dark blond hair hung loosely around her shoulders and down her back. She was dressed in only a t-shirt that hit her mid-thigh, her long legs hanging out beneath it. Her bare feet padded further into the apartment. "I wasn't expecting company. I should change."

"You're fine," I said.

She nodded her head in acceptance. "I was just packing." She waved her hand toward the boxes strewn across the apartment. "Can I get you something to drink?"

"Rissa, where are you going to go?" I couldn't leave not knowing if she was going to be okay.

She shrugged her shoulders. "I don't know yet. I might be able to crash with someone from work until I do. Tonight, I have to pack. Tomorrow I'll figure out the rest."

"Can I help?" I asked. "I may be the black sheep of the family, but I have money. I can make this easier for you."

She shook her head. "I won't take your money, Zack. That's not who I am."

God, she was stubborn. There had to be something I could do. "Can I at least help you pack?"

Rissa gave me a sad smile. "Sure." She led me to their bedroom. "You should go through Wes's things and see if there's anything you want before Malcolm gets rid of everything."

"What about you? Don't you want it?" I asked curiously. It seemed a little too easy for her to give his stuff away.

"I've sorted through the things that mean the most to me. I can't take much. Where would I put it?"

I ran my hand through my short hair. "I don't know. I guess I didn't think about it."

"You should start with his dresser." She motioned to the tall set of drawers.

Next to the dresser were a couple of guitar cases. "These Wes's?" I asked.

She walked over and picked up the two cases, placing them on the bed. She opened one of the cases. "The Fender is his." Then she opened the other case. "The Gibson is mine. He always insisted his was better, but I disagreed. I'm a Gibson girl all the way. You can't beat it for acoustic."

I took the Fender out of its case and threw the strap over my head. I plucked at the strings. "Ahhh, you may be right, but a Fender is better for electric. Where's his amp?"

"Spare room." Rissa picked up her guitar and led me to the spare bedroom that had been transformed into a mini studio.

I loved this room. It made me long for the days I used to play. I hadn't made a lot of time for my music over the past few years, just dabbled occasionally. I saw the amp in the corner and plugged the guitar in. I ran my fingers over the strings with one hand while the fingers of my other hand danced skillfully on the fretboard. "God, this is nice. Only the best for my brother."

Rissa cocked her head to the side. "Wes said you didn't play anymore."

"I haven't in a while, but I haven't forgotten either." I started playing "Stairway to Heaven", it was a Led Zeppelin classic that every guitarist learned. After a few bars, Rissa picked up her Gibson and joined in. The sound of the electric and acoustic guitars blended together beautifully. We played through the first verse and into the chorus, ending the song prematurely.

I lifted the guitar up over my head and set it on the stand. "You're good," I told her.

She smiled at me. "You're not so bad yourself. You should take that home. I strictly play acoustic, and Wes would want you to have it."

I nodded my head appreciatively at her. "I think I will." We stood there awkwardly, and I glanced at my watch.

"If you need to go, it's fine. I can handle all this."

I shook my head. "No, it's not that. I'm getting hungry. Have you eaten?"

"No," she said. "Food hasn't really been on my mind."

34

"Well, I'm starved. Do you have a Chinese place around here that delivers?" I asked.

She let out a little laugh. "Yeah. Come on. I've got the take-out menus in the kitchen."

I followed Rissa to the kitchen. She riffled through a drawer, pulled out a menu, and handed it to me. I scanned over my choices. "I'm going to get the General Tao Chicken. What do you want?" I pulled my phone out of my pocket.

"I'll have chicken chop suey. White rice, please. Tell them not to forget the fortune cookies. Last time they forgot."

"Got it." I chuckled. I made the call and placed our order. "It'll be here in 30 minutes."

"Thanks. You should go through the dresser while we wait," she suggested.

Rissa and I headed back to their bedroom, and I started going through the drawers. We worked silently as she continued to pack some boxes with her clothes, and I sifted through the contents of Wes's drawers. The only things I found of interest were a gold chain with a cross pendant, a notebook that looked like some sort of journal, and an envelope full of pictures. I pulled the items out and laid them on the bed.

I returned to the bottom drawer and lifted out a pair of jeans. Underneath them sat a small glass vile full of white powder. "What the fuck?" I held it up for Rissa to see.

She stormed over and snatched it out of my hand. "Goddamn him!" I followed her to the kitchen and watched her dump the cocaine down the sink. She set the bottle on the counter and searched for something in the drawers. She pulled out a mallet and smashed the bottle. I heard the glass break with the first hit, but she kept at it. "How long, Wes? How long did you lie to me?" she screamed.

I wrapped one arm around her and used the other to grab the mallet from her hand. "Hey, it's okay," I said soothingly.

"It's not okay. How is any of this okay?" she cried. I pulled her to my chest and rubbed her back. I held her for only a minute before the doorbell rang. She untangled herself from me and wiped her face. "Our food is here." She reached for her purse and pulled out her wallet.

I frowned at her. "Put your money away. I've got it."

"Zack," she huffed.

"Rissa? Seriously, you can at least let me buy you dinner." I left her in the kitchen and went to answer the door.

When I got back to the kitchen, she was using a towel to brush the glass from the counter into the trash can. She threw the towel in too and started pulling out plates and silverware. "So, when are you going home?" she asked.

"Maybe tomorrow. Maybe the next day if you need me to stay. I'm not sure." I filled my plate with a healthy portion of food and started to dig in.

Rissa waved her fork at me. "I'm sure you want to get back to your life."

"It's nothing that can't wait. I can stay."

"Okay," she agreed. That shocked me. I was sure she was going to put up a fight. "Let's see what we get done tonight and play it by ear."

I smiled at her. "I can agree to that." We finished our dinner with small talk. She talked about growing up in Oklahoma and I talked about my time in the Marines. The conversation flowed easily between us, and it was… nice. It was really nice. The longer we talked, the more she relaxed and occasionally she would slip unconsciously into her Oklahoma accent. She was damn adorable.

After dinner and clean-up, we returned to the bedroom, and I finished going through Wes's things. It was late when she sat on the bed with a photo album perched on her lap. "Come look at these with me?" she asked.

I sat next to her, and she opened the book. The pages were filled with pictures of Wes's rise to almost stardom. "I took pictures at all of his shows," she said. Occasionally, Rissa was in one of the photos. They looked so happy together. My eyes welled with tears as we flipped through the pages. "You look like him," she said. Silent tears fell down her cheeks as she went down memory lane. "I miss him already. I don't want to be alone again."

She rested her head on my shoulder and cried. I wrapped my arm around her as the tears continued to fall. I missed him too and the emotions I tried to keep at bay filled my chest. I lifted her chin with my fingers and my green eyes locked to her blue ones, our faces only inches apart. "You don't have to be alone."

She swallowed down the lump in her throat and moved closer. I could feel her warm breath on my lips and the smell of the light floral scent that lingered on her skin. I closed the gap and pressed my lips to hers. I placed my hand on the back of her head and pulled her in closer. She opened her mouth and our tongues gently tangled together. It was soft and sensual.

She pulled back slightly and whispered, "What are we doing, Zack?"

"I don't know," I whispered back. "Do you want to stop?"

"No."

"Me neither."

I kissed her again and it became desperate. We both needed this. I laid her back on the bed and massaged her breasts over her t-shirt. She was so soft and perfect. Her nipples hardened beneath her shirt. Her hand rubbed over my ass and gently squeezed. My cock hardened even more. "I want you."

"Just for tonight," she whispered.

"Just for tonight," I agreed. I wasn't expecting to have sex. "I don't have a condom."

"You don't need one." Of course, she was on birth control. I'd never had sex without a condom, but tonight I didn't care.

I rose from the bed and untied my boots, slipping them off my feet. My jeans came off next, along with my shirt. She laid on the bed in only her t-shirt that had risen to reveal her lace panties. She was beautiful.

I crossed the room and dimmed the lights, then returned to her. I crawled up on the bed next to Rissa and kissed her again. My one hand ran through her silky hair while the other rubbed up her long, soft legs. I reached under the hem of her shirt and rubbed her soft tits. She let out a little moan. The sound was so sexy, and it stirred something deep inside me. I wanted more.

I lifted her shirt over her head to reveal her round, full tits. She watched me take her in. Her eyes were full of desire and lust. I knew mine were the same. I lowered my head to one of her tits and sucked her hard nipple into my mouth. "Oh, God," she whispered. I moved to her other tit and her hand moved under my boxer briefs rubbing my bare ass. Her nails

37

scraped along my skin, and I let out a groan of my own. I kissed her lips again. I pushed my tongue inside her mouth. Her tongue met mine and they twisted together, needy and desperate.

My hand skimmed down her flat stomach and slid beneath her panties. My fingers ran through her folds and down between her legs. She was so damn wet. I pushed two fingers inside her. Her back arched off the mattress and she barely made a sound, except a soft moan that escaped her lips.

Her hand caressed down my back and wound around the front of me. She slipped her hand inside my boxer briefs and gently rubbed my hard cock. Her hand felt so good. "More," I whispered. She gripped tighter, jacking me up and down. This woman knew how to use her hands.

Keeping my fingers inside her, I used my thumb to rub slow circles on her clit. The pleasure she was giving me made me want to please her just as much. I increased the speed and pressure of my thumb. She tightened around my fingers and let out a soft mewl. If I hadn't felt her clench my fingers, I wouldn't have known she had come at all. "I need inside you," I told her.

She slid her panties down her legs, and I removed my boxer briefs. We laid together naked on the bed. I moved between her legs, caging her in with my arms. "Are you sure about this?"

"I'm sure," she whispered. "I need to feel you."

I gently pushed inside her. She was warm and wet and felt like heaven. I slid in and out of her using long, deep strokes. The feel of nothing between us was unbelievable. This was emotional sex. It had everything to do with the loss we both suffered. It wasn't about carnal desire, although it was more than physically pleasing. I kissed her as I fucked her, I needed to feel the connection.

Rissa wrapped her arms around me, using my shoulders as leverage to move with me, thrust for thrust. "Zack," she whispered. I felt her pussy clench around my dick, as she dropped her head back and let out another soft moan. My balls tightened as I neared my climax.

Every muscle in my body seized tight and then I came inside her. Rissa wrapped her legs around me and gripped her hands on my ass to pull me in closer. She couldn't get close enough to me. And I couldn't get close enough to her.

I pulled out and laid on my side, staring at her sad, pretty face. A single tear ran from her eye and into the pillow. "Stay with me tonight. I don't want to be alone," she said quietly.

"I'll stay for tonight," I answered her. We crawled under the covers. She laid on her side and I laid behind her, pulling her soft body tight to my hard chest with my arm. "Sleep, Rissa."

I should have felt bad about what I had done. I betrayed my brother. But as hard as I tried, I couldn't feel bad. We had both wanted it, if only for tonight. Then an aggravating thought crossed my mind. Maybe my father was right. Maybe I was falling for Clarissa Lynne Black.

Chapter 6
Rissa

I laid in Zack's arms, feeling safe and secure. It had been almost a week since I had felt that way. I had used Zack for my own selfish reasons. To ease the loneliness. To erase, if only for a few hours, the sadness that filled me. To make me forget what tomorrow would bring. To pretend that I wouldn't be homeless in a couple days. To make me feel like Wes was still here with me.

He wasn't.

And never would be again.

I missed him so much. And despite the strong arms that held me, I felt alone.

I laid awake, tucked to Zack's chest, his warmth permeating my body. What we had done was wrong. But if something was so wrong, why did it have to feel so right? I couldn't keep him. Tomorrow he would leave, and I'd never see him again. I wasn't sure if that was a good thing or not. Regardless, it was going to happen.

I heard Zack's soft snores behind me. He was out like a light. The past few days had taken their toll on both of us.

I glanced at the clock. It was nearly four in the morning, and I'd barely slept. It seemed sleep was going to evade me tonight. I lifted Zack's arm from me and slipped from the bed. Grabbing my black, silk robe off the chair, I wrapped it around me. I went to the one place that always brought me peace.

I slid onto the bench of my piano and began to play. My fingers knew the notes, I didn't have to think. The sound of Evanescence's "My Immortal" filled the room. My heart knew the words. My voice started soft, then started to crescendo. *I'm so tired of being here. Suppressed by all my childish fears. And if you have to leave, I wish that you would just leave. Your presence still lingers here, and it won't leave me alone. These wounds won't seem to heal. This pain is just too real. There's just too much that time cannot erase.* I finished the song and dropped my head to the top of the piano.

"That was beautiful." Zack's voice came from across the room. I looked up to see him leaning against the doorway in only his boxer briefs. The tattoos on his muscular chest and arms made him even more attractive than he was in a suit and tie. I felt another pang of my betrayal for even noticing.

I ran my hand along the keys. "Wes bought me this piano. It's going to kill me to leave it behind."

Zack pushed off the wall, slowly making his way towards the piano. He slid onto the bench next to me. "Wes could play anything. He was so fucking talented."

"I know. I miss him. I was so damn lonely before he came into my life. I'm not ready to be alone again." My fingers aimless danced over the keys, not really playing anything.

Zack ran his hand along the side of my face, then gently turned it towards his. "Come home with me, Rissa."

I dropped my chin. "You don't owe me anything, Zack. I know what last night was."

"I know what it was too. We were both emotional. We were drowning our grief in each other. But you don't have to do this alone. We can help each other get through this."

"I might not be okay for a long time."

"That's all right."

I couldn't believe I was actually considering this. But where else would I go? It could be my chance to make a new start away from the memories of this place. I could take this chance, but... there were so many buts. "What happened last night, can't happen again."

"I know," he answered. "But we could be friends. We could help each other."

"It would only be until I got back on my feet. I'll get a job and find my own place as soon as I can." I was already putting stipulations on his proposal.

41

"There's no hurry. You can stay with me as long as it takes," he offered.

"Let me have until the morning to decide?" I asked. His offer was more than appealing, but was it the right choice? Zack was a Kincaid. Although he seemed nothing like Malcolm, there could be strings attached to this arrangement. Wes was a Kincaid too. There were never any strings with him. I'd like to think Zack was more like Wes, but what if I was wrong?

I couldn't deny the immediate attraction I felt towards Zack. Getting involved with him would be wrong. I didn't know if I would be able to have a platonic relationship with him. What if he wanted more? What if I did? Then what? What would he think when he found out I was carrying his brother's baby?

"I can see your wheels turning," Zack said. "Just think about it." He stood from the piano bench and took my hand. "Come back to bed with me."

I didn't say a word. I just let him lead me to bed. We crawled back between the sheets, and I rested my head on his hard chest. His strong arm wrapped around me. I fell into a blissful sleep and dreamed everything was right in my life.

♫♪♫♪

I woke to an empty bed. The space beside me was cold and I wondered if last night was all a dream. It seemed too real to not have happened, but my mind was a mess.

I grabbed my robe to put on, then scooped my hair up on top of my head and fastened it with a clip. I was sure my mind had gone rogue. Dreaming about Zack was nothing but an illusion my brain had created to help me deal with my reality. Why would Zack ask me to move home with him? It was ridiculous.

I left my room and headed for the kitchen. Coffee. I definitely needed coffee. When I entered the kitchen, I stopped dead in my tracks. "You're here," I said.

Zack turned from the counter where he was whipping something up in a bowl. "Good morning, Rissa."

My face scrunched up in confusion. "So, last night wasn't a dream? We... you... me... it really happened?" I asked pointing between us.

He set the whisk in the bowl and leaned back against the counter. "It wasn't a dream. It was very, very real," he said with a smirk.

I set my hand on my hip. "Huh."

Zack returned to whipping whatever was in the bowl. "Do you want onions in your omelet?" he asked.

He acted like it was no big deal. Maybe I needed to do the same. "No onions for me, but extra cheese." I moved towards the coffee pot that was already filled and grabbed myself a mug from the cupboard. I poured myself a cup, then went to the fridge to get my French vanilla creamer. After preparing my coffee, I faced Zack again. "Are we going to talk about last night?"

Zack poured the eggs in a pan, and they started to cook. "There's nothing to talk about. It happened. I don't regret it. We both needed it."

I waved my hand wildly in the air. "Is it that simple?"

"Don't complicate it, Rissa."

"It is complicated," I insisted. "How can I go home with you after what we did last night?" Zack was dressed in only his jeans. His tattooed chest and arms were very distracting. So were his bare feet. How could I find his feet sexy? What was wrong with me?

He crossed his arms over his chest and leaned back against the counter again. "Very easily. Do you want a fresh start?"

I stared down at my coffee. "I need one."

"Then come home with me." He made it sound so damn easy. It was anything but easy.

I decided to stop hemming and hawing. I let out a sigh of frustration. "We had sex, Zack."

His lips curled up. "I'm very aware of that."

"I enjoyed it," I admitted. I could feel the heat rising up my neck at my confession.

"So did I. Very much so."

"Is it wrong?" I asked. "I feel like it's wrong."

Zack stepped toward me. He ran his hands up and down my arms. "I can honestly say, I don't know. Maybe it was a one-time thing. Maybe not.

How about we start over as friends and see where it goes?" He kissed the top of my head and looked down at me. "What do you say? What have you got left here?"

I shrugged my shoulders. "Memories?"

Zack was still holding my arms. "You can bring them with you. And I can guarantee you'll make more memories."

"Where will I stay? Do you even have room for me?" I asked. I had so many questions.

"I have an extra bedroom," he answered.

"What if you get sick of me? You're used to living alone."

He laughed. "I don't think you realize how much I work. I'm hardly ever there."

"What about a job? Where will I work?" I continued.

"You can start by running the front counter of my shop. I've been meaning to hire someone, and you'd be perfect. If you don't like it, I have lots of connections and there are a ton of businesses within walking distance. You could probably even get a gig playing music at one of the bars."

I nodded my head. "You've given this a lot of thought, haven't you? You seem to have all the answers."

"You might not know this about me yet, but I'm a problem solver. Any more questions?"

I shuffled back and forth on my feet. "Two. How will I get my stuff there?"

Zack returned to the eggs cooking on the stove. He flipped the omelet in one skilled move. "We'll put what we can in my car and ship the rest. Easy. What's your other question?" He turned back to me.

I looked at him with pleading eyes. "Are you really sure about this? I mean really, really sure? It wasn't just an impulsive offer after last night?"

"I'm more than sure, Rissa. Come home with me," he said again.

"Okay." I closed my eyes and took a deep breath. "I'll do it."

Zack's face turned from serious to extremely happy. "It's going to be good. I know it will be."

That was it. My decision had been made. I was going to move to Michigan. I didn't know much about where Zack lived, but I didn't know anything about New York before I came here either. It was going to be a big adventure.

It was going to become an even bigger adventure in about eight months. I should have told Zack about the baby, but I didn't. Now, I almost felt like it was too late to tell him. I was spinning a tangled web I wasn't sure I would be able to escape. But, instead of being the spider, I felt more like the fly.

Chapter 7
Zack

Was I sure about moving Rissa home with me? Not really, but it felt right. It wasn't like she and my brother had broken up and I was swooping in. He was gone. And he was never coming back.

I thought about the sex Rissa and I had last night. Those little sounds she made… drove me crazy. I was falling fast and hard for her.

The sex I'd been getting lately was from my regular booty call, Gina. Gina was wild and untamed in bed. Fucking her was always more than pleasing. But Gina and I would never be anything more. We were convenient. We fulfilled a need for each other, and it had been enough.

Until now.

Rissa was the kind of girl I could see myself settling down with. She was sweet and sexy and stubborn. It was an enticing combination. Maybe it would turn into nothing. Maybe we would end up just being friends. But I couldn't pass up the opportunity to find out if it could be more. Keeping my hands off her was going to be challenging, to say the least. I foresaw a lot of cold showers in my future.

Rissa and I sat at the table eating our omelets and all she had on was a damn robe. I fought hard with myself to keep my eyes at her neck and above. After we finished, I excused myself to call my mom and sister. I needed to see them before I left town. There was no telling when I would be back again.

I found Rissa packing a box in her closet. I leaned against the doorjamb. "Hey."

She looked up at me, her hair a mess and no makeup, but still beautiful. "Hey. When do you want to leave? I still have quite a bit to go through."

"Take your time. We'll leave tomorrow morning." This was getting very real. "I'm going back to my hotel to shower and change. I'm meeting my mom and sister for lunch. Do you need anything before I leave?"

"No. I'll be fine. Are you coming back, or should I plan on seeing you in the morning?" she asked.

"I'll be back," I assured her.

She nodded. "Have a good lunch. I'll see you later."

I wanted to lean down to give her a kiss good-bye, but that wasn't what friends did. Instead, I shoved my hands in my pockets and left.

♫♪♫♪

I was dressed down, my tattoos on full display and my piercings back in place. My ears adorned small silver hoops, I had a barbell through my eyebrow, and one through my tongue. The last one wasn't for me. The women loved it. It made them crazy when I went down on them and rubbed that silver ball all over their girly parts. And who was I to deny a woman pleasure? I was willing to bet that Rissa would love it when I finally got to put my skills to use on her. But we were friends, and friends didn't do that.

I shelved the thought before entering the restaurant, filing it away for later. I walked into the upscale bar and grill where I was meeting my sister and mom. I had planned to talk to my sister before my mom showed up. Ronni was sitting at a corner table and waved me over. My sister and mom always accepted me for who I was. I didn't have to pretend with them. I made my way to her table and kissed her on the cheek. "Hey, sis."

"Hey, big brother. I'm glad you called. I wanted to see you before you left. I miss you."

"I miss you too, but you know I can't stay."

Ronni folded her hands on the table. "Mom said you had a big blow out with dad." Clearly, she was fishing for information, and I wouldn't lie to her.

I ran my hand through my hair. "Yeah, we did. He kicked Rissa out of the apartment. Gave her three days, starting yesterday."

"Shit. What's she going to do? Where will she go?" Ronni asked.

The waitress came over to take our drink orders. I ordered a beer for myself, and Ronni got a martini. Obviously, she was stressed to be having a martini mid-afternoon. "That's what I wanted to talk to you about. I found a place for her to go."

Ronni let out a sigh of relief. "That's great. Where is she moving to?"

I rubbed my hands over my face and steepled my fingers. "Michigan. I'm taking her home with me."

Ronni shook her head as if she hadn't heard me correctly. "Excuse me?"

"I'm taking her home with me," I confirmed.

"Are you fucking crazy? Why? Why would you do that?" Ronni asked.

I took a deep breath. "I think I'm falling in love with her."

Ronni shook her head. "Wait. What? This is crazy, Zack. What the hell are you thinking?" The waitress arrived with our drinks and Ronni downed half her martini in one gulp. "You're supposed to be the smart one. I don't even know what to say."

I knew she would react this way. "I don't know," I said. "Maybe it's nothing, but what if it is? I can't let her be homeless. What kind of person would that make me?"

"This isn't your responsibility, Zack." Ronni cringed before she let the next words leave her lips. "What if dad was right about her? I mean, I like Rissa. Don't get me wrong. But what if she's using you?"

I leaned back in my chair. "I understand your concern. She's going to get her own place as soon as possible. We already discussed it. But what if this is my chance to find happiness? What if she's the one?"

"Fuck, Zack! I hope you know what you're doing. I'm going to be calling you, to make sure you're not being stupid."

I smiled. "I wouldn't expect anything less. Do me a favor and keep this between us. Okay? Mom doesn't need to know, for now."

"Your secret is safe with me. I hope this works out the way you think it will. Not just for you, but for Rissa too."

♫♪♫♪

After lunch with my mom and Veronica, I headed back to my hotel room. It felt so empty. I dropped my keys by the front door and wandered to the bedroom. I laid back on the bed and wondered if I was making the right choice.

I closed my eyes and thought about Clarissa Lynne Black. She was so goddamn perfect. Everything about her was everything I never thought I deserved. But why couldn't I have her? It was doomed from the start. I knew that. She was still hurting from losing Wes. She was fragile, and I was taking advantage.

I needed sleep. Maybe things would be clearer after I got some rest. I curled up on my side and soon I was out.

Chapter 8
Rissa

I had packed my last box an hour ago. I glanced at the clock on the wall. It was almost ten o'clock. All I could think, was that Zack had changed his mind and was too chicken shit to tell me. I picked up my phone and called Tina at The Hot Spot. Regardless of what happened with Zack, I needed to be out the day after tomorrow. It weighed heavily on me.

The phone rang twice and then she answered. "Hi, Tina. It's Rissa."

"Hey, girlie. How are things going?"

I choked down my pride. "That's why I'm calling. Wes's dad is kicking me out. Do you think I can crash with you for a week? I just need a place to go until I find something I can afford." I tried to keep the hitch out of my voice but failed miserably.

"Motherfucking bastard! Rissa, you're the best bartender I have. My place isn't that big, but we'll make it work."

I breathed out a sigh of relief. "Thanks, Tina. I don't know what I would do without you. I'll call you tomorrow and we'll figure out a plan."

"For you, anything. I remember when you first walked into my bar. You needed a job, and I needed a bartender. You've been my friend ever since. Let me work my magic. We'll find you a place in no time."

"Tina, you're a life saver. I owe you big time. I thought I had a plan, but it seems to have fallen through. You don't know how much I appreciate this."

She let out a little laugh. "You don't owe me a thing. I'm glad to help. I'll talk to you tomorrow."

I hung up with Tina feeling better about where I would end up. I had been looking forward to moving in with Zack. However, it was after ten and I still hadn't heard from him. I could only assume he had gotten cold feet. I didn't blame him. I was nervous too. I only wished that we had exchanged phone numbers. That way I could call and tell him to forget the whole thing. Unfortunately, I had the feeling he had already forgotten about me.

I knew it was too good to be true. Knights in shining armor didn't really exist, except in childhood fantasies. I wasn't a child anymore and no one was going to save me. There wasn't going to be a white horse, I was going drive into the sunset in the back of a taxi. My castle was going to be a teeny apartment I could barely afford. I was only fooling myself to think I could ever be more than the poor white trash I was born into.

There was some security in that thought. I was free to be who I was. There was no need to impress anyone anymore. I could let my Oklahoma twang run free and no one would care that I liked jeans more than little black dresses.

I carried the last box and set it beside the front door. Tomorrow was a new day. The start of a new life. I looked around at our apartment and the life I would be leaving behind. Out of everything, the piano pained me the most.

I sat down on the bench and thought about the day I met Wes.

I was working at The Hot Spot. It was early, before the dinner crowd came in. We were having live music that night, but right now the stage was empty. I asked Tina, "Do you mind?" as I motioned to the stage.

"Knock yourself out," she said.

I finished wiping down the bar and approached the empty stage. I sat down at the old piano sitting there and began to play. My fingers danced over the keys, and I began to play "Titanium" by Sia. The words poured from my lips, as I sang softly. That song had become my own personal anthem. I was determined not to let anything knock me down. Being in New York was scary and exciting at the same time. I formed a barrier around myself where nothing could hurt me.

When I finished, soft applause erupted around me, Tina leading the pack. My cheeks blushed. It felt good playing my music, but I hadn't had much of a chance since I arrived.

I left the stage and returned to my place behind the bar.

"That was amazing." The compliment came from a good-looking guy sitting on a bar stool. He had a guitar propped against his leg. "How am I supposed to go on after that?" he asked.

"It was nothing," I said shyly.

"It was everything." His eyes searched mine and there was an instant connection. What I didn't know was that over the next few weeks, I would get to know that guy very well. Wes and I hit it off right from the beginning.

And now, I sat here at my piano playing that same damn song. I would be okay. Nothing could hurt me. Not losing Wes. Not Malcolm. And sure as hell, not Zack. I was resilient. I was going to make it on my own. It wasn't going to be easy, but I was used to taking the difficult path. The only time in my life that had been easy was my time with Wes.

Until the last couple of months. Those months had been challenging, but I was stronger for it. His addiction ate away at our relationship, one little piece at a time. I thought having a baby on the way would straighten him out, but that was just my own naïve wishful thinking.

The reality was I was alone again. I would find a way to make it work for me and our baby. I would start again and make a life for us.

I closed the top over the keys of the piano. It was like saying good-bye to an old friend. I left the piano and changed into my pajamas. Pajamas consisted of one of Wes's long-sleeved shirts and a pair of shorts. I brushed my teeth and looked in the mirror. I barely recognized the girl that stared back at me. She had dark circles under her eyes, and she looked lost. *Pull yourself together*, I told her. *You're better than this.*

I didn't know if it was true, but the girl in the mirror needed to listen to what I told her. It was time to pull up her big girl panties and face reality. Every day was a new opportunity. Tomorrow I would move in with Tina and start my search for a new apartment. *Tomorrow*, I told myself.

I crawled beneath the cold sheets of my bed and waited for darkness to take over. I laid awake for a long time before my eyes got heavy. Eventually I drifted into a peaceful sleep.

A bang on my front door startled me awake. I glanced at my phone. It was past midnight. Who the hell would be at my door? Before I had time to answer my own question, the banging came again. More insistent this time.

It had to be Malcolm. He was probably here to kick me out. From the letter that had been attached to my door, I knew I had one more day. Now, I was pissed. I stormed from my bed to the front door, ready to rip him a new one. Without looking through the peephole, I jerked it open. "I have one more day asshole!"

The last word froze on my lips. It wasn't Malcolm. Zack stood there looking nervous. "Can I come in?"

I crossed my arms. "What for?" I didn't realize how pissed I was at Zack, until now. He had built up my hope, just to drop me flat on my face.

"Please," he said, almost begging.

"Fine." I opened the door wider and let him through.

He slipped past me and looked at the boxes stacked by the door, "Rissa…"

I held up my hand. "I get it. You changed your mind and it's fine. I've made other plans, so you're off the hook."

"Fuck," he muttered. "Let me explain."

"There's no need. It was a stupid idea from the beginning. Why would I move halfway across the country with a man I barely know? It doesn't even make sense."

"Rissa…," he started again, but I cut him off.

"No, Zack. You don't have to say a thing. We had sex. It meant nothing. People do it all the time. It was my mistake to think that your offer was real. But I've got it all handled now. You can go home and forget about me. I'm not your obligation or responsibility. Let's just call it an indiscretion. We both go our separate ways and maybe I'll send you a Christmas card."

He stepped toward me. "Is that what you want?"

I stepped back. "I want to move on."

Zack cupped the side of my face. "I didn't change my mind. I went back to my hotel and fell asleep. I'm so sorry. My offer still stands. I want you to come home with me."

Well, shit! His explanation made sense. Neither one of us had gotten much sleep the night before. I was running on pure adrenaline. But I couldn't understand why he was pushing this so hard.

I backed up further and threw my hands in the air. "Why? Why would you want that? You barely know me." I needed answers and I needed them now.

"I know enough. You're a strong, sexy, independent woman. I find that combination incredibly attractive. I want to get to know you better. And unless I've read you totally wrong, I think you're curious about me too. We owe it to ourselves to find out if there could be something more between us."

I walked over to the couch and plopped down. I held my head between my hands. I felt like my head was going to explode. Zack had just admitted he had feelings for me. I couldn't deny I was attracted to him too. It was too soon, wasn't it? Wes was barely cold in the ground, and I wanted to climb his brother like a spider monkey. It was sick when I thought about it. "I have a life here," I said.

Zack sat down next to me. "You're a bartender. You can do that anywhere. Is staying here going to make you happy or will you always wonder what could have been?"

I turned my head and stared into his captivating green eyes. "I thought we were just going to be friends."

Zack took ahold of my hand. "I want that with you first. I'm just not closing the door to the possibility of more than friends."

I could agree to that. I bit my lip. "I felt humiliated," I blurted out. "When you didn't show, I felt stupid for believing you. I thought you lied. I didn't realize how much I wanted to go home with you until I realized it wasn't going to happen."

Zack wrapped his arms around me, and I rested my head on his shoulder. "I'm sorry. I promise you I'm a man of my word. I don't say things I don't mean. Do you trust me?"

My eyes welled with tears. "I trust you." Why did I trust him? I wasn't sure, but I did.

He tilted his head to the side. "We have a long day tomorrow. I already checked out of my hotel and my suitcase is in the car. Can I stay the night?"

I smiled at him. "On one condition."

He smiled back at me. "What's that?"

I teasingly pointed a finger at him. "No kissing and keep your hands to yourself."

Zack stood from the couch, his hands up in surrender. "No kissing. I promise. And my hands will stay right here." He slipped them in his pockets. "Think you can open the door for me, so I can get my bag?"

"I think I can do that."

Chapter 9
Zack

When I had woken to a dark room, I knew I fucked up. It was after eleven when I woke up. I should have called her, and I would have, except that we hadn't exchanged numbers. How could I have been so stupid?

I wasn't surprised at the greeting I got when Rissa opened the door. I figured she assumed I had abandoned her. I didn't. I wouldn't. I wasn't my father.

She was scared. I could see it written all over her face. I would bet she'd hardly slept at all over the past few days. Rissa's eyes looked tired. All I had done was ratchet up her anxiety another notch. I was supposed to be making things easier for her, not harder.

When I finally got her to accept my apology, we climbed into bed. She rolled all the way to the edge and laid on her side. "You stay over there. I mean it."

I chuckled at how damn adorable she was. "Scout's honor, I'll stay on my side."

Then she squinted her eyes and pointed at me. "Were you ever a boy scout?"

I shook my head.

"Didn't think so. No funny business, mister." Then she snuggled into her pillow and pulled the blanket up to her neck. "Good night, Zack."

"Good night, Clarissa."

We laid in the dark for a long time and then I heard her whisper, "Zack?"

"Yeah?" I turned and faced her.

"Nobody's ever called me Clarissa before," she said quietly.

"Hmmm. That's your name, isn't it?"

"Well, yes. But I've always either been Clarissa Lynne or Rissa. Never just Clarissa."

"Are you okay with me calling you Clarissa?" I asked.

"I guess so. It's different is all," she answered.

"New beginnings, sweetheart. New beginnings," was all I said.

"Zack?" she whispered again.

"Yes?"

"Just you, okay? You can call me Clarissa. Nobody else."

"Okay. Go to sleep now. We've got a long day tomorrow." I leaned over and kissed her on the cheek.

"Thank you, Zack," she said sleepily.

"You're more than welcome, Clarissa."

I laid there in bed thinking. I liked that no one had ever called her Clarissa before. It was something special, only for me. I was definitely falling for her.

♫♪♫♪

I woke early, but Clarissa was dead to the world. I let her sleep as long as possible before we had to get on the road. I packed what I could in my car. I took the rest of her boxes to the front desk and arranged for them to be shipped to my apartment. With any luck, they would arrive in a day or two.

Seeing that Clarissa was still sleeping, I walked down the block to a coffee shop to get us breakfast. When I got back to the apartment, Clarissa was dressed in a pair of shorts and a red, sleeveless blouse. Her hair was pulled back in a ponytail, and a few curls fell loosely around her face. She looked young, and I reminded myself that she was only twenty-one. She'd been through so much and I wanted to make everything better for her.

I set the box of pastries and coffee on the counter in the kitchen. I held out a cup to her. "I got you coffee."

"Thanks," she said, taking the cup from my hand. She took a small sip and smiled. "Mmmm. French vanilla. You remembered."

I winked at her. "I've been paying attention. There're doughnuts too. I didn't know what you liked, so I got a little bit of everything."

She opened the box and pulled out a jelly-filled doughnut. "These are my favorite." She took a bite and strawberry jelly squirted out onto her lip.

I reached over and wiped it off, then licked the jelly from my finger. "You had a little something on your lip."

"Thanks." She wiped at her mouth. "How long is the drive? Should we get going?"

"Finish your breakfast first. It's about ten hours. Longer if we stop for lunch."

She popped the rest of the doughnut in her mouth. "Last chance to change your mind. My boss, Tina, said I can stay with her for a while."

"Not a chance in hell, sweetheart. I've already packed the car and arranged for everything else to be shipped to Michigan. You're stuck with me now."

She wrinkled up her nose. "Actually, I think you're stuck with me." She picked up the box of pastries from the counter. "Can we take these with us?"

I laughed. "Of course. I wouldn't want you to starve."

She looked around at her apartment. "I feel like I'm forgetting something."

"We can get whatever you need when we get there. Believe it or not we have stores in Michigan."

"Yeah, I know. I came here with nothing. This should be easy, but it's not. It feels like the end. Like I'm abandoning him."

I stepped toward her and brushed a curl from her face. "You're not abandoning him. You were forced out. It wasn't a choice, but a necessity. Wes wouldn't want you to be struggling on your own. He would want you to take this chance. He would want you far away from my father."

She tilted her head to the side. "That's true. Should I leave a note or something? I feel like I should."

I shook my head back and forth. "No. He doesn't deserve anything from you. Walk away with your head held high. Don't give my father the satisfaction of thinking he won."

"But he did," she said softly.

"That remains to be seen. He only wins if you let him," I told her.

She nodded, accepting what I was telling her. "Can I take my pillow? I really love my pillow."

I laughed. "Go grab it and then we're out of here."

She bounced to her bedroom and came out with her pillow clutched to her chest. She grabbed the small overnight bag from the floor and hooked her purse over her shoulder. "I'm ready. Let's go."

Once we were settled in the car, Clarissa slipped her flipflops off and sat cross-legged on the seat. "Sooo…. have you told anyone that I'm moving home with you?"

"My sister, Ronni," I said.

"What'd she say? Did she think it was a mistake?" she asked.

I loved that Clarissa wasn't afraid to ask tough questions. Ever since I arrived, she been very blunt with me. I didn't have to wonder what she was thinking. If she was willing to ask, I owed her the truth. "She's concerned," I said vaguely.

"She probably thinks I'm some kind of whore, jumping from one brother to another." Rissa looked absently out the window.

I grabbed her hand. "Hey. Don't say that. I don't want to hear you ever refer to yourself that way again."

She pulled her hand away and twisted the rings on her fingers. "Why? It's kind of the truth, isn't it? What will you tell people when they ask who I am? There are going to be questions. You left alone and are returning with your brother's…" She waved her hands in the air. "What do you call the fiancé of someone who died? He's not my ex. We weren't married, so I'm not a widow. What am I?"

I took her hand back in mine and laced our fingers together. "You're a friend who needed a new start. No one needs to know anything else. What we are or who we become is nobody's business but our own. I've never worried about what people think about me and I'm not going to start now." I lifted her hand to my lips and kissed the back of it.

I dropped our hands so they rested on the center console. She didn't pull away and I liked the feel of her hand in mine. We fit together perfectly.

"I guess you're right. That was the point of all of this. A fresh start. No one there knows me, and I don't know them. I can be anybody I want to be."

I smiled at her. "You absolutely can."

We drove in silence for a while, and I could see her eyes getting heavy. "Why don't you try to get some rest. I'll wake you when we stop for lunch."

"I think it's the car ride that's making me sleepy. You don't mind?" she asked.

"Not at all." I reached over the seat into the back and grabbed her pillow.

Clarissa took it from me and made a little nest against the door. "Don't let me sleep too long."

"I won't."

♫♪♫♪

About halfway through the drive, I pulled off I-80 into a service plaza with a bunch of restaurants. We had lunch, gassed up, and were ready to get back on the road.

"Can I drive?" Clarissa asked out of the blue.

I quirked an eyebrow up. "I don't think so." There was no way I would let her drive my baby.

She put her hands on her hips. "Why not? Don't you trust me?"

That was exactly it. I'd never trusted anyone to drive my car. She was a classic and couldn't be easily replaced. "I trust you," I lied. "But it's a stick shift," I reasoned.

"Yeah? I drove a stick all the way from Oklahoma to New York. I know how," she persisted.

I rolled my eyes. "This ain't a pickup, sweetheart. There's a lot of power in this engine." I rubbed my hand lovingly along the hood. *Don't worry Betsy, I won't let her drive you.*

Now she rolled her eyes. "I can handle it."

I chuckled. "I bet you can, but you're not driving."

"So, you don't trust me."

I let out a sigh of aggravation. "I trust you, just… she's my baby."

"Admit that you don't think I can handle her." Clarissa shook her head. "I grew up in Oklahoma. There's not much to do there as a teenager

60

except drive fast cars and mess around in the back of 'em. They may not have been pretty, but no one cared what the outside looked like, it was what was under the hood that was important. I've driven my share on the dusty back roads. Let's just say no one balked at me being the driver in more than a few races. I could hold my own, but if you don't trust me that's fine." She walked around the passenger side and opened the door.

This girl. She was something else, that was for sure. I tossed her the keys. "Okay, big talker. Let's see what you've got, but I'm telling you right now, if you crash my baby…"

She bounced on her toes. "I won't. I promise." She skipped around to the driver's side and kissed me on the cheek.

I looked at her flipflops. "You don't exactly have driving shoes on."

She dismissed me with a wave of her hand. "Oh, please! I could drive this thing barefoot." She eased into the seat, I shut the door and hurried around to the passenger side. She adjusted the seat and the mirrors. She started the engine and smiled. "God, I love that sound."

She was making me nervous. "Just ease her out onto the expressway."

"Yeah. All right." She eased my Chevelle towards the entrance of the expressway. She checked her mirrors and looked all around her. "Looks like we're clear." She punched the gas and fishtailed the car onto the entrance ramp, quickly straightening it out.

I held on to the door handle with a death grip. This was a bad idea. We were going to die for sure. "Clarissa Lynne!"

"Relax. I'm just gettin' a feel for her." She sped down the entrance ramp and expertly merged into traffic. She swerved around cars, moving to the far-left lane.

Her feet moved quickly over the clutch and her hand shifted the gears fluidly. I watched the speedometer jump from 70 to 100 in a matter of seconds. All the while she handled my car like a pro, weaving in and out of traffic. We were flying, and she was scaring the shit out of me. "You can slow down now!" I shouted so she could hear me above the wind whipping through the car.

Clarissa let off the accelerator and slowed to a respectable 80 mph. "God, that was fun. You can't drive like that in New York."

I scowled at her. "You shouldn't drive like that anywhere." My heart was finally returning to a normal rate after damn near pounding out of my chest.

She laughed at me. "You're kind of acting like a pussy for a bad boy. I didn't kill you."

"Bad boy? What makes you think I'm a bad boy?" I huffed.

"Shall I count the reasons. One, you were in the Marines, which means you know how to handle yourself. The Marines is not for wussies."

I smiled at that. It was true.

"Two, you turned your back on your family to start your own tattoo shop. Three, you're all tatted and pierced, which I find very sexy. Four, you've got a great body, so I know you work out. Five, this car is a thing of beauty. And if I was a betting woman, I'd say you probably own a Harley too."

I rubbed my hand over my face to contain my laughter. "You think you've got me all figured out, don't you?"

She shrugged. "I'm good at reading people. But you don't fool me at all. Underneath all that bad, is a guy with a huge heart. You're a softy on the inside, which is why you brought me home with you."

I didn't know what to say. Everything she said was true. "I do own a Harley, but you're not driving it," I said definitively.

"I knew it!" She smiled. "I rather be on the back anyways, so don't worry about that. Cars are more my thing."

I turned in the seat, so I faced her. I was finally comfortable with her driving. "My turn, since you think you know me so well. I know you grew up in Oklahoma and you didn't have a lot of money."

"True," she said.

"Your mom was sick, so you probably took on adult responsibilities early."

"I worked in a diner and helped pay the bills, so yeah."

I looked her up and down. "You want a better life for yourself but aren't sure you deserve it. You work hard, just to prove everyone wrong. You're not sure if moving to Michigan is the right choice, but you're willing to take a chance. You're stubborn and a fighter. You'd like to be taken care of, but at the same time won't let yourself be dependent on anyone."

"I don't want to be taken care of. I'm not going to leech off you, Zack. I'll pull my own weight." She let out a sigh. "What I had with Wes was a partnership. Yes, he bought me nice things, but I didn't expect it."

She was getting defensive and that wasn't what I wanted. Me and my damn mouth. "I didn't mean it like that. I never thought you were taking advantage. Everyone needs to be taken care of sometimes. It doesn't make you weak."

"Who takes care of you?" she asked.

"That's different. I've been on my own a long time. I don't need to be taken care of."

"I'll take care of you. I'm gonna take such good care of you, you're going to wonder how you ever got along without me."

Damn, I was in trouble.

Chapter 10
Rissa

It was late when Zack pulled through the gate at the back of his shop. He parked next to the back door and cut the engine. "Are you ready for this?" he asked.

I bit my lip. "I'm nervous. Do you have clients in the shop?"

He smirked at me. "I'm not sure. I kind of just got here. Most likely, but it's almost nine on a weeknight. They should be finishing up shortly."

"I don't think I'm ready to meet anyone tonight. Is there a way for me to sneak upstairs?"

Zack exited the car and came around to my side. He opened my door and pulled me out by the hand. Then he pulled me close and wrapped his arms around me. "I won't let anything happen to you. You're safe here. Everyone is going to love you."

It felt good being nestled in his arms. "How do you know?"

He stared down at me. "Because you're very lovable."

"As friends," I reminded him. I was reminding myself too. Falling for Zack would be way too easy. I could feel it already happening. *It doesn't matter how sweet his kisses are or how I feel being held by his strong arms, just friends.* That's what I told myself, even if it was a lie.

"With the option for more. We see where this goes. We decide our future," he said. I nodded my acceptance of his statement. Zack released me and took my hand. "Come on, you can at least meet Layla. She and Chase ran the shop for me while I was gone. They're good people and very non-judgmental."

"Okay, but then I want to unpack the car and see where I'll be living."

"I promise you'll have time. I won't have any appointments tomorrow, so I can help you. We'll get everything done," he said.

64

"I don't want to take you away from your work. I can do it myself," I insisted.

"You could, but you don't have to. Now, come inside." Zack pulled me forward and I tried to tame my hair with my other hand. He opened the back door and we stepped into a hallway. He pointed to a door on my right. "That leads to the stairwell and straight ahead is my shop."

I had been here once before, a couple of years ago, but I had never been upstairs. He pulled me forward into an open area. Along the sides were small studios with doors. Each room had a large chair and work area. Up front was a lounge with couches and chairs. Tables held magazines and photo albums. There was also a front counter, where clients would check-in. The walls were covered in artwork, including framed portraits of tattoos. It was a lot to take in all at once.

Standing at the front counter was a short girl with jet-black hair tied up on top of her head. She wore dark black eyeliner that formed perfect cat eyes. Her arms were covered in tattoos.

"Hey, Layla. I'm back. How'd everything go?" Zack asked.

Layla looked up from what she was working on and smiled at Zack. Then her eyes scanned me from head to toe, zeroing in on my hand that Zack was holding. She frowned. "Just awful. There was a flood in the basement and a fire in your apartment. I don't know how we survived without you." She grabbed her chest dramatically.

"We're you able to save my cat?" Zack asked without concern.

Layla gasped. "You have a cat? If I had only known, perhaps we could have saved the furball." Layla threw her hand up on her forehead. "Oh, the tragedy!"

"Seriously, you did remember to feed her, right?" Zack asked. I didn't know Zack had a cat. It reminded me how little I knew about him.

Layla held up two fingers. "Twice a day like clockwork. She missed you."

"I missed her too." Zack pulled me forward. "Layla, this is Rissa. She's going to be staying with me for a while." I wondered what *a while* meant. How long would I have to figure my shit out?

I gave Layla a little wave. "Hi. Nice to meet you."

Layla leaned forward and gave me a hug, taking me by surprise. "We hug here. It's nice to meet you, Rissa."

I hugged her back, because what else could I do?

"So how do you know Zack?" she asked.

"We're friends from New York." I shrugged. It wasn't a total lie. "I needed a fresh start and Zack suggested I come home with him. I'm going to see if I can make a life for myself here."

"Well, if Zack ever gives me a day off, I'll show you around this town. He's a slave driver, you know?" she said hiking her thumb at Zack.

"That would be great," I said appreciatively. I liked Layla already. She was easy going and could be my first new friend here.

"Everything went smoothly then?" Zack asked Layla.

"Except for the flood and the fire, everything was perfect. I was just finishing up tonight's receipts."

"Thank you. Thank you for being here when I couldn't. Go home. I'll finish everything in the morning."

Layla quirked up an eyebrow. "You're working tomorrow?"

"I'll be in and out. I'm going to help Rissa get settled, but I'll be available," he said.

Layla grabbed her purse from under the counter. "I'll be on my way then. Tootles." She waved. "Don't forget to lock up."

Zack winked at her. "I got it. See you tomorrow."

Layla left through the front door, leaving Zack and me alone. "I like her," I said.

"Told ya. Let me show you my apartment and introduce you to Miss Priss." He started walking toward the door we had passed.

"I didn't know you had a cat."

He looked over his shoulder at me. "There's a lot you don't know about me. I hope I don't scare you off."

"That's highly doubtful. I like what I do know."

Zack opened the door and ushered me inside. It was an industrial stairway that had stairs going both up and down. He pointed downward. "The basement." Then he pointed upward. "My apartment."

I followed him up the stairs to another door. He took out his keys and unlocked it. There were more stairs going up. I pointed at them. "Where does that go?"

"Rooftop access. I'll take you up there tomorrow." He opened the apartment door and led me inside.

I couldn't have been more surprised at what I saw. The building was old, and I expected the apartment to look old as well. I was so wrong. The walls were brown brick, but the apartment was beautiful. It had hardwood floors with area rugs scattered around. The furniture was leather and there was a huge flat screen TV hung on the wall. I moved into the kitchen to find granite countertops and stainless-steel appliances. Sometimes I forgot that Zack was wealthy. Very wealthy.

"Miss Priss," Zack called.

A long-haired black cat jumped up onto the counter and let out a loud meow. Zack went right to her and picked her up. "There you are, girl. I missed you." The cat nuzzled into Zack and started purring loudly. "You're not allergic to cats, are you? I probably should have asked before."

I shook my head. "Not allergic, but cats make me nervous. They don't seem to like me." I reached out a tentative hand to pet her. Miss Priss rubbed into my hand with her head.

"She likes you," Zack said. "She's a good girl. There's nothing to be nervous about with her."

We would see about that. As long as she didn't hiss at me or pee in my shoes, we'd be good. Zack set Miss Priss on the ground and motioned for me to follow him. We walked into a dark room, and he flipped on the light. "This is my room."

It was very manly. A king-size bed sat in the middle of the room, covered with a black comforter. There were two dressers made of dark wood and nightstands on both sides of the bed. Framed drawings hung around the room. "Did you draw these?" I asked touching one of the frames.

"Yeah. Drawing is my true passion."

"They're really good." I was impressed. Zack was super talented.

"Thanks," Zack said. "Wes was the only one who really appreciated my artwork."

Wes. I had hardly thought about him all day. I felt a stab in my heart. I was a shitty girlfriend. Or ex-girlfriend? I didn't know how to classify it.

"Let me show you the other room. Don't be scared. I didn't know I was going to have company. It's not really ready for guests yet."

I swallowed down the worry in my chest. "Okay."

Zack led me to the other bedroom. It was set up as his art studio. It wasn't as big as Zacks's room, but it was more than spacious. A drawing table sat in the middle, with a lamp clamped to the side. Bookshelves lined the walls, holding a variety of art supplies and books. The walls were covered in drawings. Some of them complete, others were works in progress.

"You're giving me your art studio?" I asked incredulously. "Where will you work?"

Zack placed his arms on my shoulders. "Don't worry about that. I'll have Chase help me move this stuff tomorrow and then you and I will go furniture shopping. It'll be fine. I want you to feel at home here."

"This is going to disrupt your life. I can sleep on the couch until I find my own place." I already felt guilty about infringing on Zack's personal space.

"Nonsense," he said. "You're not sleeping on the couch. We'll get this fixed up in no time. If anybody is sleeping on the couch, it'll be me."

"You're not sleeping on the couch," I said insistently.

He gave me a sly smile. "Then I guess we'll have to coexist in the same bed for a couple more nights. Think you can handle it? You're not going to attack me in my sleep or anything?"

"I can handle it." I rolled my eyes. I looked around at Zack's studio. It didn't have much furniture and the space was big. "What if I just got a futon? It would fit in here and then you wouldn't have to move all of your stuff out?"

Zack shook his head. "Those are horrible to sleep on. You're going to need a dresser too. Where will you put all your clothes?"

"I can live out of boxes for now. It seems silly to redo this whole room for me when I'll be moving out eventually." That was supposed to be my goal. To live on my own. I was afraid that if I got too comfortable here, I wouldn't ever want to leave. "I'm serious, Zack. I don't need much room. My first apartment in New York wasn't much bigger than this room. It barely had a kitchen, and the bathroom was so tiny I could hardly turn around in it. I could literally brush my teeth at the sink while taking a shower."

Zack scowled. "You're not living like that here. How about we get the car unpacked and revisit this in the morning?"

I sighed. Zack was going to be difficult. I don't think he realized all I had to my name was a few hundred bucks. I couldn't be spending money on furniture when I needed to find my own apartment and buy some type of car. My first priority was to find a job that paid well. I could bartend for a while, but in a few months, that wouldn't be an option. No one wanted a pregnant woman slinging drinks behind the bar.

"I guess unloading the car would be a good idea," I conceded.

We went back down the stairs and started unpacking the car. I couldn't believe how much stuff Zack had been able to fit in the Chevelle. By the time we finished, I was dead on my feet. It had been a long day. All I wanted to do was sleep. "Do you mind if I take a shower before bed? I feel gross."

"Of course. Here, let me show you the bathroom. I'll clear out a couple of drawers in there for you." He led me to the bathroom, which wasn't huge, but it certainly wasn't small either. And it was pristinely clean. He opened the linen closet. "Clean towels are in here. Wash clothes, bath towels, whatever you need."

It was organized neatly. In fact, the whole apartment was. More than I would have expected from a single man. "Do you have a cleaning lady?" I asked.

Zack laughed. "I have someone who comes in once a month to do all the big stuff, but I clean in between. Why do you ask?"

I shrugged. "I don't know. Everything is perfect. I think I could eat off the bathroom floor."

"Linda, my cleaning lady, was here yesterday, but I'm not a slob. My mom insisted I keep a clean room as a kid and spending three years in the military helped," he said.

"I'll try to be neat. You'll hardly know I'm here."

"I'm not worried," he said. "I'm going to go down to the shop to look over some paperwork. Make yourself at home."

Zack left me alone in the apartment. I was starving, but I didn't want to tell him. I didn't want him buying me food too. He'd already paid for my lunch. I'd only ordered a salad because it was cheap. I opened the box of leftover doughnuts I'd brought up from the car. This would have to do for now. There was no way I was going through his cupboards in search of food. I quickly scarfed down a hard custard-filled doughnut, even though it wasn't my favorite, and washed it down with a glass of water. At least my stomach would stop rumbling.

I went to Zack's studio and searched for my shower things. After securing what I needed, I headed for the shower. The hot water felt divine, and the water pressure was phenomenal. I spent longer than usual letting the spray soak into my sore muscles and wash the day away. Before leaving the bathroom, I pulled on a pair of shorts and a tank, then ran a comb through my wet locks and fluffed out my natural curls. I collected all my belongings, wiped down the counter, and hung my wet towel on the hook.

When I opened the door, there sat Miss Priss. She stared up at me as I stared down at her. "Are we going to have a problem?" I asked her.

She let out a big yawn and showed me all her teeth. "Got it," I said. "This is your house and I'm the guest. Can I come out of the bathroom?" She stared at me with her yellow-green eyes. "Please?" I begged her.

Miss Priss wagged her tail and moved to the side, letting me out. "Thank you," I said to her. Now I was talking to a cat. All of this was so screwed up. I shook my head as I returned my things to the spare bedroom. I grabbed my pillow and tried to decide where to sleep. The couch would make the most sense, but Zack's bed looked really comfortable.

"Fuck it." I headed to Zack's room and looked at his bed. I wondered which side he usually slept on or if he starfished and took up the middle. I made a decision and went to the far side. Pulling back the covers, I slipped between the sheets and pulled them up to my neck. I laid there on my back staring at the ceiling. This felt so weird. I was laying in Zack's bed when I should have been on Tina's couch. I rolled on my side and tucked my pillow under my head. I closed my eyes, but there was no way I would fall asleep. It was too damn quiet. Living in New York, there was always the sound of a horn honking or a police siren wailing.

I rolled to my back again. Miss Priss jumped up on the bed and was giving me the evil-eye. "I suppose I'm lying in your spot," I said to her. She walked around in a circle and sat with her back to me, giving me the cold shoulder. "So, that's how it's going to be, huh?" She started licking her paw, not giving me a second thought.

I got out of bed and left her there. I grabbed my pillow and found my favorite blanket that I had packed in a trash bag. I took them both to the couch and looked for the TV remote. I tucked my pillow into the corner of the couch and covered myself with the blanket. I flipped through the channels, searching for anything that would help put me to sleep. I stopped when I came across *How to Lose a Guy in 10 Days*. I loved this movie. Matthew McConaughey was so stinking cute.

I curled up in the corner and began watching. My eyelids got heavy, and I let myself fall asleep.

Chapter 11
Zack

It was after one when I finally made it back upstairs. I wanted to give Clarissa time to settle in without me hovering over the top of her. I quietly opened the door, not wanting to wake her. I expected it to be quiet, but I could hear the TV. An infomercial for pots and pans played on the screen. Clarissa was sound asleep, tucked into the corner of the couch. Miss Priss laid by her feet, curled into a fluffy, black ball.

I left her there and made my way to the kitchen. The box of doughnuts sat partially open on the counter. "Shit," I mumbled. I opened the box and touched the pastries. They were hard on the outside. I dumped them in the trash with a sigh. She was probably hungry, and I didn't think enough to feed her. She'd only had a small salad for lunch. I wasn't used to thinking about anyone besides myself. I made a peanut butter and jelly sandwich and finished it off in a couple of bites.

I needed a shower bad. I went to the bathroom, expecting to find Clarissa's shampoo and stuff in there. It wasn't. She'd left nothing behind. If it wasn't for the wet towel on the hook, I would have never known she'd been in there.

I stepped in the shower and let the water run over me. I really liked Clarissa. She was so goddamn perfect. And beautiful. And sexy. I leaned one hand against the wall and grabbed my dick in the other. I didn't know how we were going to live together without me touching her. I squirted shampoo in my hand and started to stroke myself. The worst part was I already knew what she felt like, inside and out. So soft. So sweet. I wanted to taste her more than anything. I pictured her perky nipples and her soft pussy. My hand moved faster over my cock, stroking hard and fast.

I imagined her pushed up against the shower wall while I fucked her from behind. I imagined the soft little sounds she made when she came. Her clenching my dick with her pussy. All of it was too much. I stroked harder and faster. I heard my name on her lips. My balls tightened, and my muscles constricted. I felt everything tense up before I came all over the shower wall. "Fuck!" I took a couple of deep breathes and finished off my shower. I couldn't believe I had jacked off while she slept on my couch. I was a fucking perv, but at least I wouldn't go to bed with a hard-on.

I usually slept in only my boxer briefs, but I threw on a pair of shorts. I went to the couch and lifted Clarissa into my arms. She smelled like strawberries and vanilla. She didn't wake but curled her head into my chest. I carried her to bed and tucked her in. I set my alarm for seven and crawled onto my side of the bed. I laid there staring at the ceiling with my hands tucked behind my head. I didn't want her to leave. I didn't want her to find her own place. I wanted her to stay in my bed. With me.

Clarissa started to murmur in her sleep. I couldn't tell what she was saying. It didn't matter, because within seconds, she had moved toward me and rested her head on my chest. She wrapped an arm around me and snuggled in. I wrapped my arms around her tiny body. "Sleep, baby," I whispered.

I was so damn fucked!

♫♪♫♪

The next morning, I woke up before my alarm went off. Clarissa was still snuggled into my side. I kissed the top of her head and rolled out from underneath her. She tucked her pillow up under her head and nestled into it. She looked angelic with her dark blond curls fanned out around her on my black sheets.

Miss Priss was curled up on the end of the bed. I scooped her up and cuddled her to my chest. "Come on, girl. Let's get you some breakfast," I whispered to her. She purred as I rubbed the fur along her back. "Did you miss me?" I set her on the kitchen counter and opened a can of food for her. Scooping it into a glass bowl, I placed her food on the floor and filled her water bowl. She eagerly jumped off the counter and started eating her breakfast. "Did Layla take good care of you?" I rubbed Miss Priss's head. She purred contentedly as she ate.

I started the coffee and pulled bacon and eggs from the fridge. I laid the strips of bacon in a frying pan and started cracking the eggs in a bowl. I assumed Clarissa like scrambled eggs since she ate an omelet the other morning. I needed to go grocery shopping. The fridge was pretty empty, and I wanted to make sure Clarissa had food to eat. I felt an overwhelming need to take care of her. I wanted to pamper her. Living with me, there was no need for her to want for anything. And she certainly shouldn't have been eating stale doughnuts at midnight.

I added grocery shopping to my mental list of things to do today. I had cleared my schedule for a week, so I didn't have any appointments. That left today and tomorrow to get Clarissa settled in. I needed to clear out my studio and get her some furniture. I wanted her to stay in my room, but I didn't want her to think I expected it because I was letting her stay here. I wanted her to have her own space. The last thing I wanted her to feel... was trapped. If she slept in my bed, it would be because she wanted to.

Clarissa emerged from the bedroom as I was putting our eggs onto the plates. She stretched her arms up over her head as she meandered into the kitchen, her nipples showing through her white tank top. She plopped down onto a bar stool at the counter. "Good morning."

"Good morning." I smiled, trying not to look at her breasts.

Obviously, I wasn't too sly. She looked down at herself. "Oh crap." Clarissa folded her arms over her chest. "I'll be right back."

She rushed off to the bedroom. "It's not like I've never seen them before," I called after her, laughing.

She returned with a black t-shirt on. "That's not the point. I can't walk around here like that, especially if we're trying to be friends."

I quirked an eyebrow up at her. "It actually seemed very friendly to me. I don't mind."

"I bet," she huffed. Miss Priss jumped up on the counter and sat right in front of Clarissa. She pulled back. "Well, hello there, kitty. I thought we had an agreement. I'll stay out of your way, and you stay out of mine." Clarissa reached out a tentative hand and tapped Miss Priss on the head like a dog.

I laughed. "She likes you. She was all curled up at your feet last night on the couch."

Clarissa scrunched up her nose. "I don't think it's like. I think she's keeping an eye on me. Making sure I understand this is her house."

I scooped Miss Priss up and set her back on the floor. "She likes you," I reaffirmed. "If she didn't, she'd be hiding under the bed." I crossed my arms over my chest. "Which leads me to something else we need to discuss."

Worry crossed her face. It was cute, and I kept her waiting a few more moments. "What'd I do?" she asked.

I held up two fingers. "Two things."

"Okaaay."

I held up one finger. "First of all, doughnuts."

She dropped her head. "Crap. I left the box on the counter, didn't I? The cat didn't get into them, did she?"

"No, she didn't," I said. "Do you know why?"

She shook her head.

"Because they were hard as a rock. Not even my cat would touch those, but you ate one anyway. I have food here. Granted, I need to go grocery shopping, but I'm sure you could have found something else to eat."

"I wasn't that hungry. It was fine," she said.

"It's not fine and if you do it again, I'll never buy you another doughnut as long as you live."

Clarissa rolled her eyes. "Okay. What's the second thing?"

I placed a plate of eggs and bacon in front her and leaned on the counter. "Why were you sleeping on the couch?"

She took a bite of her eggs and swallowed them down. "I tried the bed first."

"And?"

"It was too quiet. In New York, there was always background noise. Even in Oklahoma, there would be crickets chirping or coyotes howling." She shrugged her shoulders. "I'll get used to it."

I bet she got scared being in a new place by herself. I took her hand over the counter. "I'm sorry. I shouldn't have left you alone."

She took a bite of bacon and waved it at me. "Don't apologize. I don't want to interfere with your job."

"But it was your first night. I should have been here."

"I'm a big girl. The last thing I want you to have to do is babysit me." She finished her piece of bacon. "Do you have orange juice?"

"Yeah, but I made coffee. Do you want that instead?"

"I'm giving up coffee. OJ is better for me anyway."

"Suit yourself." I went to the fridge and pulled out the orange juice. I poured her a glass and some coffee for myself. I'd have to remember to put OJ on the grocery list.

"Thank you. What's on the plan for today?" she asked.

"I have to go downstairs for a little bit, then we'll go grocery shopping and to the furniture store. Make a list of whatever you'll need. We can go to Target too."

Clarissa cocked her head to the side. "What the hell is Target?"

"Are you serious? They don't have a Target in Oklahoma?" I asked.

She shook her head. "Not where I lived. I don't remember one in Brooklyn either."

I racked my brain to think of something to compare it to. "You know what Walmart is?"

"Of course. Everyone knows Walmart."

"It's like that, only better. We have a Walmart, but I prefer Target."

"Oh. What time do you want to leave?"

I looked at the clock on the microwave. "How about ten? That will give you time to get ready and figure out what you need."

She nodded. "Leave the dishes. I'll do them since you cooked."

"Are you sure?" It felt strange leaving the dishes unwashed.

"I've got it. Go do what you need to do."

I finished my breakfast, changed and went down to the shop. I checked our inventory and made a list of supplies to order. Next, I straightened out and cleaned the reception area. Then, I checked over the appointments for the next week. I had a late one on Tuesday.

I had a lot of high-profile clients, mostly pro athletes, but a few well-known local musicians too. They came to me for two reasons. One, I was damn good at what I did. Two, I kept their shit private. They knew whatever was said here, stayed here. I always accommodated them after hours, so there was no fanfare. They could sit back and relax without worrying about crazy fans or the media.

Tuesday, I was inking a player from the Pistons. He'd been here plenty of times and I wondered where I'd be tatting him. He didn't have much open real estate left on his body. I pulled the design I'd drawn for him from his file. It was a hawk with a serpent in its beak. The hawk's wings were spread wide, and its talons were dagger sharp. It was badass. He was going to love it. I tucked it away, as I heard a key in the front door.

"Hey, Layla. You're early."

She squinted her eyes at me. "Yes. Yes, I am." She came behind the front desk and locked her purse in the safe there.

I lifted my chin to her. "What's up?"

She planted her hands on her hips. "You tell me."

She had behaved herself last night, but I knew it wouldn't last. "What do you mean?" I asked innocently.

"Oh, for Christ's sake, don't give me those puppy dog eyes," she scolded. "Who is she?"

"Who? Rissa?" I knew damn well who Layla was referring to.

"Yes, Rissa. Who else would I be asking about?"

I needlessly shuffled some papers on the desk. "She's a friend who needed some help."

Layla shook her head back and forth, pursing her lips. "A friend?"

"Yeah."

"Well, the way you looked at her last night, I'd say she's more than a friend. I haven't seen you look at anyone like that since you had the hots for Kyla."

I crossed my arms over my chest in defiance. "I didn't have the hots for Kyla."

Layla laughed. "You're such a fucking liar. You totally did. You were in a funk for weeks after she and her boyfriend got back together."

"Husband. She's married now with twins on the way." It was true. I did have a thing for Kyla. When I met her, she was so broken, and I tried to help her, but it wasn't until she and Tyler got back together that she finally healed. He was the one her heart truly wanted. Now she designed for me and we were just good friends.

"Anyway… you look at Rissa the same way. So, what's the story?" she asked.

I resigned to the fact that Layla wasn't going to let this go. "I'm not sure. We're friends for now. If it were to turn into something else, I wouldn't be opposed." That was as much as I would give her.

A cheesy smile took over Layla's face. "So, you like her? Did you two do it yet?"

I threw my hands in the air. "What are we? Sixteen?"

"You totally did!" she squealed. Then she threw her arms around me in a tight hug. "I'm so happy for you!"

I unwrapped her from me. "Don't get too excited yet. It's not like that. She's been through a lot."

Layla held her crossed fingers up in the air. "I'm keeping my fingers crossed. You so deserve this."

I rolled my eyes at her. "Try to keep your enthusiasm at a dull roar. I don't want you to scare her off."

I heard the door to the stairwell open and Clarissa peeked her head around the corner. "Is it okay if I come down here?"

I waved her over. "Of course. You can come down here anytime you want. You don't have to stay upstairs."

"I just didn't want to bother you."

"You're not a bother," I assured her. Clarissa came around the door and approached Layla and me. She was wearing a yellow sundress that showed off her shoulders, legs and all the curves in between.

"You're in so much fucking trouble," Layla whispered to me.

"I know," I huffed out.

"So, what are you two kids doing today?" Layla asked playfully.

"Zack's going to take me grocery shopping and to the furniture store." Clarissa stared out the front window of the shop. "Maybe later I'll go exploring. I need to find a job."

"I told you, you can work here," I said.

"I know," Clarissa answered. "But I'm going to need more than that. I want to check out the bars. Maybe someone needs a bartender. I can make good money in tips slinging drinks."

Layla clapped her hand together. "I get off at six. I can show you around if you want."

Clarissa smiled warmly. "That would be great."

78

It kind of bummed me out. I wanted to be the one to show her around. But she was going to need more friends than me, so I let it go. We'd spend most of the day together. It would have to be enough. "We're going to get out of here. Chase will be in at eleven. Call if you need anything."

"Are you kidding? This place practically runs itself," Layla said, shooing us away. "Get out of here."

Clarissa and I walked out the back door to the garage. I pressed in the code and the garage door opened. "I didn't even see this last night."

"I had it built when I bought Betsy."

"Betsy?"

"Betsy," I said motioning to my Chevelle.

"Oh…she has a name?"

"Yes. All worthy cars should have a proper name." I opened the door for Clarissa, and she slid inside.

Once we arrived at the grocery store, I grabbed a cart for us. Clarissa got her own cart. "What are you doing?" I asked.

"Ummm, getting a cart."

"We don't need two," I said.

"Yes, we do. I'm paying for my own groceries."

"Why? I don't mind. You're staying with me, so it's part of you being my guest."

"Please, Zack. This is step one of me not taking advantage. I can feed myself," she insisted.

I wasn't going to fight with her in the grocery store, but we would be discussing this later. "Fine," I said.

We walked through the store together, and my cart was quickly filling up. Clarissa was very selective about what she chose, inspecting labels and prices. By the time we got to the check-out, my cart was full and hers was pitifully almost empty. I internally cringed. I knew what she was doing. Money was tight for her, but I wouldn't let her starve.

I put my items on the conveyer belt and paid with my Amex card. When it was Clarissa's turn, she carefully counted out her cash for the cashier. Her total was less than forty dollars.

When we got back in the car, I turned to her. "Is this the way it's going to be?" I couldn't keep the irritation out of my voice.

79

"What do you mean?" she asked, clearly taken aback.

"Why won't you let me help you? I can afford it. This shopping trip was ridiculous. You're being ridiculous," I said harshly.

Her eyes welled with tears. "Wow," she said softly. "I'm sorry the poor girl from Oklahoma doesn't meet the standards of the rich boy from New York. Maybe I should just buy a bus ticket home."

Fuck! I didn't want her to feel less of a person just because she didn't have the same means I had. I tried to never pass judgement on others. I was fortunate, and I knew it. "And where is home, Clarissa?" I softened my tone.

"I don't know!" she yelled. "I'm trying to figure that out. I'm trying to do the right thing, by not taking advantage of you. You're already putting a roof over my head. I want to pay my own way."

I sighed. "Clarissa, be honest with me. How much money did you come here with?" I needed to know what I was dealing with and why she was being so unreasonable.

Clarissa looked out the window. "I don't want to tell you. It's embarrassing."

I gently took her by the chin, so she had to face me. "Tell me."

She closed her eyes and refused to look at me. "Three hundred dollars. It was my tip money from the few nights before Wes died. Everything else was in the bank." Tears rolled down the sides of her face.

Shit. No wonder she was so damn frugal. She was dirt poor and scared to death. I wrapped her in a hug, and she buried her head in my chest. "It's okay, sweetheart. You're going to be okay," I said softly.

"I don't know how to do this," she admitted. "It's never been this bad before."

"You just got here. Give it some time. You're putting way too much pressure on yourself. Will you please let me help you?"

She snuffed back her tears. "Okay. I'll try."

I pushed her hair over her shoulder. "No more stale doughnuts. No more five-dollar salads. If I want to take you out, I will. If I want to spend money on you, I will. You're not taking advantage. It's my choice."

She pointed her finger at me. "You can't go overboard."

"Again, my choice. I didn't bring you home with me for you to struggle. I want you to be happy here," I told her.

"I think I could be," she said. "You're here."

Chapter 12
Rissa

I was so embarrassed. I never wanted Zack to know how bad it was. I didn't want to depend on him, but I didn't have a choice.

Part of this was my own stupidity. When Wes and I had gotten engaged, I started depositing my checks into his account. At the time, it made sense. He paid all the bills, and my checks went to pay my share.

My daddy taught me better than that. I should have kept my money separate. I didn't expect Wes to die and Malcolm to seize the account.

I should have known better. I was mad at myself for being so naïve and trusting.

It was why I was having a hard time letting Zack help me. Nothing in life was free. Everything came at a cost. I just didn't know what it would cost me this time. I felt like the stakes were higher. I was going to build up a debt there was no way I could pay back.

One day at a time, I told myself. Zack was right. I was putting a lot of pressure on myself, but I knew a day would come when he would walk away, and I had to be prepared. It was inevitable. He wouldn't stay with me when he found out what I was hiding.

I had my reasons. Number one being Malcolm. That man scared the shit out of me. He was the reason why I left when Zack offered me a way out. Staying in New York would have been a huge mistake. If nothing else, moving to Michigan bought me time. Zack hating his father, worked in my favor. And I would take full advantage of that fact.

After Zack and I unpacked our groceries, he took me to lunch and then the furniture store. I didn't fight with him when he picked out a bed and dresser that was way more than I needed. I let him take control and pay with his fancy credit card.

However, when we went to Target, I paid for my own sheets and comforter. It was the least I could do. And one less debt I would owe. I was keeping a running total, so I could pay Zack back for every dime he lent me.

The kindness he showed me was something I would never be able to repay. Without him I would be in deep trouble.

♫♪♫♪

Layla was getting off at six and she had promised to show me around. The first thing I wanted to see was the bars. I needed a job.

I took my makeup bag to the bathroom and laid the contents out on the counter. I let out a deep breath because Zack had never seen me dolled up for work. He'd only seen the subtle side of me which was on display at the funeral.

I made my eyes dark and smoky then lined them with black. I painted my lips a deep burgundy. Big silver hoops adorned my ears, complimenting my hair that was piled on top of my head. I looked older than my twenty-one years.

I crept to my room and pulled out a tight pair of jeans and a sparkly black tank top that showed off just enough cleavage. Sky-high heels completed my outfit. I took a look at myself in the mirror. Gone was the timid girl from Oklahoma. In her place stood a worldly woman from New York.

I grabbed my purse and headed down the stairs where Layla was waiting. I walked to the front of the building, passing Zack on the way.

"Clarissa?" he called out.

I turned on my heels in his direction. "Hey, Zack."

He blinked his eyes a couple of times. "You look…wow." He rubbed his hand over his scruffy chin. "I thought you were just checking the town out."

I looked down at myself and then back at him. "You don't think I look nice?"

"Ummm… nice isn't exactly the word I would use. Sexy?" He scanned me from head to toe. "Yeah. Definitely sexy. Are you going looking for….?"

I couldn't help but laugh. "A job, Zack. I'm looking for a job. No one is going to hire me as a bartender if I look like I just stepped off the bus from Oklahoma." I kissed him on the cheek. "I'm here with you. I'm not looking for anyone else. Once I secure a job, I'll scrub all this off if you don't like it."

Zack eyed me again. "I didn't say I didn't like it. I like it a lot. As a matter of fact, I think I love it. I'm just afraid everyone else is going to like it too."

I winked at him. "I'm not interested in everyone else. I'm only interested in you and making decent tips. Do you want to come with us?" I offered. I kind of liked this jealous side of Zack.

"No," he shook his head. "I have things to do here. You girls go and have fun."

Layla approached us with her purse over her shoulder. "You look hot," she said to me. Zack visibly cringed. "You ready to go?"

I stood tall. "Absolutely. Let's go find me a job."

We walked toward the front door when a male voice stopped us. "Whoa! Hold up. Layla, are you going to introduce me to your friend?"

We turned toward the voice. It belonged to a guy covered in tattoos with shaggy, dark-blond hair. He looked a little unkempt in his baggy jeans and black tank top.

Layla rolled her eyes. "Chase, meet Rissa. Rissa, this is Chase."

He held his hands up. "Wait, you're Rissa? The girl who came home with Zack?" He let out a long whistle.

I thrust my hand out. "That's me. It's nice to meet you."

He took my hand and kissed the back of it. "Nice to meet you too. Very nice. You're not at all what I was expecting."

I pulled my hand back as Zack approached. "And just what were you expecting?" he asked.

"I...ummm," Chase stuttered.

"You might want to think about the fact that I sign your paychecks before you answer," Zack threatened.

"Nothing. Nothing at all. You girls have fun," he said.

I waved at Zack over my shoulder. "See ya later." Layla and I walked out of the shop and onto the sidewalk.

She hooked her arm with mine. "You're going to kill him, you know that?"

I feigned innocence. "I don't know what you're talking about."

"Oh, you're good. But you two don't fool me a bit. He's got it bad for you. And you, missy... you're just as smitten as him," she said.

"It's not like that with us," I insisted. "We're friends. He's helping me out. That's all."

Layla quirked up one side of her mouth. "Maybe for now. But I think there's more to it."

"So, tell me more about Zack. How long have you known him?" I asked, trying to take the focus off my relationship with him.

"I started working for Zack about four years ago. He's a great boss. He's totally devoted to his job. It doesn't leave room for much else," she said.

"No girlfriends?" I asked.

She shook her head. "Nope. I thought it might happen once, but it never panned out."

"Why do you think that is?" Curiosity was getting the best of me.

"I'm not sure. He's good-looking, sweet, and generous. I think he's been burned, has trust issues. My advice... don't lie to him. He can look past just about everything but lying," Layla said.

"I'll remember that." It was great advice, but it was too late for that. I'd already lied to him. Technically, I'd omitted the truth, but it was all the same.

We had walked about a half block down from Forever Inked. Layla stopped in front of a bar called The Locker. "If you want a job as a bartender, this is your place. Let's go in. I know the owner."

I smoothed down the front of my top. "Okay. Let's go."

Layla opened the door for me, and we walked up to the bar. "Hey, Lou!" she called out.

"What's up, Layla? Early for you to be out," Lou said. He looked gruff, with graying hair and a goatee.

"I'm not drinking. Yet," she smirked. "You fill Kari's position?"

"Naw, I'm still one bartender short. Why? You know somebody?" he asked.

"Yep. Lou, meet Rissa. She just moved here from New York," Layla introduced me.

I stuck my hand out over the bar and mustered up my courage. "Nice to meet you, Lou."

He shook my hand. "So, Rissa? Do you have any bartending experience?"

"Three years in Brooklyn. I worked at a place called The Hot Spot," I told him.

"Brooklyn, huh? The ball game is just about to end, and this place will be crazy in about fifteen minutes. Want to do a trial run?"

"Ball game?" I asked.

"Yeah," Layla answered. "There's a minor league stadium down the street."

"Wow. I've got to check out this town." Then I turned to Lou. "I'm your girl. Just give me a quick rundown."

Lou nodded his head and showed me around the bar. "Think you can handle this?" he asked.

"I've got it." Lou wasn't kidding. Within minutes people started pouring through the doors. Pulling beer and mixing drinks was easy, the only thing I had to ask about was prices. I had a great memory though and soon I was working flawlessly next to Lou. Courtesy of some harmless flirting, my tips were piling up. Before I knew it, it was almost midnight. The bar had been busy for a Sunday but was starting to empty out as people made their way home to start the work week.

Lou clapped me on the shoulder. "I didn't expect you to stay this long, but I'm glad you did. We were slammed tonight. You want a job, you've got one here," he offered.

I bounced on my toes. "Thank you. When can I start?"

Lou laughed. "You already have." He handed me a fistful of cash, "Here's your tips for the night. Be here at five tomorrow?"

"Absolutely. Thanks again!" I left the bar and stood outside on the sidewalk. It was fairly empty on the street. I looked left and right, unsure which way to go. I didn't have to think for long, because Zack stood leaning against the lamppost just outside the door.

"Hey," I said. "What are you doing here?"

He smiled at me, "Layla called. She said you got a job. Congratulations."

"Yeah, I did. Made good tips too. Lou wants me to come back tomorrow at five."

Zack slung his arm over my shoulder, "I'm proud of you." He kissed me on the forehead. "I came to walk you home."

I slipped off my shoes, taking the pressure off my aching feet. "You didn't have to do that. I would have found my way."

"Not a chance, sweetheart. You're looking way too pretty to be walking out here after dark all alone." He grabbed my hand and swung it between us, as we walked back toward Forever Inked. "How was your first night?"

"Fantastic. I thought Lou was just trying me out, but we got so busy that I ended up staying. I should have called. I'm sorry," I apologized.

"No need. I knew where you were." Zack reached in his pocket. "I got these made for you. One opens the front and back doors. The other opens the apartment and the roof access. I want you to come and go as you please." He handed me two brass keys. "I'm still going to walk you home at night, but just in case."

I leaned up and kissed him on the cheek. "How did you get so sweet?" I pocketed the keys. "I didn't get a chance to really walk around down here. Maybe tomorrow morning I'll do that. If it's okay?"

"Tomorrow's my last official day off. I can show you around," Zack offered.

"Aren't you the boss? Can't you take off any day you want?"

Zack laughed. "I guess in theory I could. I just usually don't. That's how I've made my business successful. My clients expect me to be there, so I usually am."

"I think you should take some time for yourself once in a while."

"Says the girl who got a job on her first official day here."

"That's different. I don't have a choice. I need to get a car and find an apartment. Those things aren't going to happen by magic," I reasoned.

Zack frowned. "There's no hurry, Clarissa. You can stay with me as long as it takes. Or longer. I like having you here."

I couldn't help but smile. "So noted. I do want to see one thing tonight. Can I see the rooftop access? I bet it's peaceful up there."

"It is," Zack confirmed.

We reached the front of his shop, and he opened the door for me. Then he reset the alarm. "If you come in here at night alone, I want you to use the front door. You don't need to be out back alone. I've got it lit up, but still."

"You do realize I lived in Brooklyn? I bet this place is ten times safer. It's kind of small townish," I said.

"That's true, but there's no need to take any chances. Bad shit can happen anywhere."

"I'll use the front door," I assured him.

We made our way toward the stairs. We walked up one flight and then continued to the roof. Zack undid the deadbolt, and I walked out onto the roof. I could see the lights from the stadium down the street and the bars that lined the downtown area. I spun in a circle with my arms spread wide and stared up at the stars. "I love this!"

Zack smiled at me. "You can come up here anytime you want. You look so happy."

I stopped spinning. "I am. I really, really am!" I grabbed ahold of Zack's hands. "Is it wrong to feel so happy?"

"No, sweetheart. You deserve happy. I want to show you what I did while you were gone. Come inside."

We went back to the apartment and Zack led me to the spare bedroom. It was cleared out of all his art supplies. "What happened to all your stuff?" I asked.

"I had Chase help me move it down to one of the studios in the shop. I also got cable installed in here and in my room." He pointed to the flat screen TV that now hung on the wall. "No more falling asleep on the couch because it's too quiet. Your furniture will be here tomorrow. That doesn't mean you can't sleep in my bed, but I want you to have your own space."

Zack was too sweet for his own good. Everything he had done for me, was more than I ever expected. "I think you're too good to be true. What is this between us Zack? What's happening?"

"I don't know, but I don't want to question it, Clarissa. Seeing you happy, makes me happy. It's enough for now."

I nodded my acceptance of his words. I wanted to be with Zack, but it was too soon. I felt my emotions jumbling together. I loved Wes, and now I was falling for his brother. I felt like I was betraying Wes. It wasn't fair to either of them. "I'm going to take a shower and then I'll be to bed shortly." I needed to put some distance between us because if I didn't, I wasn't sure what would happen.

I gathered my shower things and headed to the bathroom. "Clarissa?"

"Yeah?"

"You can leave your stuff in the bathroom. You're not a guest. You live here. I cleared out the left side of the vanity. It's all yours."

I looked at him from under my lashes. "Thank you." Then I went to the bathroom and shut the door behind me. I was so confused. Zack was damn near perfect. Was I replacing my memory of Wes with Zack? They looked so much alike, yet they were so different. I was afraid I was filling the hole in my chest with whatever would soothe the pain. And right now… that was Zack.

Chapter 13
Zack

I was falling hard for Clarissa. It made me crazy knowing she was behind the bar all night. I'm sure the guys were all over her. When she left to find a job today, I had to do a double-take. I had never seen her look so beautiful. She was gorgeous in her robe with her hair a mess and no makeup but seeing her dolled up for work... it was on a whole other level.

I wasn't sure hanging out with Layla was a good move, but I trusted Layla. She had my back. And damn if she couldn't see through all my bullshit. Layla was right, I was a mess when Kyla had gotten back together with Tyler. I thought she could have been the one, but she only saw me as a friend, and I never pushed it any further. I hadn't been with anyone serious in a long time. Gina was my only constant. It wasn't about anything but sex with us, and I liked it that way. Zero complications.

Clarissa had "complications" written all over her, but I didn't care. I had only put my heart on the line once in the last five years and that had ended badly. When I moved here five years ago, I started seeing Megan. I thought we had something good, until I found out she was seeing her ex-boyfriend behind my back. She'd gotten pregnant and tried to say it was mine. It wasn't. I was just a payday to her.

Since then, I'd been cautious. Maybe the name Kincaid didn't hold as much weight here, but it wasn't a secret that I had money. Clarissa knew I had money, but so far, she had done everything possible to ignore that fact. She hadn't once expected anything from me.

I heard the shower turn off as I slipped into bed. She knocked lightly on the door. "Can I come in?"

"You don't have to ask," I told her.

She peeked her head in. "I'm trying to respect your privacy." Clarissa was dressed in shorts and a bright pink tank. She tentatively entered my room and pulled back the sheets on her side of the bed. "Zack? Can I ask you a question?"

"Sure."

"What's the story with you and your dad? Why do you hate him?" she asked.

I wasn't prepared for that question. It wasn't a simple answer. "We don't see things the same way. I was a disappointment to him. He wanted me to take over Kincaid Industries. He was pissed when I dropped out of Yale." It was as simple of an answer as I could provide. It was the root of our problem, but the hate went much deeper than that.

Her eyes got huge. "You went to Yale?"

"Yeah. One year and then I dropped out to join the Marines."

"But you're super smart, right? I mean, you have to be smart to go to Yale," she said.

"I don't know. I always got good grades in school, but it wasn't for me."

"I'm not that smart, Zack," she said as she dropped her head. "I know how to survive, but that's it. I was raised in a hick town. I didn't even graduate high school. I needed to work, and school became a second priority. Your dad was right about me. I'll never be anything more than what I was born into. Why would you want to be with someone like me?"

I saw a tear fall down her cheek and wiped it away with my thumb. "Where you came from, doesn't define you. You're a strong woman. Why wouldn't I want to be with you?"

"Because you could do so much better."

"Actually," I said. "I think you're wrong about that. I think you're pretty damn smart. I don't care about your past. All I care about is what I see in front of me. And I like what I see. I'm not saying we have to rush anything, but give this a chance, Clarissa."

"I will," she said. "Friends first, right?"

"Friends can cuddle," I told her.

Clarissa wiggled her body next to mine and snuggled in close. "Good night, Zack."

"Good night, sweetheart." I kissed the top of her head.

She lifted her head from my chest and pressed her lips to mine. She smelled like strawberry shampoo and tasted like mint toothpaste. She kissed me slowly and passionately. My lips moved with hers, as we devoured each other. I poked my tongue out and she opened for me. Our tongues twisted together tentatively. I wanted to fuck her so bad. I cupped her ass in my palm and squeezed.

She pulled back and rested her head against my chest again. "I'm sorry," she whispered. "I shouldn't have done that."

"Don't be," I whispered back.

♫♪♫♪

When I woke in the morning my bed was empty, but I could smell breakfast cooking. I rolled out of bed and followed my nose to the kitchen. Clarissa stood at the counter in her shorts and tank, her ass wiggling to the music she had playing on her phone while she flipped the pancakes on the gridle. I stood at the counter smiling, as I watched her dance while she cooked.

"Good morning."

Clarissa startled and grabbed at her chest. "Oh, God! You scared the bejeebers out of me."

I laughed at her dramatics. "Sorry. Something smells good."

"It's just pancakes and coffee." She took a mug down from the cupboard and filled it. She slid the mug across the counter to me. It had been a long time since someone made me coffee.

"Thanks," I said, taking a sip.

"I fed Miss Priss too, but she seems way more interested in pancakes than cat food." Priss sat on the far side of the counter and watched Clarissa from afar.

"Did you try petting her?" I asked.

"I did. Watch. She just sits there and stares at me." Clarissa stretched over and tapped her on the head. "Good kitty."

I covered my mouth with my hand to hide my laughter. "That's not how you pet a cat. You look scared to death. No wonder she's standoffish."

92

Clarissa plated the cooked pancakes and poured more onto the gridle. "I told you cats don't like me."

I walked around the counter and picked Priss up. I rubbed the long fur on her back. "Hold your arms out," I said.

"Nuh-uh. She has claws and teeth. I like her just fine over there," she insisted.

"Quit being a baby," I teased her. "She doesn't have any claws and she's never bitten anyone. Now hold your arms out."

"Fine," Clarissa huffed. She held her arms out like I was going to put a sack of potatoes in them.

I chuckled again. She was ridiculously cute. I carefully set Miss Priss in her arms and wrapped them around my cat's furry body. "Now rub her back."

Clarissa ran her hand up and down Miss Priss's back and soon her tail was moving like crazy. "She likes that," I encouraged. Clarissa kept rubbing and Priss stretched her neck up to rub on Clarissa's chin. Soon soft purring filled the silence.

"Take her, please," Clarissa begged. I reached over and took my cat from her arms. "She was kind of close to my face."

I set Priss on the floor. "It was progress. You two will be friends in no time."

Clarissa returned her attention to the stove. "Maybe." Placing the last of the pancakes on the plate, she moved to the fridge in search of butter and syrup. She put everything on the counter between us, along with plates and silverware.

I dug into my pancakes, and they were delicious. "There's something different about these," I said pointing to the plate with my fork. "They're really good."

"It was my mama's secret recipe." She smiled. "My mama always added a bit of cinnamon to the batter. She said it was because her baby girl was made of sugar and spice and everything nice." Clarissa shrugged her shoulders sadly, "Now when I make pancakes, I always add cinnamon too. It's something I'll pass on to my daughter one day."

"I'm sorry. I didn't mean to make you sad."

She bit her lip. "You didn't. It's a good memory. I have a lot of good memories. My mama taught me how to cook and how to play the piano. She was a great mom."

"And your dad?" I asked.

"My daddy was the best. He taught me how to drive." She wiggled her eyebrows up and down. I had to laugh at remembering how nervous I was to let her drive my Chevelle, but she had proved me wrong in seconds. "My daddy also taught me how to play the guitar. The two of us would sit on the back porch for hours, strumming our guitars and singing at the top of our lungs."

"I've heard you play the piano, but I haven't really heard you play the guitar. Only that first night when we were messing around. Would you play for me sometime?" I asked. I wanted to know everything there was to know about Clarissa Lynne Black. Music was a big part of her life, so I would start there.

Her cheeks flushed. "Maybe later. Right now, I want you to finish your breakfast. Then, you promised to show me around."

She was embarrassed, and it was cute. "Fair enough. Do you mind if I sneak in a workout first?"

"Not at all. I don't want you to change your routine for me. I have plenty to do. I need to wash my sheets and comforter. Is there a laundromat close to here?" she asked.

It rubbed me the wrong way, because her wanting to wash her new sheets meant that she probably wouldn't be sleeping in my bed. I brushed it off and led her to the utility room. "Waalah! We have a washer and dryer here. Help yourself."

"This is awesome. Thank you." She faced me with her hands on her hips, "Now run along and do what you have to do. I'll clean up and be ready when you are."

"You cooked. I should clean up," I said,

"Nonsense. Go. I got this," she insisted.

I held up my hands in surrender. "Okay, okay. I'll be about an hour or so and then I'll need to shower."

Clarissa pointed at me. "Go!"

I headed toward my bedroom and changed for my workout, then headed to the basement. I had it set up with a weight bench, heavy bag, and a treadmill. It had been a while since I worked out. With my trip to New York, I had let it go. I cranked up the music and got to work. I had more of an incentive since Clarissa had moved in. I wanted her to find me irresistible. I wasn't blind to how she looked at me and I wanted to give her a reason to continue looking.

I spent more time working out than anticipated. I pushed myself hard, and it felt good. I went back upstairs to shower. Clarissa was locked in her room, and I wondered what she was doing. All the towels from the bathroom were freshly washed and hung back on the hooks. The bathroom was wiped down and cleaned. She had been busy.

While taking my shower, I couldn't help but think about her. Again, I took matters into my own hands. It was becoming a pattern I was finding hard to break. I couldn't stop thinking about her soft skin and the kisses we had shared. I needed to pull it together and fast.

After my shower, Clarissa and I headed out. I showed her everything that was worth seeing in the historic district. We had a great lunch together and before I knew it, it was time for her to get ready for work.

She dolled herself up and was out the door. I hated watching her leave like that. It was like she was two different people. Natural and carefree during the day and smoking hot at night. I knew she was trying to make money and I tried not to let it bother me. But it did. I didn't want other men looking at her. I knew what they would be thinking, and it killed me.

If anyone was going to get biblical with Clarissa, it would be me. I was trying to adhere to our "friends first" policy, but I couldn't deny that I wanted more with her. Everything about Clarissa Lynne was totally addicting.

♫♪♫♪

Clarissa's furniture arrived shortly after she left for work. The delivery guys set everything up in her new room. She didn't know I ordered the complete bedroom set, not just the bed and dresser. She was going to be pissed when she got home, but I didn't care. I wanted her to have what she needed.

Growing up with a sister, I knew what girls liked. She had chosen a light green comforter and sheets. I ran up to Target and got to work buying accessories for her room. I picked out a fancy curtain rod and curtains to match her bedspread. I found a lamp I thought she would like, a couple of throw pillows and a music inspired wall hanging.

I took everything home and hung the curtains over the plain blinds that covered the window. I attached the music notes to the wall. Then I made her bed with the freshly washed sheets and plugged in her lamp. Lastly, I stood her guitar up in the corner next to the floor length mirror.

When I was finished, I looked at her new room. There were boxes stacked in the corner, but it looked comfy and welcoming. I hoped Clarissa would like it. I hoped she would want to stay. She was going to say it was too much. It wasn't.

I didn't give two shits about the money. I had plenty. I just wanted her to be happy. I wanted her to be happy here.

With me.

I went down to the shop and found Layla. "You busy?" I asked her.

She smiled at me. "My next appointment isn't for twenty minutes. What's up?"

I stuffed my hands in my pockets. "I need your opinion. Can you come look at something for me?"

She narrowed her eyes. "Sure."

I led her up to my apartment and we stood outside Clarissa's shut door. I took a deep breath and opened the door. "What do you think?"

Layla stepped inside. "Wow. What happened to all your art stuff?"

"I moved it downstairs. Do you think she'll like it?"

Layla moved through the room inspecting everything. "I think she's going to love it. You did all this for Rissa?"

I nodded. "Yeah. Is it too much?"

Layla shook her head. "No. It's perfect. So… does this mean you're not sleeping together?"

"Not like that. We've been sharing the same bed, but that's it. I wanted her to have her own space."

"I love you, Zack. You've been a great boss and friend. I just hope you're not setting yourself up for heartbreak. I worry about you," she said.

"I know, but I have a good feeling about this. It just feels right," I told her.

"You deserve this. I hope you're right. She'll love it. I mean, how could she not? No one else would do this for her."

"Thanks, Layla. Keep your fingers crossed for me," I said.

Layla winked at me. "Been crossed since the day I met her."

Layla left, and I knew I had one more thing I needed to do.

I called Gina.

She answered on the second ring. "Hey, Zack. You're back. You want to get together?"

"Hey, Gina. I'd love to see you, but I met somebody," I told her.

"No way! I thought you and I would be single together forever. Who is she?" Gina asked.

"Someone from New York. She moved back here with me. I'm not sure what it is yet, but I want to give it a chance. Are you mad?"

"Zack, you and I have always been what we are. The goal was always for us to find someone lasting. I'm not mad, but I will miss you. I won't lie about that."

I laughed. "I'll miss you too, but I really want to give this a chance. Still friends?"

"Of course," she said nonchalantly. "If it doesn't work out, give me a call. You're going to be hard to replace. No one gives me an O like you."

"Well, I aim to please."

"And please, you do, darling. Keep me updated."

"Will do, Gina. I love ya, girl," I said. And I meant it. Gina was one of a kind, but we were never meant to be more than fuck buddies.

"Love you too, Zack. Good luck."

We hung up and it felt good that I had cut ties with Gina. We would always be friends and I'm sure I would see her from time to time. It was inevitable. But we had always wanted more for each other than a meaningless relationship.

♫♪♫♪

I keep busy doing paperwork and what not until Clarissa got off work, then I walked down to The Locker. I got there a little early and watched her work behind the bar. She effortlessly filled orders with a smile. This was her comfort zone. She shined, and I could see why Lou had hired her so fast. She was a ray of sunshine behind the bar.

When she was finished for the night, I made my presence known. "You ready to head home, sweetheart?" I asked.

She looked at Lou questioningly.

"Go on. Get out of here. I'll see you on Wednesday."

"Thanks, Lou. I'll see you then," she answered. Clarissa grabbed her purse from behind the bar and we walked out together.

"Good night?" I asked.

"Everyone has been so nice. Yes, it was a good night," she said.

I grabbed her hand as we walked back toward Forever Inked. "I've got a surprise for you and I know you're going to get mad, but just go with it. Okay?"

She scowled at me. "What did you do?"

"Nothing you don't deserve," I said.

"Hmmm. Now, I'm curious. Our opinions on that vary drastically."

I unlocked the front door and led her upstairs. "Don't be mad."

"Okaaay."

Then I led her to her room and opened the door. Her hand came up to cover her mouth. "Oh. My. God," she whispered.

"Are you mad?" I asked.

"It's beautiful, Zack. I don't deserve this. It's... I have no words." Clarissa walked in and ran her hands over the freshly made bed, then checked out everything else. "You did this for me?"

"Yes. I want you to be happy here," I answered.

"You're making it hard for me to not be happy. Thank you. I never expected this."

"You are so very welcome."

Clarissa crinkled up her nose. "Does this mean I have to sleep alone now?"

"Not in the least. That is entirely up to you. I wanted you to have a choice. I'm fine with whatever you choose," I said honestly. I hoped she would choose to still sleep in my bed, but I didn't want to sway her one way or the other.

She walked over to her guitar and picked it up. "Do you still want to hear me play?"

"More than anything."

She carried her guitar to the front room and sat on the couch cross-legged. "I'm not used to playing for an audience of one. Do you mind turning the lights down?"

"Whatever you want." I was just happy that she was going to play for me at all. I dimmed the lights and sat on the floor in front of her.

Clarissa strummed a few notes and then started into a song. I didn't know this song, but from the lyrics, I surmised it was called "I'm Not an Angel". Her beautiful voice filled the room. The words she sang were filled with emotion. She had the voice of an angel, even if she thought she wasn't one. The lyrics hit me like a freight train. There was an underlying message in the words that flowed from her. Was it a warning? She didn't scare me, but I think she was trying to.

I had no illusions of who she might be. She was trying to warn me off. I was sure of it. It wasn't going to work. I didn't scare that easily.

When she finally finished, I asked her, "Who sings that?"

"Halestorm."

"You have a beautiful voice and you're super talented. But you know what?"

"What?"

"You don't scare me. Not one little bit. Was that the point of that song?" I asked.

Clarissa shook her head in resignation. "You don't know me, Zack. I'm not a good person. I'm not who you think I am."

I took the guitar from her hands. "Why don't you let me be the judge of that. I can handle you. There's nothing you could tell me that I couldn't handle. I'm not afraid of this."

She closed her eyes and swallowed down the lump in her throat. "I'm not so sure that's true."

I took ahold of her hand. "Then tell me. Tell me what's holding you back from trying to make this work."

99

"I can't. I'm not ready. You have me built up to be something I'm not. I'm not ready for you to look at me differently."

I didn't know what she was hiding, but whatever it was, it was big. An anchor she was allowing to hold her down. I didn't give a shit about her past. All I cared about was what our future could be. If she would just let us have a chance... "I'll wait for you. I'm not giving up without a fight."

"I don't want to disappoint you," she said honestly.

"I'm here. When you're ready. Until then, there's no pressure. We can continue to build our friendship. I'm okay with that for now. And if you want to kiss me in between, I'm fine with that too." I smirked at her.

"How did I get so lucky to find you?" she asked.

"It wasn't luck," I insisted. "It was fate. The last thing I ever expected to be doing last week, was attending my brother's funeral. Finding you outside sitting on a bench was our destiny. I would have never gotten to know you had it not been for that moment. My father being a prick, only helped me to get to know you better. I hate him. But if it weren't for him being such an asshole, I would have never driven you home that night. Everything happens for a reason. I can't help but think that Wes's death had a bigger purpose. Maybe that purpose was you and me." I laid it all out for her. I bared my soul and hoped she was listening.

Clarissa rubbed her lips together nervously. "I'm not over him," she admitted. "We were together for two years. I can't help but think I'm betraying his memory. I don't want to forget Wes."

"You don't have to forget him. I wouldn't expect you to. But don't you think he would want you to be happy? He died. You didn't."

A tear escaped her eye. "I want to be happy. I just need you to be patient with me."

I pulled her from the couch and into my lap. I wrapped my arms around her. "I'm a very patient man. Especially when it's worth waiting for." I rocked her in my arms. "You're worth waiting for."

We went to bed, and I held her close. She held onto me like I was going to disappear. I wasn't. There wasn't a chance in hell that I was going anywhere.

Chapter 14
Rissa

I tried to scare Zack off, but he could see right through me. I didn't want him to give up on me, but it would be easier if he did. I knew getting attached to him was a bad idea. It was a horrible idea. Eventually my world was going to come crashing down around me.

But until that time came, I was going to bank as much money as possible. I started working for Zack, running the front desk. I thought he had created the job especially for me, but I was really busy scheduling appointments and dealing with clients. It let Zack get back to doing what he did best, being an artist.

We settled into an easy routine. I worked for Zack during the day and worked at the bar at night. I was making good money. Every night, I took my tips and stuffed them into the Mason jar my dad left me. I hid the jar in the bottom of my dresser.

I don't know why I felt the need to hide my money, but I did. Maybe I didn't trust Zack completely. I should have, but I didn't. All I could remember was what happened the last time I trusted someone else with my finances. I had ended up broke and alone. I wouldn't let that happen to me again. I couldn't. This time I would be smarter. Stronger.

I didn't just keep money in that Mason jar. Sitting at the bottom of it was my engagement ring from Wes, along with the diamond earrings and necklace he had bought me. I wasn't ready to get rid of them, but if I needed to, I would. They had to be worth a pretty penny. When the time came that I needed money, I wouldn't hesitate to pawn them.

Next to the Mason jar, I kept a notebook. In it I logged every dime that Zack spent on me. There was line after line of debt I owed. Every so often, I would run a subtotal and cringe at the numbers I saw. I owed him so much; rent, utilities, lunches, dinners, and all the little things most people didn't give a second thought to.

I scheduled another appointment into the book and closed it. I was supposed to work late for Zack tonight, since it was my night off from the bar. I looked out the front window and watched the people walking by on the sidewalk. I wished I had time to enjoy what this town had to offer, but so far all I had done was work. It was a means to an end. Living in New York wouldn't have been any different, except that I would be living in a shitty apartment. Alone.

Zack snuck up behind me and rubbed my shoulders. "Want to get out of here for a while?"

I smiled up at him. "How did you know?"

"Because you haven't had any fun since you've been here. I think we're due for some fun."

"What did you have in mind?" I asked.

"You'll see. Go throw some jeans on and your boots." I gave him a questioning look and he swatted my ass. "Go on. I'll wait by the back door for you."

"So bossy," I teased. I didn't know what he had planned, but I didn't really care. I needed to get out. I ran up to the apartment and changed my clothes, then met Zack by the back door.

He was waiting for me at the bottom of the stairs. He held out a leather jacket for me, "Try this on," he said. I quirked an eyebrow at him but turned my back and let him slip it on over my arms.

I ran my hands down the front of it. The black leather smelled of him and fit me perfectly. I turned around and Zack was smiling. "That looks good on you."

Zack slipped on his own jacket then led me by the hand, out the back door. We walked over to the garage, and he opened the door. "Betsy or Harley?" he asked.

I looked between the two. It was a tough choice, but I had been dying to get on the back of his bike. "Harley," I said without hesitation.

"I figured that was what you would choose. Have you ever ridden on the back of a motorcycle?" he asked.

"A few times," I admitted.

Zack grabbed two helmets off the shelf and tossed one to me. I was so excited to get on his bike. I pulled the helmet over my head and fastened the strap under my chin. It was a little loose and Zack tightened it up for me. "Get on," he ordered.

I climbed on the back of his bike without a second thought. "Where are we going?" I asked.

"It's a surprise," he answered. Zack climbed on in front of me and I grabbed onto the back of the seat. He started the engine and eased us out of the garage. He looked over his shoulder at me with a smirk. "You should wrap your arms around me."

We cruised out of town and onto the main highway that ran through the bustling suburban area. We passed the Target we went to my first day here and then the furniture store. We crossed over some railroad tracks and Zack took a left. Within ten minutes the scenery changed drastically. Gone were the busy roads, department stores and restaurants. In their place was a two-lane road surrounded by open fields with an occasional farmhouse. Not farmhouses like we had in Oklahoma, these were much fancier, but they were set back on large expanses of land. We rolled through a small town with a corner bar and café. A big banner hung across the intersection, reading *Welcome to Armada.* It reminded me of home.

Zack drove a little further and I saw the lights of a Ferris wheel high in the sky. I hadn't been to a carnival since I was a teenager. Zack pulled through a gate and parked in a huge field amongst dozens of cars. "We're going to a carnival?" I asked.

He pulled off my helmet then removed his own. "Oh, it's much more than a carnival, I assure you. I think you're going to like it."

"I haven't been to a carnival in years. I used to go all the time when I was a kid. I haven't thought about that in forever," I said, climbing off the motorcycle.

"I figured if you haven't been back to Oklahoma in three years, you might be missing it. This was the closest thing I could think of besides flying you there."

I stretched up and kissed Zack on the cheek. "Thank you."

He laughed. "Don't thank me yet, you haven't even seen it."

"It doesn't matter. The fact that you brought me here is enough." I held out my hand for him to take and he didn't hesitate to twine his fingers with mine. "So, what did you mean by this is more than a carnival?"

Zack winked at me. "You'll see." He paid our admission and led me toward a long row of barns.

"They have animals here?" I asked excitedly.

"Uh- huh."

I pulled his hand a little harder, rushing him forward to the first barn. In Oklahoma, we had a small farm. Nothing huge. The animals were a way for us to supplement our income. Most of them ended up on the dinner table. When my mamma got sick, my daddy sold them all. No one had time to take care of the animals and we needed the money.

"Slow down," Zack chuckled. "They're not going anywhere."

I could hear the grunting before we entered the first barn. Inside were rows and rows of corralled pigs. I dropped Zack's hand and covered my mouth. "Oh, my god!" I went to the first pig sticking his nose through his containment and rubbed him on the head. He grunted at me happily. "You like that, don't you boy?"

Zack crossed his arms over his chest. "You'll pet a huge-ass pig, but you won't pet Miss Priss. That's messed up."

"Cats don't like me. Pigs do. I used to have a pig when I was ten. I raised Homer from the time he was a piglet. We took him to the 4-H fair. I didn't know at the time that he was going to be sold to be eaten. When I realized Homer was going to become bacon, I cried and cried. My dad gave in, and we brought him home." I walked down the line of pigs and stopped in front of a pink and black one. I rubbed his head. "He looked just like this."

Zack was finding humor in my excitement. "What happened to Homer?"

I shrugged my shoulders. "When I was twelve, he ran away. I cried for days."

He quirked his eyebrow at me. "Your pig ran away?"

"I was twelve. I didn't know any better. I still like to think that's what happened, even if it isn't." I kneeled in front of the pig and rubbed his wet snout through the bars. "Want to know a secret about me?"

Zack kneeled next to me. "Sure."

I smiled at him. "I'm a pig-whisperer. Watch." I reached between the bars and started to rub him behind the ear. "Hey, baby," I cooed. The pig closed his eyes. Within seconds, he laid down and turned his head to the side. "That feels good, doesn't it?"

I looked up at Zack and he was smiling down at me. "That's kind of amazing."

"Told ya. We had pigs, chickens, and a cow when I was growing up." I stood and wiped my hands on my jeans. "What else do they have here?"

"Lots. Come on." He motioned to me with his head. We walked through the goats and the sheep. They weren't my favorite, but then we got to the cows. I loved cows. Their big brown eyes and long lashes always melted my heart.

At the end of the row was a mama with her newborn calf. The sign overhead said the calf was only three weeks old and her name was Nora. I motioned to the old man sitting nearby in a chair. "May I?"

"Go right ahead," he answered.

I approached the calf and rubbed the back of her neck. "She's so sweet. Hey, sweetheart." Nora nudged her head into my body as I pet her. I rubbed down her nose and her long, wet tongue licked me. I moved my fingers to the tip of her nose. She reached her head up and began to suck on my fingers. I couldn't help but giggle, as I used my other hand to pet her head.

"That's so gross," Zack cringed, scrunching his nose up.

"It's not gross. She's just a baby," I defended.

"You have cow slobber all over your hand," he cringed again.

"Meh. What's a little cow slobber? I can wash my hands." I stood from Nora and thanked the old man for letting me get my baby cow fix. Zack and I walked outside, and I washed my hands at one of the several hand-washing stations. "That was amazing," I said, as I dried my hands.

"You know what's amazing?" he asked, and I shook my head. "Watching you be so happy." He kissed the top of my head and took my clean hand in his.

I grinned up at him. "Please tell me they have horses."

"Next barn over." Zack pulled me behind him. Dozens of stalls lined the barn, each one containing a single horse.

I walked along the row stopping now and then to rub one of the horses along the nose and talk softly too it. "I always wanted a horse," I said.

"How come you never had one?" Zack asked.

"My dad said they were too expensive and required more land than we had, but I still wanted one anyway."

"What happened to all the animals when you moved to New York?"

"When my mom got sick, my dad sold them all. We needed the money. Everything was gone way before I left," I said sadly.

"I'm sorry, sweetheart."

"Don't be. We did what we had to do, but I have great memories. Thank you for bringing me here. I love it."

Zack gave me a sad smile. "There's more. You can't come to the Armada Fair without getting a corndog. You do like corndogs, don't you?" He eyed me questioningly.

"Of course. Who doesn't like corndogs?"

Zack threw his hand against his chest in a dramatic gesture. "Whew! I thought that was going to be a deal breaker." He led us over to one of the several food trucks selling everything from pizza to bratwurst and ordered us two corndogs and a couple of drinks. We were walking toward a picnic table when I heard someone call Zack's name.

Zack turned around and clasped hands with another guy. "What's up, Tommy? You driving tonight?"

"You betcha. I've got a winner this year," he answered. "You staying for the derby?"

Zack looked at me and then back at Tommy. "I'm not sure. Maybe."

I nudged Zack. "Are you talking about a demo derby?"

"Yeah," Tommy answered for him. "I'm car number eight. A black beauty with a skull painted on the hood."

"We're in!" I exclaimed.

Zack looked from me to Tommy. "I guess we'll be there." They clasped hands again. "Good luck tonight."

Tommy backed away. "Luck's got nothing to do with it. It's all about the skill. Have fun with your girl."

Your girl. I liked the sound of that. I smiled internally as we finally made it to a picnic table.

106

"We don't have to go, if you don't want to. It's not like he'll know the difference," Zack said.

"Are you kidding? Cars and dust and mud? I love that stuff. It's not like I got to go to a demo derby in New York. Unless you don't want to?" I questioned. Maybe he was ready to call it a night.

"No, I think it'll be fun. It's just that most girls aren't into that kind of stuff."

"Most girls aren't from Oklahoma."

Chapter 15
Zack

I had hoped that Clarissa would like the fair, but I didn't expect to see this other side of her. She was so sweet with the animals. Deep down she was more country girl than anything else. I could see now, that even though she tried, she never really fit into New York.

After we finished our corndogs, I asked if she wanted to go on some rides. She rubbed her stomach and said it probably wasn't the best idea. Yeah, corndogs and spinning rides really didn't go together. We walked through the fairway anyways. We passed a game where you shoot a water pistol at a frog's mouth. "Wanna play a game?"

"I've got good aim," she warned.

"I've got better aim. Marines, remember?" I winked at her.

"Oh, you're on." She scooted onto one of the stools, while I paid the guy.

"Best two out of three," I challenged.

"I'm ready," she said seriously.

When the bell rang, we fired our water pistols at the frogs. It was close, but I won round one. She won round two. "This is it, sweetheart. Winner takes all."

Despite her effort, I won round three by a landslide. Clarissa pouted cutely.

"Pick a prize," the guy said.

I looked around us and saw a small pink pig hanging from the ceiling. "That one," I said pointing. He took the pig down and handed it to me. "You're very own Homer," I said placing it in Clarissa's hands.

She looked down at it and started talking to the pig. "Homer, where have you been? I've been looking everywhere for you. Thank goodness you came home," she said hugging it to her chest.

I slung my arm over her shoulder pulling her close to me. "Come on, silly girl. We better get our seats for the derby."

I led her toward the grandstand and found us a spot on the bleachers. The derby would be starting in less than a half hour. We chatted and people watched as we waited for it to start. Clarissa and I rarely got time to just be. She was working a lot. I knew she wanted to make money, but tonight was just what we needed.

When cars started to drive into the arena, Clarissa sat up tall and moved to the front of her seat. I loved watching her. Her excitement was contagious. When they started the countdown, she yelled out, "Three, two, one!" She watched attentively, commenting on the crashes and which cars she thought had a chance to win.

When the third heat drove onto the track, she pointed to a black car with a skull on the hood. "There's your friend."

"He's not really a friend, just someone I've done work on," I said.

"From all the way out here?" she asked.

"I've got clients from all over. Some famous ones too," I answered proudly.

"Really?" she asked in surprise. "Anyone I would know?"

"Maybe. I can't tell you though. They like their privacy."

"Oh, come on," she huffed. "Who the hell am I gonna tell? I don't know anyone."

She had a point, and honestly, I wanted to tell her. I leaned down and whispered their names in her ear.

She leaned back in surprise. "You're shittin' me!"

"Nope. Maybe if they come in, I could introduce you," I said smugly. She was impressed, and I loved that she was.

"Nuh-uh. I don't want to ruin what you have going on. Maybe I'll just sneak a peek," she insisted.

"We'll see. I don't have anything scheduled right now, so it's really a non-issue."

We watched the final heat of the derby and Clarissa cheered for Tommy, even though she didn't know him. He ended up coming in second because another car slammed him into the wall, hitting him on the driver's side. "That was bullshit," she proclaimed. "That shit would never fly in Oklahoma. You're not allowed to hit the driver's side door."

I laughed at her enthusiasm. "Let it go, sweetheart. It's just for fun." We walked out of the grandstand, and I grabbed both of her hands in mine. Night had taken over and the lights from the carnival pulled my attention. "Go on the Ferris wheel with me?"

"I haven't been on a Ferris wheel in forever. The last person I went on a Ferris wheel with was Bobby Joe," she said.

"Who was Bobby Joe?" I asked with a tinge of jealousy.

"My boyfriend, until I caught him making out with Bobbi Sue. He was an asshole. She got pregnant and they named their baby Bobby Ray. It was stupid and so were they," she huffed.

"How about you give me a chance to replace that memory with something better?" I laughed.

"I think that's an excellent idea," she agreed.

I bought our tickets and headed towards the Ferris wheel. It didn't take long for it to be our turn. We climbed into the seat together and the carnie secured the safety bar over our laps. I put my arm over her shoulder, and she rested her head against me. I loved having her close to me like this.

The ride raised high into the sky, the sounds from below faded and Clarissa looked around. "It's so peaceful up here," she said.

I pushed her hair over her shoulder. "I've had a great time with you tonight."

"Me too. I needed this more than I knew. It felt good to have some fun."

"You know I care about you, right? I would do anything for you." I pressed my lips to hers and she kissed me back. We made out like two teenagers in the back of a car. I ran my hand up her side, under her jacket and she stopped me.

"I care about you too," she admitted, pulling back. "I don't want to hurt you, but I need more time. I'm not saying no, I'm just saying not yet."

My heart deflated at her admission, but I wasn't giving up. "I'll be here when you're ready." I pulled her to my chest and held her tightly. She nuzzled into me and I breathed in the smell of her strawberry shampoo. I would wait. I just hoped she didn't keep me waiting too long.

110

After our ride on the Ferris wheel, we headed back toward the parking lot. Music blared from the huge red and white tent to our left. "What's in there?" she asked.

"That's the beer tent," I told her. "Usually, they have a live band and dancing too."

"Can we?" she asked. "I don't want beer, but I wouldn't mind seeing the band."

"Sure," I said leading her toward the tent. It made sense. Music was a big part of her life and lately she hadn't been able to indulge that side of her. "Do you drink at all?" I asked. "I haven't seen you even have a sip of beer since I've known you."

She waved her hand at me. "I've never been a big drinker. I guess working in a bar and seeing drunk people night after night killed it for me. I don't need to act stupid to have fun."

We entered the beer tent and music blared from the band on stage. I saw Clarissa's eyes light up. "Do you mind if I grab a beer?" I asked.

"Of course not," she said, clearly more interested in the band.

I made my way to the bar as she made her way to the stage. I watched her as I waited for my beer. Her ass began to wiggle, and she was singing along to the music. I crept up behind her and wrapped my arm around her waist. She may not have been mine, but she sure as hell wasn't up for grabs. I was shamelessly making my claim. I leaned down toward her ear. "You really love this, don't you?"

She threw her hands against her chest. "I do. I really do. It feels like home."

We listened for a few songs, and I saw how much she missed being up on stage. "You should ask them if you could sing?" I suggested. Selfishly, I wanted to see her in her element. I'd seen her play before, but never on stage.

"Oh, I couldn't," she protested.

"Sure, you could." I unwrapped my arm from around her and approached the stage. Clarissa pulled on my arm to stop me, but I was on a mission. I snuck up on stage and whispered in the guitarist's ear. He got a wide smile and nodded his head. I jumped off the stage. "You're up next."

"Are you shittin' me? Oh, my god! I'm so nervous!" she exclaimed.

"Go! Do your thing, sweetheart." The band finished their song and then waved her up on stage.

Clarissa took the guitarist's hand and hopped up on the platform. She quietly whispered to him, and he consulted his band mates. He gave her a thumbs-up. "Anyone got a guitar I can use?" she asked. She took the one offered to her and then turned her attention to the crowd.

"How y'all doin' tonight?" she spoke into the microphone. Her accent was thick, and the crowd responded accordingly with hoots and hollers. "You might know this one by Miranda Lambert called 'Gunpowder and Lead'." More shouts of encouragement erupted around her. "This goes out to all the women who've been wronged by their man. One, two… a one, two, three, four…" She began strumming her guitar and the band picked up behind her.

Her voice was strong and confident. I watched her jump around on the stage while never missing a note. She walked the stage like she owned it, giving the crowd exactly what they wanted. I didn't know this song, but I quickly became a fan. She was mesmerizing.

When the song was over, the crowd went wild. "Thank y'all. Thank you for lettin' me be a part of your evening." She pulled the strap of the guitar up over her head and hugged the band members. The smile on her face lit up the whole tent.

She hopped off the stage and ran toward me. I caught her in my arms and spun her around. "That was so much fun!" she shouted.

"You were great!" I complimented. "Everybody loved you. That's what you should be doing, not bartending."

Her smile was so big, her cheeks were bursting. "One day, maybe. For now, it's just a pipedream. But that was fun," she admitted.

"You ready to go home?" I asked.

"Yeah. I've had enough fun to last a while," she answered.

We headed back to where my bike was parked. I secured her helmet and then my own. This time I didn't have to tell Clarissa to wrap her arms around me. She held me securely and rested her head on my back. I loved the feel of her wrapped around me and the peacefulness of our quiet ride back home.

After I pulled into the garage, we headed inside. Clarissa pulled Homer from inside her jacket. "Thank you for tonight. I'm so happy Homer and I have been reunited. This was the best time I've had in... well, a long, long time."

I was still upset that she refused me on the Ferris wheel, but she was worth waiting for. Tonight, was amazing. Seeing her sing on stage had been the icing on the cake. I just had to keep showing her how good we could be together. I had connections. I could open doors for her, she just had to be willing to walk through them. My brain started whirring, as possibilities wove in and out of my mind.

"I'm going to jump in the shower. I'm sure I smell like a damn farm." Clarissa headed for the bathroom and shut the door behind her. I needed to get in there after she was finished. My hand was going to get a good workout tonight. That was for sure.

♫♪♫♪

The next night, everything went back to normal. Clarissa went to work behind the bar while I tattooed a young kid who had brought in the most ridiculous image I'd ever seen. It was the Mr. Peanut man making a lewd gesture, with the words *I'm nuts for you!* I won't even say where he wanted it. If he thought it was going to get him chicks, he was seriously mistaken. Sometimes I hated my job. Did people not realize this shit was permanent?

After he left, I decided to head over to The Locker. I sat in the back and out of Clarissa's line of sight. I ordered a beer from the waitress and watched Clarissa behind the bar. She shamelessly flirted with more than one customer, sticking her tips into her bra. I knew she was working to make money, but she seemed to be selling herself out. It pissed me off. She was better than that.

After my first beer, I needed something stronger to deal with what I was watching. I ordered a double shot of Jim Beam and another beer. A few minutes after my drinks were delivered, Chase walked in with his arm hanging over a brunette. He spotted me, and they made their way to my table.

"Zack, man, whatcha doing here alone? Couldn't find a chick to hang out with?" he teased.

I lifted my chin towards the bar and motioned to Clarissa. "I'm waiting to walk her home."

Chase and his friend invited themselves to sit at my table. I didn't want to chit-chat. I wanted to sit and stew in peace. "That's cool," Chase said. "This is Becca. Becca, Zack. He's my boss."

Becca leaned forward on the table, putting her cleavage on display, "So you do tattoos too? I want to get one, but I don't know what."

"I own the place. You come up with an idea and we'll draw it up for you. I'm sure Chase would do a great job." I shifted to the side to get a better view of Clarissa. I wasn't interested in small talk. It didn't go unnoticed.

Chase peered over his shoulder at Clarissa. "Nothing yet, huh? I thought you had that in the bag. You losing your game?"

"I'm not losing shit," I answered defensively.

"Then what's the problem? She seems into you," Chase questioned.

"You don't know what the fuck you're talking about. She's been through some shit. It's gonna take some time."

"It's been weeks and all you two do is dance around your feelings for each other. I see the way you two look at each other. Have you told her how you feel?"

"She knows how I feel," I said harshly. "I'm not gonna push her. And since when is my love life your concern?"

"Since you're fucking grumpy when you're not getting any," Chase said. "Isn't Gina putting out these days?"

"Gina and I are on a break and you're dangerously close to getting fired. You need to shut the fuck up."

Chase held his hands up. "Fine, dude. I'm just saying you're more fun when your dick's getting wet."

He was right, but hell if I was going to admit it. I focused back on the bar. I watched some slimeball write something on a napkin and slide it across the bar. Clarissa picked it up and stuffed it in her bra next to her tips. I was going to need a hell of a lot more alcohol to deal with this shit. This was exactly why I usually stayed away from Clarissa while she was working. I didn't need to see her flirting with random guys.

When the waitress came back, I ordered two more doubles of Jim Beam. I felt the need to get fucked up. I thought we had a good time last night and now she was acting as if it was nothing. That's what I needed to know. Was she acting, or did I mean nothing to her?

The longer I sat, the drunker I got. When Clarissa's shift ended, I headed to the bar. "Are you ready to go home?" I asked.

She took her tips out of her bra and stuffed them in her purse. She crumbled up the napkin the slimeball had given her and threw it in the trash. At least that was something. "Yeah. I'm ready. When did you get here?"

"A while ago," I answered vaguely.

She came out from behind the bar and took my hand. I swayed on my feet. I hadn't been this drunk in a long time. "How much have you had to drink?" she asked.

"A lot." It came out harsher than I intended.

"Ummm. Okay. Let's get you home. Are you pissed about something?" she questioned as we left the bar.

"No, no. I'm fine watching the woman I love flirt with everyone. It's awesome." God, I was drunk. I regretted the words as soon as they left my lips.

"Are you serious right now?" she asked. "I'm doing my job, Zack. I'm sorry if you don't approve, but you know what it takes to make tips. It's all harmless. Last time I checked, I've slept in your bed every night."

We were back at Forever Inked. I pulled out my key but couldn't seem to get it in the keyhole. Clarissa took the key from me and opened the door. She let us in and then set the alarm. "I thought we had a good time last night," I said. God, I sounded pathetic.

Clarissa wrapped her arm around my waist and helped me up the stairs. "We did."

"Then, what the fuck? Why would you take that guy's number?" I asked as she let us into the apartment.

"Because I'm trying to make money and he was tipping me well. I know that's hard for you to understand."

Next thing I knew, she was laying me down on the bed and taking off my boots. "I have money. You don't have to whore yourself out," I said. I was serious too. Why wouldn't she let me take care of her?

"I'm going to forget you just said that because you're drunk. I'm going to take a shower. Good night, Zack."

She left me alone in the dark and the room started to spin. I closed my eyes and that was the end of it.

♫♪♫♪

I woke with a throbbing head. I looked over and the bed next to me was empty. Not only was it empty, but I could tell no one had slept there last night. This was the first time Clarissa and I hadn't slept together since she had gotten here. I rubbed a hand over my face. "Fuck!" I couldn't remember a damn thing I said to her last night. I didn't even know how I got into my bed. The fact that I was wearing last night's clothes wasn't a good thing.

I stumbled to the kitchen, dumped a couple of Motrin in my hand and washed them down with a glass of water. I looked at Clarissa's closed door. I assumed something happened last night that she was pissed about. Something that had everything to do with me.

What I did know was that my mouth tasted like shit, and I needed a shower. I went to the bathroom and attempted to make myself feel human again. I dressed for the day and Clarissa still hadn't emerged from her room. Every minute that went by made me feel shittier and shittier.

I made myself a bowl of cereal and sat at the counter in the kitchen. All I could hope was that Clarissa would come out and talk to me. Miss Priss hopped up on the counter and rubbed against my arm. She was waiting for me to finish eating so she could drink the milk. "Be patient, girl," I said rubbing her back.

Music started to fill her room. Clarissa was awake. I crept next to her door and put my ear to it. I knew the song she was playing, and it broke my heart. She wasn't singing and then she struck a bunch of random chords that were not part of the song. She let out a scream of frustration and the playing stopped. I heard soft crying from the other side.

I did this to her, and I couldn't have felt worse if I tried. I went to my room and grabbed my own guitar. I wasn't as good as her, but I had to try. I knocked softly on her door and let myself in. She sat in the middle of her

116

bed, guitar cradled on her lap. "I really want to be alone," she said not looking at me.

"I know I fucked up last night and I'm sorry. I don't remember what I said, but I'm guessing it wasn't very nice," I admitted.

"It doesn't matter. I think I should look for a new place to live. This isn't working," she said.

I crawled up next to her on the bed. "Please don't. I'm sorry."

"You don't even know what you're sorry for. It would be best if I moved. Maybe I'll go back to Oklahoma. I don't fit in here or anywhere." A tear fell down her cheek.

"No. I don't want you to go." I wiped the tear from her face. "Play with me," I held my guitar up and started to strum the same song she was playing before. The song was fitting.

"I don't want to," she said.

"Please. Give me another chance." I continued with "Broken" by Seether. I started to sing Shaun Morgan's part and hoped that she would join in singing Amy Lee's part. My voice was shit, but that wasn't the point. I wanted her to hear the words, not my voice. *I wanted you to know, that I love the way you laugh. I wanna hold you high and steal your pain...*

I kept singing and she picked up where I left off. Her voice was like an angel and when we joined together on the chorus, we didn't sound half bad together. We finished the song, and she dropped her head. "Please stay," I begged. "Don't leave. Give us a chance."

"I don't want to leave, but you can't call me a whore or make disparaging remarks about my job. I need that job more than you know." She wiped at her face.

"I wouldn't," I defended.

"You did. And it hurt, Zack. It hurt a lot."

Now, I felt like a fucking asshole. No wonder she didn't sleep with me last night. I put my guitar aside and took hers from her hands. I wrapped my arms around her tiny body. "I'm so sorry, Clarissa. I shouldn't have gotten drunk last night. I should have never said those things."

"If this is ever going to work, you have to trust me. I work in the bar for one reason and that's to make money. I don't have any other skills. It's all I know," she said.

"I trust you," I said. "I want this to work. Please stay. Please don't leave," I begged.

"I promise you, as long as we're doing whatever this is, I won't be with anyone else. My heart is still healing. But if you're going to go and break it all over again…"

"I won't," I promised.

Chapter 16
Rissa

Since that morning, Zack and I had come to an understanding. I knew he felt awful about the things he said, and he tried even harder to accept my job for what it was. A job.

When I was working for him, we playfully bantered back and forth. It was comfortable and easy. He didn't pressure me about committing to a relationship. He didn't have to. We we're already in one, whether I admitted it or not.

I had been in Michigan for a month. Every night, Zack and I slept together. I would crawl in bed with him, or he would crawl into mine. It didn't matter which one we slept in. I wasn't alone. Zack and I still hadn't had sex. We'd only had that one night together after Wes's funeral. It was getting harder and harder to resist temptation.

I had fallen in love with Zack. I didn't think it would be possible with Wes's memory clouding my mind, but it happened. Zack was so kind and generous and everything that was good. He saved me when I thought no one could. Everything was going well, except that I was avoiding the fact I was pregnant. It was the biggest barrier holding me back from committing completely to him.

I walked by Dr. Peterson's office a dozen times. According to Layla, he opened his practice forty years ago and became the small-town doctor people depended on. He wasn't interested in being in a big medical building. He liked his small practice and the personal connections he had with his patients.

Small towns were notorious for gossip. I knew that first-hand from growing up in Oklahoma. Everyone knew everyone else's business. But I hadn't bought a car yet and my options were limited.

I sauntered past Doc Peterson's office and casually glanced through the window. The sign on the door said he was closing at five. It was almost five now. Soon the receptionist and medical assistants would be leaving. I sat outside his office on a bench and waited. Shortly after five, a group of women left his office and went their separate ways. I waited patiently for the doctor.

Around five-thirty, he exited the office and locked the door behind him. My nerves kicked up a notch, but I had to do this. I stood from my spot on the bench and approached him. "Dr. Peterson?"

"Yes?" He looked at me curiously.

I took a deep breath, "I need your help."

"You can call and make an appointment. We open at nine tomorrow," he said with a smile.

My eyes welled with tears. "It can't wait. And it's private. I really need your help."

He took one look at me and nodded his head. He unlocked the door and led me inside to his office. "What can I do for you?" he asked kindly.

"I've gotten myself into a mess." My first tear fell down my cheek and I quickly wiped it away. I didn't want him to think I was a basket case, even if it was the truth.

He sat me down in a chair across from his desk and handed me some tissues. "How can I help you, Miss...?"

"Black," I said, blotting the tears from my eyes. "My name is Rissa Black."

He patted my hand. "It can't be that bad, Rissa."

I swallowed my pride and told him my secret. "It is to me. I used to live in New York. I was engaged to a very wealthy man there. His father never accepted me because I was poor. I found out I was pregnant and two weeks later my fiancé died. He left me alone to have this baby. I ran away from New York after he died. I'm afraid his family will try to take this baby from me because I don't have any money. I know I need to do what's best for my baby, but I don't have any insurance. I don't know what to do." The tears poured down my face. This was the first time I had acknowledged the realty of my situation aloud.

"You don't have anyone?" he asked sympathetically.

I shook my head. "I moved here with a friend. He's been absolutely amazing, but I can't tell him I'm pregnant. It's complicated. I need to do this myself. I've been working, and I've saved some money."

"How far along are you?" he asked.

"About nine weeks, I think. Nobody knows. The only person who knew is dead. I can pay you, but I don't have much. I just want to do what's best for my baby."

"I can help you, Rissa. We can work out a reasonable payment plan. My staff is very discrete. I insist upon it. Come in tomorrow and we'll do an ultrasound to make sure everything is going well. It's going to be okay. We'll take care of you."

I thanked Dr. Peterson profusely and left his office. I had an appointment at ten o'clock in the morning. I was going to get to see my baby. That little bit of knowledge put a smile on my face. I wished I could share this information with Zack, but I wasn't sure he would understand. I also didn't trust him one hundred percent. I wanted to. I really did. He'd been nothing but good to me, but he was a Kincaid. That one small fact made me leery.

I got back to Forever Inked to find Zack talking to a very pregnant woman. She was beautiful with long blond hair and bright green eyes. I instantly felt jealous.

"Hey, you're back." Zack slung his arm over my shoulder. "I want you to meet a very good friend of mine and probably one of the most talented girls I know. Rissa, this is Kyla."

I reached my hand forward to take hers. "Hi, Kyla. It's nice to meet you." I forced a smile.

"Hi. Zack said you just moved here from New York. How are you liking it?" she asked.

"I've only been here a few weeks, but so far so good."

"Well, Zack said you don't know many people here. I thought maybe we could go for lunch tomorrow," she offered.

"That would be great, but I'm supposed to work tomorrow. I don't want to leave Zack short-handed."

Zack looked at me and shook his head. "You should go. I can handle everything here. You've been working like a dog since you got here. It'll be

121

good for you." He kissed the top of my head and I saw the curiosity about our relationship float across Kyla's face.

"I'll pick you up at noon," she said. There was no room for arguments. It had been settled. I was going to lunch with Kyla tomorrow, whether I wanted to or not.

"I'll see you then," I said. I excused myself and made my way upstairs. I sat on my bed cross-legged. I was such a jumbled mess of emotions. In one respect, I was looking forward to my doctor's appointment tomorrow, but I also knew that it was going to make the pregnancy I'd tried to ignore very real. I had to make a decision about Zack. I was either going to let him in or I was going to be alone. The whole point of me coming here was to not be alone. I would have to tell him eventually. Today was not that day. Nor was tomorrow, but eventually.

I didn't want to be alone. And that started with letting Zack into my heart. The rest would come with time.

I decided to take my guitar and go to the roof. I'd sat up there a lot over the past few weeks. It provided me with an escape I desperately needed. I sat up on the ledge with my legs dangling over the wall and played my guitar. The late August sun warmed my skin. My fingers danced over the strings, and I let my voice break free.

Chapter 17
Zack

My last appointment of the night had just left. I walked to the front desk to check my schedule for tomorrow. The sun was starting to set, and the last rays of the day shone through the front window. Everyone had left for the day, so I decided to lock up early and spend some time with Clarissa. She'd been working so hard and tonight she had the night off from the bar.

I approached the front door and noticed all the people standing on the sidewalk. Instead of turning the sign to *Closed*, I stepped outside to see what was attracting so much attention.

As soon as I opened the door, I heard it. Her voice was loud and clear. I instantly looked up and saw her feet dangling over the ledge. I walked across the street to get a better view and there was my girl, guitar in hand. She was playing and singing like nobody was watching. She had no clue what was going on down here on the sidewalk.

I couldn't keep the smile from my face. I strode back to my shop and locked the door behind me. Jogging up the stairs two at a time, I went right to the rooftop. The door was propped open with a big rock I'd left up there. I watched as she finished the song she was playing, then sat down next to her on the ledge.

"Hey, sweetheart."

"Hey, Zack. You don't mind that I'm playing up here, do you? I just needed a little time to myself."

I shook my head. "I don't mind and neither does anyone else."

She looked at me curiously. "What do you mean?"

I pointed down to the sidewalk. "You have an audience."

Her eyes looked to where I was pointing. "Oh, crap."

The people on the sidewalk started clapping and whistling. Her cheeks turned pink as she gave the crowd a little wave.

"They love you," I said. "You should start playing in the bar again. I want you to get back to what you love."

"Speaking of love, do you think they'd mind if I did an encore," she asked shyly.

"I think they would love it."

Clarissa settled the guitar back on her legs. She began to strum, and she closed her eyes. I knew this song. She started singing 'Wicked Game" by Chris Isaak. It was a song that had been remade several times. My favorite version was by Stone Sour. Until now. Now, Clarissa was my favorite version of this song.

After she played the last note, Clarissa stared into my eyes. "Yes."

I ran my hand down the side of her face. "Yes, what?"

"Yes, I want to do this with you. I've fallen in love with you, Zack."

"I love you too, Clarissa." I cupped her face in my hands and crushed my lips to hers. Her mouth opened, and I devoured her. Our tongues twisted together with need and desire. We were lost in the moment.

Our bliss was shattered by applause and cat calls. "Kiss her again, Zack!" someone shouted. Clarissa buried her head in my shoulder in embarrassment.

"I think we should take this inside," I whispered.

"Yes, please."

I backed off the ledge, then took her hand and pulled my girl to her feet. I had been waiting for this moment for what seemed like forever. In the few short weeks I'd known her, Clarissa Lynne Black had captured my heart.

I led her down to our apartment, took the guitar from her hand, and set it aside. Pushing her back against the door, I attacked her lips with mine again. Clarissa's arms wrapped around my neck. I squeezed her ass and lifted her into my arms. Her legs wrapped around my waist without hesitation. It was raw and carnal. Everything we'd been suppressing, came to the surface as I devoured her against the door.

"Your bed or mine?" I asked.

"Yours. I want you so bad."

My hard cock twitched in my pants, pushing against my zipper. I couldn't wait to get inside her. "God, I've been waiting for you to say that. I've wanted to fuck you again since that first night."

I carried her to my room and set her in the middle of my bed. We both pulled our shirts up over our heads and threw them to the side. Clarissa crawled up on her knees and walked herself to the edge of the bed. Her hands ran over my chest and down my abs. She traced over my tattoos with the tips of her fingers. "I want to know all about these," she said breathlessly.

I grabbed her wrists and kissed her palms. "Another time. Tonight, all I want to do is let our bodies do the talking. I love you, Clarissa."

"I love you, Zack. I tried to fight it, but I can't. I don't want to anymore. I want this life with you."

"Then let me give it to you," I whispered, while laying her back on the bed. I laid over the top of her and kissed her with everything I had. I was gentle but firm. There was no mistaking my intentions. Her arms wrapped around my shoulders and pulled me in closer. My chest was pressed against her breasts. Her soft against my hard.

I groaned into her mouth and then kissed down her neck and the valley between her breasts. My tongue traced a path down her stomach to the top of her jeans. I quickly worked open the button and zipper and pulled them down her legs.

I always thought black was my favorite color. But seeing Clarissa lying on my bed wearing a red satin bra and matching red panties changed my mind. Red was definitely my favorite color. "God, you're beautiful."

I quickly undid my belt, pushed my own jeans down my legs and kicked them aside. I had waited so long for this with her. Part of me wanted to fuck her so hard she'd be feeling me tomorrow, and part of me wanted to savor every single inch of her and sink into her slowly. One thing was for sure though, I was going to taste her. I was going to claim every part of her as mine.

"You're looking at me like I'm dessert," she giggled.

"You know what my favorite part of dessert is?" I asked.

She shook her head back and forth, her curls shaking loosely. "What's your favorite part?"

"The filling." I leaned forward and grabbed the top of her panties. I quickly stripped them off her legs. I took one leg in my hand and kissed from the arch of her foot to the inside of her thigh. Then I did the same with her other leg.

125

The whole time, her eyes never left mine. "I'm going to eat your pussy so good you're going to wonder why you told me no for so long."

A little whimper left her lips. "Say it again."

"I'm going to stick my tongue deep inside your pussy. I'm going to lick and suck every part of you," I promised.

"Do it. Please! Do it now," she begged.

I wasted no time. I laid between her legs, putting one over each of my shoulders. "You have no idea how long I've dreamt about this." I licked her from bottom to top. She was already so goddamn wet for me. It clung to my tongue and invaded my senses. The taste was better than anything I had imagined. I inhaled the scent of her and ingrained it into my memory. "Fuck, sweetheart, you taste so damn good."

I dove in again. Pushed my tongue deep inside her and lapped her up. I had her squirming, but I wanted her coming. I backed out enough to slide two fingers inside her wetness. I slid them in and out of her pussy, curling them inside her, searching for that magical spot that would make her scream. "Oh God, oh God, oh God," she panted quietly.

She was hovering on the edge, barely hanging on. I used my other hand to separate her folds and find that little bundle of nerves that would push her over. I latched onto it and sucked greedily. Her hips raised off the mattress and I felt her tightening around my fingers. She was so goddamn close.

I teased her with the tip of my tongue and the silver ball that I knew would drive her crazy. With one long, hard suck, I went in for the kill. It was her breaking point. She threw her head back and let out the softest scream I had ever heard. "Zack! Oh, oh…oh my God!" She clenched my fingers and I continued to please her, letting her ride out the waves of ecstasy.

I kissed my way up her body and back to her lips. "That was the most beautiful thing I've ever seen."

"That was amazing," she panted breathlessly.

"It's only the beginning," I promised her. "We're going to be amazing together." I ran my finger between her breasts and pulled at the front of her bra. "I need this off."

Clarissa arched her back and I slid my hand behind her to release the clasp. I kneeled over her and pulled the fabric away to reveal her full, soft

126

tits. I palmed them eagerly, then feasted on her hard nipples. They'd been teasing me for a month. I sucked hard, bruising her delicate skin and running my tongue over the diamond hard points. I couldn't get enough of her or the soft little sounds she made.

Her mewling made my dick ache to be inside her. "Clarissa, sweetheart, I need you right now. No more waiting."

Clarissa grabbed at my boxer briefs and began pushing them down my legs. "Need you too, Zack. I need your dick deep inside me. I want to feel you," she begged me.

I wouldn't disappoint. I had waited too long for this. Without another hesitation I sank my cock deep inside her. She was so wet and warm and perfect. I pulled back and pushed in slowly again. Once I started, I couldn't stop. I wasn't going to last long. Clarissa grabbed at my shoulders and dug her nails in. I loved the pain. She made me feel alive for the first time in a very long time.

I kissed her ear, her neck, her chest as I sank into her over and over again. She wrapped her legs around me and we moved together in our own perfect rhythm. Her hands clawed at me, scratching down my shoulders to my back. She was a wild one and the possibilities of what we could be together sent shockwaves through my body.

But not tonight. Tonight, I would savor her and worship her like she deserved.

"I'm gonna come again," she panted. Thank God, because I was right there too. I pushed her knees to her chest and went deeper. Harder. Closer. My dick got impossibly hard, and my balls tightened. I couldn't stop now if I wanted to. I pushed in one last time and emptied everything inside her.

I collapsed on my elbows. "Jesus Christ! God, you're addicting." Clarissa giggled beneath me. I stared into her bright blue eyes. "You're not helping my self-confidence."

"Oh, I don't think there's anything wrong with your confidence. I think you know exactly what you did to me. I don't think I've ever come that hard. A girl could get used to this," she admitted.

I ran my hand down the side of her face. "You should get used to it. Because I'm gonna fuck you every day, as long as you let me."

She giggled again. "How about twice a day? I could go again. Think you could handle it?"

"Is this how it begins? You're demanding sex already. What will I do with you?" I asked, teasing her.

"Make love to me. Make me feel that all over again. Please, Zack. Don't make me beg."

"Oh, I like you begging. I love hearing my name on your lips. Every night, sweetheart. And every morning. And anytime in between."

"Maybe you'll be the one begging," she teased back. Clarissa pushed on my shoulder until I fell to my back laughing. Then she straddled me, her wet pussy resting on top of my cock. "Has anyone ever told you that you've got a great smile? And beautiful green eyes? And an amazing body? Do you know how hard it's been to resist you? Every day I had to walk around this apartment pretending not to be affected."

"Oh yeah? How long *have* you been affected, Clarissa Lynne?" I asked, pushing her hair over her shoulder.

She tapped her finger to her lips. "Probably since that day at the cemetery when you told me to get the fuck in the car. You could have left me there in the middle of the road, but you didn't. I knew right then you were something special. Something I had no business wanting or having. I knew I couldn't have you, let alone keep you. I'm still not sure I can keep you."

"What if I've already decided to keep *you*?" I asked.

"Then you can have me." Clarissa leaned forward and kissed me. I ran my hands through her long curls and gripped the back of her head. I pulled her in closer and kissed her deeply.

Clarissa pulled back and whispered, "Now. I need you now." She lifted her hips and gripped my dick tightly. Then she placed me at the entrance to her wet pussy and slid down, sheathing me in her heat. "God, you feel so good," she said softly. She rode me up and down, slow at first and then quickened her pace. Her tits bounced, and I reached up to grab them. They were a perfect fit for my large hands, and that was saying a lot.

She leaned forward and rubbed her clit on my dick. "I love you, Zack," she whispered in my ear. She kept rubbing on me, building herself up again. I felt her come around me, squeezing my dick with every pulse of her pussy.

I flipped her over quickly, making the breath whoosh from her chest. Her eyes went wide. "I'm bossy in bed," I declared, giving her a little warning. "I want what I want and right now I want you beneath me." I pushed into her hard and loved the sound that left her lips. I'd never been with anyone who could say practically nothing and say everything all at the same time. She was so quiet during sex, but every sound that left her lips lit me on fire. I felt her down to my very core. She had my heart wrapped up in everything that was her.

We slept together naked, her small body wrapped around mine. Her head rested on my chest and her leg was draped over me. I held her close and vowed that I would never let her go. I was happier tonight than I had been in a very long time. I couldn't remember a time I had been more content.

♫♪♫♪

When I woke, Clarissa was still snuggled into me. I rubbed my hand down her back and just stared at her. This sweet woman was mine. I ran a hand through her curls and let them fall through my fingers. Last night was everything I had imagined it could be, only better.

Clarissa stirred on my chest and looked up at me with those blue-blue eyes. "Good morning."

"Good morning, sweetheart."

"What time is it? I need to get up and take a shower. I smell like sex," she said.

I chuckled. "Yeah, you do. We both do. I love that smell. But it's still early, we can stay in bed a while."

"Are you sure you're okay with me going to lunch today? I don't have to if you need me," she asked.

"Oh, I need you, but not to work. You should go. It'll be good for you. Kyla's great. She's not that much older than you. I think the two of you will hit it off," I encouraged.

"Does she know? About us? Who I am and what we are?" she asked nervously.

"She doesn't know the details, but I'm sure she has her suspicions."

"Hmmm. Is this going to be an inquisition?"

I held my thumb and forefinger an inch apart. "Maybe a little bit."

Clarissa scrunched up her nose. "Ugh! You're the worst. What do I say?"

I kissed the tip of her nose. "Whatever you want. I'm not worried about it."

"I'm nervous. Is that weird? I mean, she's your friend. I care what she thinks about me."

"She's going to love you. And you know what? She's going to love that you make me happy. Because you do. You make me so happy. Can I ask you a question?"

"Of, course," she answered.

"What changed? Why now? You've been here a month."

She sighed and put her head back on my chest. "I was tired of pretending. Pretending like you didn't matter. Pretending that I didn't need you. Pretending that I didn't love you. It was time. You've been everything to me for the last month. Maybe I didn't tell you or show you, but you're the most important person in my life. I don't know what I'd do without you. And I don't mean financially. I didn't know what to expect when I came here. It was a big gamble. I wasn't sure if I could trust you, but you're everything that's good. I feel safe with you."

Her words meant everything to me. "I want you to feel safe here. You can trust me," I assured her. "Do you know how hard it's been having you sleep in my bed and never touching you? Bringing you here was a gamble for me too. I'd say it's paid off. Wouldn't you?"

She lifted her head and kissed me. "Yes, most definitely."

We got out of bed and Clarissa jumped in the shower first. I wanted to join her, but I didn't know if it was too much too soon. So, I gave her privacy and called my sister instead. It was early, but that girl was a workaholic. I knew she would be awake. Ronni answered on the second ring. "Hey, sis."

"Well, if it isn't my big brother. How are things, Zack?"

"Phenomenal. I know you were worried, but things are good. Really good," I said.

"And Rissa? How is that going? Has she found her own place or is she still living with you?" Ronni asked.

I sighed. "She's living here. We're together. It's official now." I knew I was about to get my ass reamed by my logical, business-minded sister.

"I don't like it, Zack," she huffed. "Something is not right. I saw her with Wes. They were like two peas in a pod. What they had was real. How could she up and forget about him so quickly? It doesn't make sense to me."

I started to get angry with my sister. She didn't have to approve, but she didn't have to be so cynical either. It's not like she had ever been in a serious relationship. I wanted to point that out to her, but that would just be mean, so I refrained. "What are you implying, Ronni?"

"Money," she said. "You have millions. She knows that. She's desperate."

I tried to calm myself and see it from her point of view, but inside I was raging. "Then why did she make me wait so long? Why not jump in with both feet right away?"

Ronni sighed. "I don't have the answers, but something is off. Call it woman's intuition. I don't want to fight with you. Please...just keep your eyes open. Don't be blinded by love. I don't want to see you get hurt."

"My eyes are wide open," I assured her. I heard the shower turn off and I certainly didn't want Clarissa to overhear this conversation. "Listen, I gotta go. I'll call you later."

"Zack?"

"Yeah?"

"You know I love you, right? I worry is all."

"I love you too, sis. I'll talk to you soon." I disconnected the call. I knew what she said had merit, but still, I couldn't believe Clarissa would use me. What we had was real. I was sure of it.

I saw Clarissa coming out of the bathroom with a towel wrapped around her and all I wanted to do was ravage her. Instead, I played it cool. "Did you save me any hot water?" I asked.

She smirked at me. "I did. But you know, we could save water by showering together."

"I'll keep that in mind for next time." I winked. I showered and was finally able to give my hand a well-deserved break.

By the time I got out of the shower, Clarissa was dressed and ready for the day. She was in the kitchen, whipping up breakfast. I snuck up behind her and wrapped my arms around her waist. "What's on your plan this morning?" I asked.

She leaned her head back and kissed me. "First, I thought I'd feed us, because I seem to have worked up an appetite and I'm starved. Then I want to go to a couple of stores I've been meaning to check out. All I've gotten to do is window shop. Then, of course, I'm having lunch with Kyla," she groaned.

"Come on, it's going to be fun. Don't be grouchy."

She plastered a huge fake smile on her face. "Me? Grouchy? Never. I'm totally looking forward to it."

I pulled on her chin. "Okay. Try not to make that face though. It makes you look like a Barbie on steroids. Just be yourself."

"Yeah, all right. What time is your first appointment?" she asked.

"Ten. I'm booked all day. I have a break around five and then a late appointment that's not coming in until eleven tonight."

"Anyone special?" she asked curiously.

"Maybe," I said vaguely. "I can't say. You know, confidentiality and what-not."

"Ugh! You suck! What if he's here when I get off work?"

"Then I'll have to hide him in a closet or something," I teased, kissing her on the nose. There was no way she was meeting my client tonight.

Chapter 18
Rissa

I knew Zack had an appointment at ten. It worked into my plan perfectly. I used the guise of shopping to hide my visit with Doctor Peterson.

I walked into his office a few minutes before ten and approached the receptionist apprehensively. She smiled kindly at me. "Hi, I'm Gina. You're a new patient, right?"

I nodded, and she handed me a clipboard. "I'll just need you to fill out these forms for me."

I took the clipboard from her and sat down in the waiting room. The first part of the form was easy. My name, address, phone number. Then the hard questions started. *Number of previous pregnancies:* Zero. *Father's name:* I let the pencil hover over the form. I could write Wes's name, but what would be the use of that. I couldn't write *unknown* or *none*. I knew who the father was, and this certainly wasn't an immaculate conception. I settled with writing *deceased* on the paper. It wasn't a lie. *Date of Conception:* I counted back in my mind and wrote my closest estimate. *Name of Insurance Company and Policy Number:* I wrote *cash*. I signed the form and gave it back to Gina.

"I don't have insurance, but Dr. Peterson said we could work out a payment plan," I told her.

She smiled warmly. "It's not a problem. Have a seat and the doctor will see you shortly."

I sat back down, and my nerves started to kick into overdrive. Growing up, we didn't have money. I had rarely been to a doctor, let alone a gynecologist. Dr. Peterson wasn't a gynecologist, but I assumed he was going to see all my girly bits. I had no experience in this department at all. I wanted to walk out and never come back. But I had gotten myself into this situation and now I had to be a big girl and suck it up.

I picked up a magazine from the side table and tried to distract myself with reading about the importance of prostate exams. I failed miserably. I closed the magazine and set it back on the table.

Gina opened the door to the back office. "Miss Black, the doctor will see you now." I followed her. She weighed me and left me in a room alone, with the instructions to take off my clothes and put on a paper-thin gown. I wished I wasn't alone. Thoughts of having Zack here with me fleeted through my mind. But I couldn't tell him about this baby yet.

I stripped out of my clothes and put on the gown. I sat up on the exam table and threw the thin blanket over my legs. It was freezing in the room, but I muscled through it.

A light knock came at the door. A young woman not much older than me entered. She took my blood pressure and listened to my heart. She made notes on the chart in front of her and assured me the doctor would be in soon.

When she left, I let out a breath of relief. So far, so good. A few minutes later, Dr. Peterson entered. "Hi, Rissa. How are we doing today?"

I answered honestly. "I'm scared to death. Is this going to hurt?" I asked.

Dr. Peterson patted my knee. "Don't be scared. I assure you this isn't going to hurt. Women do this every day. How are you feeling? Any morning sickness?"

I shook my head. "None. I guess I'm one of the lucky ones."

"Very lucky," he agreed. "Do you smoke?"

"No."

"How's your diet?"

I grimaced. "It could be better, but I've been trying to eat healthier. I cut out coffee and caffeine," I said, as if it made up for my poor eating habits.

"We could all eat healthier," he said with a laugh. "My wife's been trying to get me to lose weight for years. It sounds like you're making some good choices though. Where do you work?"

I grimaced again. "In a bar. I'm a bartender at The Locker."

"Drinking is not an issue?"

"Not at all. I never was a big drinker. Working in a bar took care of that for me."

He smiled. "That's good. I assume you're on your feet a lot."

"I am," I confirmed.

"It's fine for now, but as you get further along it might become an issue. Listen to your body. If you need to take a break and sit, you should. Now how about we try to see this baby and get a due date?"

"I'd like that."

"Go ahead a lie back. You can leave the blanket over your waist and just pull up the gown, so I can get to your belly."

This wasn't as bad as I had anticipated. I laid back and pulled up the gown, while Dr. Peterson rolled over the ultrasound machine. "This may be cold," he warned. He smoothed a gel over my stomach and then ran the wand over it. I watched carefully. He pointed to a small spot on the screen. "Here's your baby."

I couldn't help but smile. "I can't believe that's growing inside me," I said in awe.

"This is one of my favorite parts of this job," he smiled back at me. "It looks like you're going to be a mama in about seven months. You're due the end of March. Do you want to hear the heartbeat?"

My eyes welled with tears. "So much." He pushed a button on the machine and a soft whooshing sound filled the room.

My heart filled with happiness and sorrow. It twisted me inside. All the things I felt and had tried to suppress, rose to the surface. I remembered the day I realized I was pregnant.

I was late. There was no ignoring the fact any longer. I sat on the edge of the tub and stared at the pregnancy test I'd picked up on the way home. It felt like a snake that was ready to strike at me. Wes had just signed his recording contract and was getting home from LA later tonight. Surely a baby didn't fit into his plan. It wasn't exactly part of my plan either, but I knew we could make it work. The thought of having a baby with Wes made me smile. I hoped the baby would have Wes's green eyes.

I worked up my courage and took the test. I sat it on the counter and waited while I washed my hands. After a few minutes, I looked down at the test and saw a plus sign. A smile spread across my face.

Now I had to tell Wes. I was torn between being totally elated and scared to death.

I dolled myself up and made him a fancy dinner. I missed him like crazy. He'd been my inspiration, my encouragement, my best friend and my lover for two years. We'd talked about starting a family after we got married, this would just move the timeline up a little bit. It was bad timing for sure, but did it really matter?

Wes walked in the front door shortly after seven, dropping his bags at his feet. He wrapped me in his arms and whispered in my ear. "God, you're a sight for sore eyes. I've missed you so much, baby."

"I've missed you too. So much," I said. It felt so good being in his arms again. "I made you dinner."

He started kissing my neck. "I'm starving, but not for food. I'm starving for you. Five days was way too long to be without you."

He pulled his shirt up over his head, and then just as quickly removed mine. He lifted me up and I wrapped my legs around him. I could feel his desire through the thin fabric of my leggings. We didn't even make it to the bedroom. He carried me to the couch, where he had me stripped in seconds.

We made love on the couch. It wasn't fast and furious. It was slow and sensual. Every time he pushed into me, he whispered in my ear. "Love you, Rissa... Missed you so much... You're so sexy, baby... Never want to be away from you again."

All his words melted me inside. I loved Wes more than anything. I couldn't imagine my life without him.

When we'd finished making love and cleaned up, I led him to the kitchen. I'd made chicken piccata with potatoes and asparagus sautéed in garlic. "That smells amazing, Rissa. Not only did I miss you, but your cooking too. I can't wait until you're my wife, baby."

I smiled sweetly at him. "I can't wait to be your wife."

"You know what this dinner needs? Wine." He reached into the cupboard and pulled out two wine glasses. "Red or white?"

I took the glasses out of his hands and set them on the counter. "I have something to tell you."

"We're out of wine?" He quirked an eye up. "Did you have a party without me?" he teased.

"I'd never have a party without you. I don't want wine." I rubbed my hand over my flat stomach. "I'm pregnant."

His eyes descended from my face to my stomach. "You're pregnant?"

I bit my lip and worry furrowed my brow. "Are you mad?"

"Mad? No, I'm not mad." He rubbed his hand over my belly. "There's a little piece of you and me growing in there?"

I nodded my head. "I took the test today."

"Oh my God!" He scooped me up and spun me around the kitchen. I couldn't help but giggle at his reaction. He set me back on my feet and held my face in his hands. "Are you sure?"

I nodded again. "I'm two weeks late."

Wes planted a huge kiss on me. "I'm so excited. Everything is coming together for us. My record deal, a baby on the way... we need to move up the date of our wedding. I want to be married when our little peanut is born."

"You're really happy?" I questioned.

"Are you kidding me? I can't think of a better life than the one in front of us. I love you so much, Rissa. Forever, baby."

Forever ended way too soon. It came crashing down on me the night I had found him dead in our apartment. Not only had Wes left me, but our unborn baby too. I was left alone to do this by myself. I wiped at my eyes.

And now there was Zack. Wes's brother who had taken me in and showed me love I thought I'd never find again. And I was lying to him. Keeping a huge secret. I was sleeping with the brother of my baby's father.

I was happy when I had no right to be. It wouldn't last, and I was going to destroy both of us in the process. In the end, I would be left to raise this baby on my own. Everything would come full circle.

I wanted this with Zack until then. Being with Zack was like having a little part of Wes. I'd keep my secret as long as I could. The tears fell down my face at the thought of losing Zack, and in essence, losing Wes all over again. *How had I gotten myself into this mess?*

"Hey," Dr. Peterson tapped my hand. "It's going to be all right. You need to have faith. You can do this. My advice is to let someone else in. You're going to need the support."

I wiped at my tears again. "I wish it were that easy."

"It can be. What are you afraid of?" he asked.

"Everything." I had never spoken truer words in my life. Every single thing about this situation scared the shit out of me.

I got dressed and headed back to the front desk. Gina gave me a look of sympathy. I was guessing I looked like shit. "It'll be fifty dollars today. Do you want to pay now, or just put a deposit down? We can put you on a payment plan."

I reached into my purse. "I've got it." I opened my wallet, pulled out five tens and handed them over. "Is that the normal charge? It doesn't seem like enough." I asked.

"It's what Dr. Peterson wrote down. He's the boss and I don't question him." She smiled and took my money. "There's a bathroom right through that door if you want to freshen up." She pointed down the hall.

"Thank you. I'll just be a minute." I headed to the bathroom and gasped when I saw myself. My eyes were red and puffy. My mascara had run down my face leaving black trails on my cheeks. "Oh, hell," I whispered to my reflection.

I quickly wiped away the black from my face and set my purse on the counter. I used concealer under my eyes to erase the red. I touched up my eye makeup and threw on a coat of lip gloss. I appraised myself in the mirror. Much better.

I left the bathroom and Gina met me outside the door. "Dr. Peterson said to give these to you. They're prenatal vitamins. You should take one every day."

I took them from her and shoved them in my purse. "Thank you. How much do I owe for them?"

Gina waved her hand at me. "Nothing. We get free samples all the time. We'll see you in a month."

I left the office and wandered down the street, back toward Forever Inked. I wasn't in a hurry, so I popped into a vintage clothing store I'd been eyeing for the past month. I perused the racks and pulled out a couple of cute

138

shirts. They were a gauzy material and had a distinct boho look to them. I didn't know how much longer I'd be able to wear tight fitting clothes. These were loose and looked comfortable as well as being fashionable. I grabbed one in black and another in a dark maroon color. Thankfully, the weather would start getting cooler soon and I'd have an excuse to dress more conservatively. I figured I had a month, maybe two, before I'd start showing. Three would be optimistic. If I started buying a few things here and there, it wouldn't be so bad later.

I took them to the register and stopped to look at a display of leather wrist cuffs. I picked one up and wrapped it around my wrist. It was black with silver studs. It reminded me of something Zack would wear. I took it off and reached for a thicker one, obviously designed for a man. I picked it up and tried to decide if it would fit around his wrist. The handwritten sign read $10.00 each.

I carried the two cuffs along with the shirts to the register and paid for them. It was a small gift, but I hoped he would like it.

When I got back to the shop, Zack had just finished his first appointment. He wrapped me in his arms. "How was your shopping trip? Did you buy anything?"

"I got something for you," I said, reaching into my shopping bag. I pulled out the leather cuff. "Hold out your hand." Zack held out his hand in front of me and I fastened it around his wrist. It was a perfect fit. "It made me think of you. I got one for myself too. Do you like it?" I asked as I fastened my own on my wrist.

He held up his arm and inspected the leather cuff. "I love it. Thank you, sweetheart. You didn't have to get me anything," he said, pressing his lips to my forehead.

I shrugged my shoulders. "It's nothing, but I'm glad you like it. Do you want me to confirm tomorrow's appointments before I leave for lunch?"

"That would be great." He kissed me long and hard, right in the middle of Forever Inked for everyone to see. So, I guess we were official. No more hiding. "I'm going to get ready for my next client. Don't leave without saying goodbye." He kissed me again and turned to head back to his private studio.

I touched my lips and headed to the front desk where Layla was hanging out. "Soooo," she smirked. "You and Zack are together now?"

"I think we've been together since I got here. I just quit fighting it," I said honestly.

"So true," she said. "I knew the moment I saw you two together that it was more than friendship. Zack doesn't love easily. But, with you he was smitten from the start."

"Smitten? That word seems so… old fashioned." I laughed.

Layla sighed, "Zack's an old soul."

"In a rockin' hot bod," I whispered conspiratorially.

Layla's eyebrows shot up. "Really? I hadn't noticed. Is he hot?"

I smacked her on the arm. "You know he is. But it's more than that. He's the total package. He and his brother are so different than his dad. It's hard to believe they're related."

Layla narrowed her eyes. "You knew Zack's brother? Did you grow up with them? Is that how you know Zack?"

I froze. What the fuck had I just said? "No. I grew up in Oklahoma. I knew Wes from the music scene in New York. We played in the same bar." It wasn't a lie. It just wasn't the whole truth either.

"And Zack?" she questioned curiously.

"I met him through Wes." Again, not technically a lie. I needed to change the subject quickly. "So, what do you know about Kyla? I'm going to lunch with her today."

"You've met Kyla?" she asked.

"Yeah. Zack thinks we'll get along well and that I need to meet more people. She and Zack seem to be good friends, and I'm trying to make an effort."

"Zack did a lot of work on her. That's how they met. Turned out she's artistically gifted and now she designs for him."

Something was missing from this story. "And?" I urged her to continue.

Layla rolled her eyes. "At one time, he was head over heels for her, but she wasn't into him. She was pining away for an ex-boyfriend. He's a super-star athlete and now they're married. He's a cool guy though. Zack made peace with it a long time ago. He and Kyla are just friends."

140

"Hmmm. This is going to be awkward," I mused.

"It'll be fine. She's totally in love with her husband. They were high school sweethearts."

"So, there's no chance that Zack still has feelings for her?" I asked.

"Nope. Zack's not that kind of guy."

The bell over the door rang and in walked Kyla. "Here goes nothing." I sighed.

"Hi Rissa. Hey, Layla. How are you?"

"I'm good. How about you?" Layla asked.

Kyla rubbed her big belly. "I feel like I'm about to burst. I'll be so happy when these babies are born. I have six more weeks."

Layla scrunched up her nose. "I don't think you're going to make it that long."

Kyla laughed. "Tyler says the same thing. I want them to cook as long as possible, so I hope you're both wrong." Then she turned to me. "Are you ready to go?"

"Let me just tell Zack I'm leaving," I said, turning on my heel. I strolled back to Zack's studio and leaned my head in. "I'm headed to lunch. I didn't make those calls, so I'll do it when I get back."

Zack perked up. "Kyla's here already?"

"Yeah."

He stood up and walked me to the front. "Hey, baby girl." He hugged her tightly and a seed of jealousy sprouted in my mind.

"Hey, Zack." She hugged him back just as tight. She was a tiny thing and his size eclipsed hers.

"Where are you girls going?" he asked.

"I figured we'd head over to Partridge Creek and decide when we get there. Tori's waiting in the car, so we should get going."

"You brought Tori?" he asked. "You girls better be good. That one's got trouble written all over her."

Kyla reached over and took my hand. "Rissa is safe with us. How much trouble could we get into? Tori's got Savannah with her and I'm ready to pop. She couldn't be safer."

Zack reached in and kissed me square on the lips. "If you need rescuing, call me."

"I'll be fine. I'll be back in a couple of hours. I've got to work tonight," I assured him.

I hopped into the front of Kyla's Jeep Cherokee and looked in the back. A girl who was equally as attractive as Kyla, but with dark hair, sat in the back next to a car seat. I gave her a little wave. "Hi, I'm Rissa."

She gave me a warm smile. "I'm Tori and this little monkey here is Savannah."

I craned my neck to get a better look at the baby. "She's so cute. How old is she?"

"Almost two months," Tori answered. "She was born on the Fourth of July."

"Wow! That must have been exciting."

"Depends on how you define exciting. I was in labor for ten hours. She was a stubborn one. But she's more than made up for it," Tori said tapping her on the nose.

Kyla squeezed into the driver's seat. She barely fit behind the wheel. "Where to ladies?"

"You two decide," I said. "I don't know what's good around here."

"P.F. Chang's," Tori piped in. "Chris's mom has been bringing us food like crazy. She's a great cook, but the last thing I want is Italian. Mama wants Chinese."

Kyla looked over at me. "Are you good with that?"

"I'm up for whatever. Thanks for inviting me out. I haven't really gotten a chance to meet many people here and the only girl time I've gotten is with Layla."

"How long have you been here?" Tori questioned. "Kyla said you moved here from New York."

"About a month, but I've been working non-stop since I arrived."

"What's New York like?" Kyla asked. "I'd love to go, but with these babies on the way I'm thinking it could be a while."

I tried to think of a word to describe New York. "Fast paced. Everyone's in a rush to be somewhere. I lived in Brooklyn. I worked in a bar there and was an aspiring musician."

"Really?" Tori's interest peaked. "So, what do you do? Sing or play an instrument?"

I let out a little laugh. "Both. I can play the piano and the guitar, but I love singing. Nowadays, it's just me and my guitar sitting in the middle of my bed."

"Are you any good?" Tori asked.

"Tori! Jeez, what the hell?" Kyla screeched, eyeing her through the rearview mirror.

I laughed out loud. "It's fine. I used to play in a bar and I got paid, so I must not suck."

"That's so cool," Kyla said. "Have you performed since you've been here?"

"Not yet," I said. "I'd love to, but I haven't really had a chance."

Kyla parked the car and we headed into the restaurant. The three of us were seated at a table in the corner. Tori set Savannah's carrier on the chair next to her. The baby girl had barely made a peep since we left Forever Inked and she was sleeping peacefully. "Is she always this good?" I asked.

"No," Tori huffed. "She's saving all her energy for the middle of the night. It's like she knows exactly when Chris and I are having sex to decide she wants our attention. She's the ultimate cock-blocker."

I couldn't help but giggle at her admission.

"Oh, please!" Kyla admonished. "You two are not sex deprived. Did you even wait the recommended six weeks?"

"Four. I couldn't wait any longer. Don't judge, it was torture. We'll see how you do after you have the twins," Tori said without shame.

"The way I feel right now, I'm never letting Tyler touch me again," Kyla said.

"That's a lie," Tori said. Then she turned her attention to me and leaned across the table. "So, you and Zack, huh?"

I had wondered how long it would take until this came up. "Um-hmm."

"Don't um-hmm me, girl. Spill the details. That boy is one deliciously hot piece of man. How did you meet?"

Kyla smacked Tori on the arm. "You're a married woman. Have some restraint."

Tori rolled her eyes. "I'm happily married, but I'm not blind."

I was saved by the waitress who came to take our order. But once she left, Tori pressed on. "Well?"

I had rehearsed my answer. "We met in New York and became friends. I needed a fresh start, so I came back to Michigan with Zack."

"The way he kissed you says *more than friends*," Kyla interjected.

I shrugged my shoulders. "We started as friends, and it recently blossomed into something else."

Tori held up her hands. "Wait! Have you been living with Zack since you got here?"

"I have my own room, but yes," I answered honestly.

"How in the world did you not jump him before that? How's the sex? You two have had sex, haven't you?" Tori asked excitedly.

I could feel the heat creeping up my neck at her boldness. Kyla buried her face in her hands. "You'll have to excuse Tori. She's never been known for her modesty."

"Hey, inquiring minds want to know," Tori defended. "So?"

"It's phenomenal," I admitted.

"I knew it! God Kyla, you should have hit that when you had the chance. I always predicted he would be good in bed."

I looked at the beautiful woman in front of me. "You two never…?"

Kyla waved her hand at me. "God, no! Not that it didn't cross my mind, but I wasn't in the right place at the time. Thank goodness, we didn't. I don't think I could work for him if we had."

I sighed out a breath of relief. "I thought you two had been together."

"Nope. But Zack was there for me during a really hard time in my life. He was a friend when I needed one. Tyler and I had broken up and then my parents died in a car accident. Zack did my first tattoo. We've been friends ever since."

Kyla and I had more in common than I thought possible. And Tori, although she was bold, cracked me up. The three of us chatted like we had known each other for years and I decided that I really liked these two women. They accepted me easily. No judgement. No pretentiousness.

It was just what I needed.

Chapter 19
Zack

The buzzer on the backdoor rang. I checked the security camera and yep, my eleven o'clock appointment was here. I should have been star-struck, but I wasn't anymore. I used to be when I first started tattooing. But after chatting with them for hours while I tatted their skin, I realized famous people are not that much different than everyone else.

Being a tattoo artist was a lot like being a bartender. People seemed to open up to you, tell you their hopes, dreams, and mostly their problems. Of course, the fact I had to sign non-disclosure agreements helped loosen their lips. Nothing they told me could be repeated and I was a good listener.

Surprise, surprise, rich people had problems too. I should have known that. I had as much money as most of my high-profile clients and my life hadn't always been roses. Far from it.

I opened the door and greeted my client. "Hey, Bobby."

"What's up, Zack?" He came in and shook my hand. I led him to my private studio, and he relaxed back in the chair. "Thanks for taking me so late. I appreciate not having to deal with all the bullshit."

"Hey, we've been doing this a long time. You know I don't mind. All I ask for in return is a referral," I answered.

"I've been sending guys your way for as long as you've been tatting me."

"And I appreciate it," I told him. I pulled out the design I did for him and held it up. "What do you think?" It was a music staff with notes, a guitar, and a mic intertwined. Underneath were the words *It's a Lonely Road.*

Bobby took it from my hands and inspected it. "I fucking love it!"

"Cool. Where's it going?"

He tapped the back of his left shoulder. I motioned for him to get out of the chair and then I adjusted it, so it laid flat like a table. "You want anything to drink before we get started?"

"Man, you know I like my Jim Beam." He laughed.

I unlocked the cabinet I had for special clients. Inside was a small fridge and a stocked bar that held their favorites. It was another perk of coming to me to get work done. "I'm gonna go make a transfer. Help yourself, but you know my rule. No more than two, unless you want to bleed like a stuffed pig."

He saluted me. "Your shop, your rules."

I made the transfer and returned to find him lying shirtless on the table, drink in hand. "Comfortable?" I joked.

"Very. The drink helps too."

I placed the transfer on his shoulder and pulled back the paper. "You want to look at this before I get started."

"Nah. If I didn't trust you, Zack, I wouldn't be here."

"Fair enough." I looked at the placement on his back and was satisfied. "This is gonna take a few hours. If you decide you want to stop, let me know and we can finish it another night."

"I want to try to power through it. I'm going on tour in a couple of weeks and my schedule gets packed," he said.

"No problem."

Bobby and I started talking about his upcoming tour, music, and his family. I'd been inking him for the last three years and we were like old friends.

A couple of hours in, I glanced at the clock and realized Clarissa would be getting off work soon. I stood up and stretched my back. I tapped him on the shoulder. "I gotta take a quick break. My girl's getting off work soon. She works down the street at The Locker and I don't like her walking home by herself. I'll only be fifteen minutes."

Bobby looked at me with a smug smile. "You finally got yourself a girl? Gina?"

"Nah. Gina and I were never a couple. We just had fun together. Rissa's the real deal." I couldn't help but smile when I talked about her.

He let out a low laugh, "Look at you, all in love and shit."

"Yeah, I am," I admitted. "Listen, I'll send her right upstairs. You want me to shut the door or are you gonna sneak out back for a smoke?"

He looked offended. "What? You don't want me to meet her?"

I quirked an eye at him and crossed my arms over my chest. "She doesn't know you're here. I figured you'd want to keep it that way."

"Hell, no! I want to meet your girl. You barely ever date. You've got more trust issues than I do."

"For good reasons," I scoffed. "But Rissa's different. There's just something about her."

"Go get your girl," he ordered.

"If you're sure. She might be a little giddy that you're here. She's really into music."

"Yeah?"

"Yeah. Guitar and piano. Has a voice that can bring me to my knees."

"Go get her!"

"You're sure?"

"I'm sure. Now go!"

Clarissa was going to flip the fuck out. I was elated that I could share this with her. I didn't want to keep secrets from her, but confidentiality was a non-negotiable part of my job. Not even Layla and Chase knew who I worked on after hours.

I got there just in time. Clarissa was packing her purse with her tips and came out from behind the bar. I grabbed her hand and pulled her to my chest. "I've got a surprise for you."

She smiled up at me. "Is it sex?"

"Better than sex," I told her as I pulled her out the door.

She giggled as she tried to keep up with my long strides. "No way. After last night, I don't think that's possible."

"Okay," I conceded. "Maybe not as good as sex, but a close second."

"What is it?" She laughed. Clarissa tugged on my hand to slow down, so she could slip her heels off. In her bare feet, she moved faster. "Slow down, Zack. My feet are killing me."

I stopped and scooped her up in my arms. "I can't have that now, can I?" She wrapped her arms around my neck, her shoes dangling from her fingers, as I carried her down the street.

"Have I told you how damn sexy you are?" she asked.

"You may have mentioned it, but you can say it again. Preferably when I'm buried deep inside you," I said playfully.

"Damn! Screw the surprise. Just take me to bed."

I set her down outside the door. "I am taking you to bed, but I have to finish working first."

She raised her eyebrows. "Your client is still here? Do you have to blindfold me or something?"

I pressed my lips to hers and caressed her tongue with mine. "I like the way you think. I'll blindfold you later, but first I want you to meet my client."

"Are you serious? I thought that was forbidden," she questioned.

"Usually, it is. But I told him about you, and he wanted to meet you."

"He does? Why?"

"I told him you were into music, and I guess he was intrigued."

I took Clarissa's hand and led her inside to my studio. She froze in her tracks and her shoes fell from her fingers. "Oh! My! God! You're... you're..." she stuttered.

He reached out his hand to her and laughed. "I'm Bobby. Nice to meet you, Rissa."

She took his hand hesitantly. "Wow! It's amazing to meet you."

"Why don't you hang with us while Zack finishes up," he suggested.

"Are you sure? I don't want to be in the way. I can go upstairs."

Bobby pulled a chair in front of the table. "Stay. I want to hear about your music."

Clarissa sat in the chair. "Okay. What do you want to know?"

Bobby laid down on the table and I started up my tattoo gun. "How did you get started?" he asked.

"My mama played piano and my daddy played guitar. They taught me from the time I was little. Before I knew it, I could play just about anything by ear. I guess I had a natural talent for it. My daddy and I used to sing and play for hours on the back porch." When Clarissa talked about home, her accent always came out. I loved how damn adorable it was.

"Nice accent. Where you from?" Bobby asked.

"Oklahoma originally." She blushed. "I moved to New York when I was eighteen. I tried to get rid of the accent, but it never fully went away. I had dreams of making it big with my music, but after three years all I managed to do was perform in bars."

"First of all, don't ever change who you are to make someone else happy. Second, there's nothing wrong with singing in bars. I've played in plenty of them. Everyone's got to start somewhere."

Clarissa shrugged. "I guess. I just thought it would be easier. I'm putting it on the back burner for now."

"You're giving up?" he questioned.

"I wouldn't call it giving up. I'd call it realigning my priorities. I still love music. I just haven't had time to pursue it since I moved here."

"Have you even talked to Lou about it?" I interrupted.

Clarissa gave me a hard stare. "No. He hired me to be a bartender, not a singer."

I rolled my eyes at her. "Does he even know you can sing?"

"No. It never really came up," she answered.

"Well, make sure it does come up. You have to promote yourself," Bobby encouraged.

I agreed with him wholeheartedly. I wanted Clarissa to get back to her music. She shined so bright the night she sang at the fair and I wanted that for her. I wanted her to be happy.

An hour later, I wiped the last of the blood and ink from Bobby's shoulder. "You want to check this out?"

"I do, but I don't need to. I already know it looks fucking fantastic." Bobby got up from the table and checked out his new tat. "Amazing as always," he complimented.

"I'm just glad you're happy, man." I always took pride in my work, but on someone like Bobby it was even more important to me.

He turned to Clarissa. "Before I go, I want to hear you sing."

She pulled back in surprise. "You do?"

"Sure do. Go get your guitar," he encouraged.

"Umm... okay." Clarissa headed upstairs to grab her guitar.

I started cleaning up the area and putting my tools away. "You didn't have to do that, but you just made her night."

"She's sweet. With her looks, if she's got a voice to match, I might be able to help her out," he said. "Is she good?"

I couldn't hold back my smile. "I'm biased. I'll let you be the judge. You're the expert."

Clarissa came back down holding her Gibson. She sat on a stool and cradled the guitar in her lap. "What do you want to hear?"

"Why don't you do that angel song," I suggested.

Bobby sat back on the table and prepared to listen.

Clarissa nodded at me and began to play. Once she started it was like the rest of the world melted away for her. She closed her eyes and got lost in the song. Her voice was even better than the first time I heard her play the song. It was strong, crescendoing in all the right places and then getting softer in others. I loved listening to her when she was consumed by the music.

When she finished, Bobby started a slow clap and let out a whistle. "Color me impressed. I did not expect you to have a set of pipes like that."

Clarissa blushed fiercely, and it was cute. "Thank you," she said softly.

"You can't quit, that's for sure. Let me work on this. My connections are endless, and I have some ideas. As a matter of fact, my tour starts in a couple of weeks. I'm gonna hook you two up with VIP tickets. I want you at my show."

I reached my hand forward and Bobby clasped it. "Thanks, man. We'll be there."

"Can I give you a hug?" Clarissa asked.

Bobby's face broke out in a huge grin. "Like I'd tell a girl as pretty as you no."

She stretched up on her toes and wrapped her arms around him and he hugged her back. "Thank you. This is a night I'll never forget. It was so cool meeting you."

"I enjoyed meeting you too. No giving up, Rissa. It's not even an option," he told her.

He turned towards me with a wink. "I'll be in touch." Then he strode out the back door and disappeared into the night.

Chapter 20
Rissa

"I can't believe that just happened." I sighed, as I hopped up on the table. "Who would've thought?"

"I'm as surprised as you are. He's usually pretty private. But I'll tell you this about him, for as controversial as he is, deep down he's a good guy," Zack said. He continued to clean his equipment and tidy up the room.

"Do you think he would really help me?" I asked.

Zack crossed his arms and leaned back against the counter. "He might. He started from nothing and appreciates good talent."

"Can you imagine? What if I really made something of myself?" I said dreamily. "I've always felt like my daddy gave up his life for me and I've wasted it. What if I could make him proud of me?"

Zack came to me and stood between my legs. He held my face in his hands. "Sweetheart, your mama and daddy are watching over you and I bet you make them proud every day."

I dropped my eyes and stared at the ground. "I wouldn't be so sure about that."

What would they have to be proud about? Their daughter was stupid enough to become a statistic, an unwed mother with no education. I was doing okay now, but what would happen when I had this baby? How would I be able to work and take care of a baby?

He caressed my jaw with his thumbs. "Why wouldn't they be proud of you? You're beautiful and smart and talented. You went to New York all by yourself and you survived. Hell, you thrived. This is just a speedbump. Things will be good again. I promise you."

I raised my head and met his green eyes. "Things are good with you. I love you so much, Zack. You make everything else fade away. I need you to stay part of my life." I couldn't lose him too.

151

"I'm not going anywhere," he said softly, as he pushed my hair over my shoulder. "Come on. I think it's time we go to bed."

Zack lifted me by the waist and set me on the floor. He picked up my guitar with one hand and held onto mine with the other. He double checked the locks and alarm, then led us upstairs. He set my guitar on the couch and took us to his bedroom. He backed me to the edge of the bed. "I missed you today."

I ran my hands down his chest. "I missed you too." I grabbed onto his belt loops and pulled him closer. "Make love to me, Zack. Make me forget about everything else."

The look in his eyes held desire. Without a word, he pulled my shirt up over my head and threw it to the side. I snaked my hands up under his shirt and pulled it over his head, throwing it next to mine. My hands ran over his hard chest. "I love your body. You're so damn sexy. But I love your heart more."

Zack put a finger over my lips. "Shhh! No more talking. Let me fuck you. You make me want you so bad, Clarissa Lynne. I've never wanted anyone as much as I want you."

His hands went to the button and zipper on my pants, undoing them quickly. I shimmied them down my hips and stepped out of them. Then I undid his belt and pushed his jeans down. He let them fall to the floor and kicked them to the side. We stood before each other in nothing but our underwear.

I gripped the top of his boxer briefs and pulled them down as I sank to my knees. He was long and thick and beautiful. I wrapped my hand around his length and began to stroke it up and down. I took his head into my mouth and caressed it with my tongue.

Zack let out a groan, then grabbed me under the arms and pulled me to my feet. "I don't want to see you on your knees for anyone. Not even me. You're so much better than that. If you're going to suck me off, then we'll do it on the bed."

He turned us around and laid back into the middle of his king-size bed. I nestled between his thighs and took him in my mouth again. I couldn't stop myself. My tongue licked up and down his hard cock, while he groaned in pleasure. I tightened my lips around him and sucked harder. His hand ran

152

through my hair and pulled me down to take him deeper. I took him all the way to the back of my throat.

Zack groaned again, although this time it was more like a growl that started deep in his chest. I wanted to make him feel good. I wanted to treat him right, to give him a little back for all that he had done for me.

He pulled my hair away from my face and into a heap on top of my head. "I wanna watch you suck my dick, sweetheart. Your mouth is a deadly weapon. It feels so good."

His words encouraged me to take him deeper. Harder. Faster. He was older than me and more experienced. I wanted to show him that I wasn't some little girl. I needed him to never want to let me go. I pushed myself to take as much of him as I could. What didn't fit in my mouth, I stroked with my hand. I was relentless in my quest to make him come. I needed him to keep me.

His hips bucked beneath me, as he fucked my mouth. I wanted him to enjoy this, and his hips told me he was. "You gotta stop, baby. I'm gonna come so hard," he gasped.

I shook my head, never letting up. His hand pushed on the back of my head pushing me deeper and I felt him tense beneath me. Warm spurts shot down my throat and I swallowed every last drop of his cum. His body went limp as he ran his fingers through my hair. I eased up and caressed him with my tongue, kissing the head of his cock before I released him.

I lifted my head and peered at him over his muscular, tatted chest. "I've been wanting to do that for a long time," I told him coyly.

He pulled me up by the arms so that we were face to face. "I've wanted you to do that to me for just as long. Hell, I've fantasized about it."

"Was it as good as your fantasy?" I asked breathlessly.

I rested on his chest, still in my bra and panties. Zack cupped my face. "A million times better." He pulled my face to his and ravaged me with a kiss. His tongue pushed into my mouth and tangled with mine. If he tasted himself on me, he didn't let it show. He was a man on a mission. He kissed me passionately, as if I were the only girl in the world. As if his next breath depended on it. His hands slid up my back and in one flick of his wrist, my bra was undone. His large hands rubbed up and down my spine and slipped inside my panties. He cupped my ass and squeezed, pulling me closer to him.

"I need you naked now. I need to taste you, Clarissa. I want to eat your pussy and then I'm gonna fuck you so good."

I shivered at his words. I felt the tingle between my legs intensify. I could feel myself getting wetter with every word that left his lips. He slipped a finger inside me from behind and I whimpered at the feel of him. I knew it was nothing compared to what he was going to do to me. I whispered one word. "Yes."

He quickly flipped me over and tore my bra away from my body, throwing it to the side. Before I could get my bearing, his lips were on my breasts. He took each one in a hand and pulled them together, alternating from one to the other licking and nipping and sucking. I threw my head back in ecstasy and let out a gasp. He wasn't gentle, but I didn't want him to be. I wanted to experience him unleashed and uncontrolled. This was so different than last night. Last night we'd made love, tonight he was going to fuck me. Hard. This was the Zack hidden behind all the sweetness he showed me. I thought last night was good, but I had a feeling I hadn't seen anything yet. The anticipation was killing me.

He continued to ravage my breasts as he ripped my panties from my body. I let out a squeal of surprise at the force he used. Despite his intensity, he didn't scare me. I knew Zack would never hurt me. He plunged his long fingers inside me and stroked me hard, his thumb coming up to rub on my clit. All my nerve-endings were lit on fire. I arched into his hand, trying to increase the pressure. "Oh god, Zack! More…more…please," I begged.

He didn't disappoint. He lifted my hips and brought his mouth to my center. He lapped and ate at me with wild abandon. He was a starving man and I was his feast, willingly laid out on a silver platter for him.

His tongue piercing rubbed over my clit and I thought I would explode. It barely took seconds before I felt the orgasm rising up inside me. It started low and began to build. I felt the tension winding me tight. It erased every thought from my mind. It kept building until I felt like I was on the crest of a wave that refused to break. Zack continued his sweet torture on my body. I couldn't take anymore. It became almost painful. I was coiled so tight and desperately wanted the release. "I can't," I gasped. "I can't." But Zack never relented. He continued kissing and nipping and sucking at me, taking me to a place I'd never been before. I was being wound tighter and tighter

154

with every stroke of his tongue. I stood on the edge of a cliff. Hovering. Waiting.

And then I broke. I let out a loud scream as I fell off the edge. I free-fell into an abyss. Wave after wave of ecstasy racked my body. I felt myself jerking up from the mattress. I had lost all control, blinded by white light as a barrage of sounds escaped from my lips. Pleasure took over. There was nothing else.

Before I even came down, Zack slipped inside me. He punished my body with every thrust of his hips. He wasn't holding back. Last night had only been a preview of what was to come. I grabbed his shoulders and held on tight, afraid of what would happen if I didn't. My nails pierce his skin, but it didn't stop him. I didn't want it to stop him.

Nothing in my life had ever compared to the pleasure Zack was bringing me. I felt the familiar tightening of my muscles. I didn't know if I could survive a second orgasm like the first, but I couldn't stop it. I didn't want to stop it. Sweat coated my body and all I could hear was our skin slapping together. Flesh on flesh. It was painful, but the pleasure far outweighed the pain. I wouldn't stop him. I couldn't. I wanted this with him. A second orgasm tore through me. I felt myself clenching his cock.

I went limp under the weight of Zack and then he released everything, filling me up as he screamed my name. The muscles in his neck pulled tight as he threw his head back. Then he collapsed on me. "Holy shit!"

Our bodies were slick with sweat. His head was buried in my shoulder. I ran my fingers through the wet hair at the nape of his neck. We smelled of sweat and sex. I couldn't imagine anything better.

Zack rolled to the side bringing me with him and hugging me to his chest. "Are you okay?" he asked.

"I'm better than okay. I'm perfect."

"I knew you had it in you," he said with a smirk.

"What?"

"All those quiet little sounds you make during sex drive me crazy, but I've been dying to hear you scream."

"It was a first," I admitted, burying my head in his chest. I remembered the sounds that had escaped me and suddenly I felt shy. "You're the only one whose made me scream like that."

155

Zack tilted my head up to look me in the eyes. "Don't be embarrassed about it. It was sexy as hell. And if I have my way, it won't be the last time I make you scream."

♫♪♫♪

Zack and I slept in the next day. It had been after four in the morning before we fell asleep. Layla was opening the shop and Zack didn't have any appointments until the afternoon.

We laid in bed, my legs twining with his. Rain pelted the windows, the sky still dark from the gray clouds outside. I had been awake for a while, but I had no desire to move. My body ached deliciously. I could still feel where Zack had been buried between my legs.

Soft kisses trailed down the side of my face. My eyes fluttered open and focused on his green eyes. I reached up and ran my hand along the soft stubble on his face. He grabbed my hand and brought my palm to his mouth, placing gentle kisses on the center of it. "Good morning, sweetheart."

"Good morning," I whispered back. I ran a hand down his naked chest and up his arm. They were covered in intricate designs, some beautiful and others dark. They told a story I wanted to know. Zack watched me as I scanned his body. He'd been tight lipped when I'd asked before. He always changed the subject in an act of avoidance. "Will you tell me now?"

Zack let out a deep sigh. "What do you want to know?"

"Everything," I said softly. "I want to know what these mean to you." I traced the ink on his body, like it was a map to a treasure I desperately wanted to find.

"Why?"

"Because they're a part of you. I want to know everything about you. When did you get your first tattoo?" I asked, trying to ease him into telling me.

Zack ran his hand through his hair. "I was in the Marines. One of the guys in my unit did this for me," he said tapping his shoulder. On his upper arm was a globe with an anchor and an eagle. The words *Semper Fi* were scripted under it. "I got this one next." He rubbed his hand over the lower right side of his abdomen where two machine guns were crossed.

156

"Is that where you learned the art of tattooing?" I asked. "In the Marines?"

"Yep. I drew a lot and was eager to learn. Darren took me under his wing. He became my best friend and a brother when I was in the Middle East. While most guys would spend their nights reading or playing cards, Darren taught me everything he knew."

"Do you still talk to him?"

Zack looked up at the ceiling and let out a ragged breath. "Nope."

I ran my hand down the side of his face, urging him to tell me the rest. I could tell this was hard for him. "What happened?" I asked softly.

He ran his hand through his hair again. "A group of us were sent to check out what were supposed to be abandoned buildings. Intelligence got wind that some rebels had been moving into the area. It was supposed to be safe. Checking the buildings was a formality. The first few were empty, and we all started to relax. We let our guard down. We broke one of the first rules of the military. We got comfortable. Darren was telling a dirty joke when we entered the last structure. He was the first one to go in. In a split second, all hell broke loose. Darren was down, and bullets were flying. We lost three guys that day. Darren was one of them. I held him in my arms as he bled out."

"I'm so sorry," I whispered.

Zack tapped the inside of his left arm, where a tattoo of dog tags sat. One had the initials *D. A. R.* The other had a date. "I did this one myself. Even though he's gone, Darren is always with me."

"Do you have PTSD?" I shouldn't have asked, but I wanted to know.

Zack gave me a wary look. "I'm a Kincaid, of course not. My father wouldn't tolerate it."

"But?"

"I passed all the psych exams, but that doesn't mean I'm not affected by the shit I did and saw. It's not something I talk about."

"Fair enough. Tell me about your other tattoos." Surely, they couldn't all have sad stories behind them. Zack loosened up and told me the stories behind all the ink on his body. Some were funny, some were inspirational, and some were just for the hell of it. I soaked it all in, trying to decode everything that was Zack.

157

I pointed to the heart on his chest with a dagger forced through it. "And this one?"

"A reminder," he said vaguely.

Someone had broken his heart before. Layla had alluded to it when I first met her. I wasn't going to ask for the details, but it must have been bad.

Zack ran his hands over my shoulders and down my back. "Enough about me. I want to talk about you and all this smooth, creamy skin with not a mark on it. Part of me wants to leave it flawless and another part of me wants to take your virginity."

I laughed. "I think we're way past that. I haven't been a virgin for a long time."

He pulled me to his lips and kissed me. "Thank God for that, but I wasn't speaking sexually. I meant that I wanted to be the first to permanently mark you."

"I've already been permanently marked," I said with melancholy.

Zack raised his eyebrow. "I've kissed and touched every inch of your body and I haven't seen anything, unless it's behind your ear or somewhere else equally illusive." He playfully checked behind my ears just to be sure.

I swatted his hand away. "You can look all you want, but you'll never find what you're searching for." I sat up, straddled his legs and put my hand to my chest. "My tattoos are here. Everyone I've ever loved has left me and each one of them has left permanent scars on my heart. So, although you can't see them, I do have tattoos. I have a tattooed heart."

Zack took my hands and let out a sigh. "I'm sorry, sweetheart."

"Don't be. I wouldn't trade having them in my heart for anything. The marks they've left behind have made me who I am. They've made me stronger."

I don't think Zack knew what to say. He pulled me to his chest and wrapped his arms around me. I let his warmth seep into my skin as he held me. This man had the power to heal me or totally destroy me.

"Make me a promise," I whispered.

"Anything. I'd do anything for you, Clarissa." He held my chin and lifted my head as he whispered kisses down my neck.

I gasped at the feel of his soft lips skimming over my skin. "Don't ever leave me. Don't tattoo my heart, Zack."

158

He licked his lips and stared into my eyes. "I'm not gonna leave you. Do you know why?"

I shook my head almost imperceptibly. "Why?"

"Because I've never loved anyone the way I love you. I'm never letting you go."

"Promise?" I didn't believe him. I needed to hear him say it.

"Promise."

Chapter 21
Zack

On the outside, Clarissa was a self-assured confident woman. But on the inside, she was scared and vulnerable. It was that side of her that she didn't let anyone see. Except me. I loved that she trusted me enough to see her raw and exposed. She'd lost so much, that I could understand why she thought she'd lose me too. No way was that happening. She made me want to wrap my arms around her and keep her safe with me. Forever. I wanted to take care of this sweet, sweet girl.

"You know what we need?" I asked playfully.

"What?"

"A nice hot shower to wash away the bad memories. I want to create new memories just for us." I pulled her by the hand and dragged her to the bathroom. I turned on the shower and let the water warm.

"Is this us conserving water?" she giggled.

"Fuck conserving water. This is me getting you wet in more ways than one." I swatted her ass. "Get in."

Clarissa grabbed her ass. "I kind of like this side of you. I didn't know spanking was part of your repertoire, but I like it."

My dick instantly stood at attention. "Oh darling, you have no idea what I'm capable of." Gina and I had some very dirty times together. Filthy. All I could think about was all the dirty, filthy things I wanted to do to Clarissa. I wanted to introduce her to my world. Her pleasure would be my only concern. And her pleasure was sure to please me.

She stood under the hot water, and I watched as it rolled down her body and dripped off her luscious tits. She was so innocent looking, and I wanted to do nothing but corrupt her. She was mine and mine alone. I'd been patient. I'd been gentle with her so far. I didn't want to scare her away.

"You're looking at me like you want to devour me," Clarissa teased.

"Oh sweetheart, you have no idea. We've only explored the tip of the iceberg." I swooped down, reached between her legs, and grabbed the back of her perfect thighs. I lifted her effortlessly, slid her up my chest until her legs hung over my shoulders and her center was at my mouth.

She squealed in surprise and held onto my head as I backed her against the wall. This is where I wanted her. Pussy in my face. I kissed her slick pink flesh and swept my tongue over her clit. She moaned breathlessly, and I decided that the piercing in my tongue was the best decision I'd ever made.

I ate at her mercilessly, sticking my tongue deep inside her, tasting every bit of her sweetness. Up and down and around, returning to her clit to give it proper attention. I nipped and pulled and rubbed the silver ball on my tongue back and forth across it. She squirmed, but I held her tight. No way was she getting away from me.

Her wetness covered my lips and chin. I didn't care that she was smeared all over my face. I wanted it. I needed it. It was everything that was good and satisfying. I pulled back, because I needed to hear that she was enjoying this as much as I was. "Do you like this, sweetheart?"

She leaned against the tiled wall. One hand wrapped around my head while she used the other one to stabilize herself on the wall. "So much. Don't stop, I'm gonna come, don't stop. I'm so close."

They were the magic words I needed to hear. Her hips bucked into me, fucking my face. Her hand gripped the back of my head, pulling me in closer. I lapped at her pussy and kissed and nipped and sucked on her clit until she came all over me. She went boneless and began to pant. "Oh God, oh God..." so softly, I barely heard her.

When she came down from her orgasm, I lowered her to her feet then turned her to face the wall. "Don't fucking move," I instructed.

Like the good girl she was, she faced the wall bracing herself on the tile. "Do it, Zack. I want it so much."

I wouldn't disappoint her. I wrapped one arm around her chest and the other hand grabbed her hip. Using my knee, I pushed her legs further apart and slid into her effortlessly. She was so goddamn wet for me. And so fucking tight. She was every dream I had come true. I had jacked off to the image of her just like this so many times. I stilled inside her. "Tell me what you want, Clarissa. Tell me how you want it."

She shifted her hips up and out. I had a perfect view of my dick in her pussy. I growled at what she was telling me without any words at all. She turned her head to look at me over her shoulder. "You know what I want. Are you going to make me beg?"

I pulled back and thrust into her hard. "You know I love when you beg."

She let out a moan of pleasure. "Please."

Her innocence was more than I could take. I began to fuck her hard. I slammed into her over and over again. My balls slapped against her. The sound was the only thing I could hear. I reached between her legs and rubbed her clit furiously. I needed her to come all over my dick.

"Yes...yes...yeeeessss!" She panted. Her tight little body tensed as she threw her head back into my chest. The feeling of her coming on my cock made me fuck her harder. Her arousal slicked my dick and pulsed around me. Nothing could be better than this. I drove into her hard and fast, chasing my own release.

My balls tightened, and my neck strained. "Fuck!" I continued pounding into her from behind, until I had nothing left. I dropped my head to her shoulder and leaned against the wall. "So good, sweetheart. So good," I panted.

She turned and faced me, wrapping her arms around my neck. Her hands gripped the back of my head and she kissed me. Hard. When she pulled back, our foreheads touched as she spoke to me. "I don't just want the tip of the iceberg. I want it all. I'll be whatever you need me to be."

And if I didn't think she was perfect before, she was now. "Do you know what you're asking for?"

"Not really, but I want to find out. Teach me. Show me how to make you happy."

I ran my hand down the side of her face. "You already make me happy. Dirty sex would just be the icing on the cake."

"I wanna be the icing," she insisted.

This girl. I closed my eyes and took a deep breath. "If we do this, we do it slow. I'll teach you, but you have to promise me something."

"Anything."

"When it's too much, you tell me. We're both supposed to enjoy it. If it goes too far, I would never forgive myself. I love you too much to hurt you," I confessed.

"You would never physically hurt me. I trust you."

"It's not just physical. It's mental too. You have to trust that anything I do is for both of us. You have to trust that pleasure is the end game."

"I want pleasure," she said innocently. She had no idea what she was asking for, but I nodded my head anyway.

"Turn around," I ordered. She did as I asked as I filled my hands with her strawberry shampoo. I ran them over her head and massaged her scalp. She moaned at the feel of my hands on her head. I ran them through her long locks and then began to rinse her hair. "The first thing you need to know, is that I will always take care of you. I want you to be happy, Clarissa. There's nothing more important than that." It was the truth. My mind started reeling through all the filthy things I wanted to do to her. This was different than Gina though. Gina didn't have my heart. We were all about the physicality of it, not the emotions. Although I cared about Gina, my emotions had never played a part in our relationship.

There was so much more on the line with Clarissa. It was going to be a tough balancing act. One I wasn't sure I could pull off. I didn't need the dirty sex with Clarissa, but I craved it.

"When do we start?" she asked.

"We already have. You letting me in, was the first step. Slow, sweetheart. We'll get there, but it's going to take time," I told her.

I finished rinsing her hair then washed her body, from her sexy shoulders to the bottom of her small feet. I wrapped her in a towel and then continued my own shower.

My head was spinning. I should have never opened my big mouth. When I looked at Clarissa, I didn't just see a playground for my sexual fantasies. I saw a woman I could have a future with. Maybe start a family with.

Wait! What? Back the truck up!

Where did that thought come from? I wasn't in a hurry to have kids. It must have been seeing Kyla yesterday that made my mind go there. She seemed so damn happy, and I was happy for her. She looked so damn cute all big and round. I imagined what Clarissa would look like pregnant and I smiled. I rubbed a hand down my face and wiped the smile away. I had no business thinking that way. I wasn't ready for kids. No way, no how. That was something so far in the future it had its own zip code.

Clarissa was changing me. We were definitely going to explore this craving inside me, but slowly. Hell, I'd gone a month with barely touching her and it didn't kill me. I wanted to worship her body and always bring her pleasure. That would be my focus.

I finished my shower and got dressed. I found Clarissa in her room, sitting in the middle of her bed. She was scribbling something in a notebook. Priss was stretched out next to her, kneading the comforter.

"Hey," I said. "I'm going to head down. I've got an appointment in twenty. What time do you go to work?"

She closed the notebook and pushed it to the side. "Not 'til four. I'm going to spend some time cleaning up around here before I go."

I lifted my chin to the furball that was crawling into her lap. "Are you two friends now?"

Clarissa shrugged her shoulders as she rubbed down Priss's back. "Looks that way."

I strode into her room. "Good. I'm glad the two most important women in my life are getting along." I pecked her on the lips. "You don't have to clean. That's what I have Linda for. She's coming the day after tomorrow."

"Good to know. I'll be down a little later."

"Okay." I cupped her face in my hands. "I love you." She was the only woman I'd said that to since Megan. I'd given my heart to Megan, and she'd taken a dagger and stabbed right through it. I didn't love easily, but with Clarissa, I couldn't help myself. She was so damn perfect. So damn addicting.

"Love you, too."

♫♪♫♪

164

Later than evening, my stomach rumbled something fierce. With our late night and busy morning, I hadn't grabbed anything but a protein shake before heading down for my appointments. I was running on empty, and my fuel tank needed filling.

I headed upstairs to make a quick sandwich before my seven o'clock showed. I opened the door, and the unmistakable smell of chocolate chip cookies filled my nose. "No, she didn't," I mumbled to myself. I strode to the kitchen on a mission. Sitting on the counter was a plate covered in foil with a note on top. *I'd say these were for dessert, but I have other ideas for that. I know how much you like things with sweet, creamy filling. Consider these an appetizer.*

I groaned at her innuendo. Yeah, she went there and now all I could think about was licking her.

On this kitchen counter.

Totally naked.

Her legs spread wide.

My tongue deep inside her.

I ran my hand over my rock-hard cock. Since Clarissa had moved in, my dick had gotten a mind of his own. Even when I was trying to be good, he betrayed me. For the last month I'd walked around with a perpetual hard-on. I tried to keep it under wraps when she sauntered around here in her silky robe or left the apartment smelling so sweet, I had no choice but to think of her. Everything about Clarissa drove me crazy, from the way she looked to the way she smelled to the soft little sounds she made. My cock hadn't made it any easier. He was a total dick...pun intended.

I pulled back the foil on the plate and swiped a cookie. One bite and I was a goner. They were so soft and sweet and delicious, just like my girl. Sooo good. I groaned as I popped another one in my mouth.

Clarissa had baked me a new treat every week since she'd been here. She had some serious baking skills. And she could cook too. On the rare occasions when we were both home, she always cooked dinner. I tried to take her out instead, but she said she loved cooking. I wasn't complaining. It had been years since I'd had homecooked meals.

165

I bet she had cooked all the time for Wes. I hadn't thought about him much since Clarissa had been here. As a matter of fact, I tried not to think about him for obvious reasons. I used to talk to Wes every other day. We'd bullshit about nothing and everything. I missed those calls. Despite the four years between us, we'd always been close. I stared down at his silver skull ring on my finger. "You stupid fucker," I muttered. "What the hell were you thinking?"

I looked up at the ceiling and rubbed a hand through my hair. "I didn't mean for it to happen," I said out loud, as if he could hear me. "I didn't mean to fuck her the day of your funeral. I didn't mean to bring her home with me. I didn't mean to fall in love with her. I didn't mean to betray you."

I took a deep breath and continued with the words I should have told him before today. "You were a stupid motherfucker for choosing drugs over that sweet girl. You left her to the wolves. Or wolf, I should say. Malcolm tried to destroy her. I couldn't stand watching the way he treated her, and so I wanted to help. That's how this whole thing started in the first place. The more time I spent with her, the more I could see why you fell in love with her. She's feisty and fiery, yet so damn naïve and innocent. You had good taste in women, I'll give you that."

"So, when I see you again, if you want to kick my ass, or try to, I'll totally understand. But until then, I'm going to take care of her, because she's amazing. And she makes great chocolate chip cookies." I ended my confession, by popping another delicious *appetizer* in my mouth.

I grabbed the note from the cookies and went to my room to stick it in the nightstand. I shook my head when I turned on the light. All my dirty laundry was washed and folded on my bed. When Clarissa said she would take care of *me*, she wasn't kidding. The apartment was clean and tidy, she made me cookies, and she did my laundry.

I squinted my eyes at the clean clothes. Something was missing. Sleeping on my clean shirts was one of Miss Priss's favorite things to do. It was why I had stock in lint rollers. But she was suspiciously missing.

"Miss Priss, where are you?" I called out. Usually when I called her, she'd come running, but not this time. "Priss?" I tried again. I turned from my room and headed to Clarissa's.

I flipped on the light and sighed. "You traitor." I couldn't blame her though. Clarissa had made a nest with some blankets and laid it in the middle of her bed. Miss Priss was snuggled into the warmth, sleeping. She lifted her head and gave me an innocent look with her yellow-green eyes.

I sat on the bed next to Priss and stroked her back. "Did she make this little nest for you? She's pretty good to us, isn't she?" As if answering me, Priss set her head back down and closed her eyes. She was perfectly comfortable and not moving anytime soon.

Sitting next to the blankets, was a glittery pink notebook. The same notebook I had seen her writing in earlier. I picked it up and turned it over in my hands. Curiosity was killing me. Most likely it was a diary of sorts. If I learned anything from having a sister, it was that looking at a girl's diary was total taboo. It was as bad as going through a woman's purse, maybe worse. Definitely worse.

My phone rang, saving me from committing an act of treason. I set the notebook back in the exact place I had found it and answered the call. "Hey, Kyla. What's up?"

"Hey, Zack. I just wanted to tell you that I enjoyed lunch with Rissa yesterday. She's great."

"Thanks. I think she's pretty great too. Thanks for taking her out. She really hasn't had a chance to make many friends here." I opened the fridge and pulled out the makings for a turkey and cheese sandwich.

"That's the other reason I'm calling," Kyla said. "I was wondering if you two want to come over for a bonfire Friday night. Well, actually it would be at Chris and Tori's house since Tyler and I still live in a condo. We'll order some food, have some drinks, and just hang out."

I set the mustard jar on the counter. "I don't mean to sound unappreciative, but we've never really hung out before. It's always been business between us." Truth be told, I had always tried to keep it business, for fear that my feelings for her would be apparent.

"That's not entirely true, Zack." She sighed. "You were there for me when I needed a friend. Both of us would be lying if we denied that there were some... feelings there. But we're past that. There's really no reason we can't hang out. Besides, I think it would be really good for Rissa. She needs this."

To say there were feelings would be an understatement. I had been crazy for her, but she was right. We were past that. "She does?" I questioned.

"Yes, Zack. I know she has you, but a girl needs girlfriends. There's only so much we can talk to our man about, sometimes we need another woman to talk to. Tori and I want to be that for Rissa."

It made total sense. The only girl Clarissa hung out with was Layla. I loved Layla, but she wasn't a girly girl. Layla was tough. She had to be to make it in this business. Clarissa was definitely a girly girl.

I sighed. "Okay. It's not going to be weird though, is it?"

"Zero weirdness. I promise. Just friends hanging out and having a good time."

"I can do that. Text me Tori's address."

I hung up with Kyla and finished making my sandwich. Kyla was probably right. Clarissa needed girl time. If there was anyone I trusted her with it was Tori and Kyla. They were both one hundred percent devoted to their husbands. Not that I didn't trust Clarissa, but I didn't want her hanging out with sleazy chicks either.

I finished my sandwich, went back downstairs, and waited for my dessert to get home from work.

Chapter 22
Rissa

It was a Wednesday night, and the crowd was dying out. The after-work crew was slowly trickling. All that was left were the diehards. Those who didn't care what day of the week it was or what time it was. Normal people were headed home to tuck themselves into bed for another long day of work tomorrow.

"You know what you need, Lou?" I asked as I wiped down the bar.

Lou threw his towel over his shoulder. "What's that?"

"Live entertainment. When I lived in New York, most of the bars had bands that would come in and play. The patrons loved it and it brought in extra business." I threw out the idea, hoping I would spark some interest.

"I've thought about it, but it just seems like too much work. I'm doing okay."

I looked around at the three tables that still had customers at them. "Seriously? You're happy with this? Newsflash… the people who play in bands have friends. Friends that will come to see them, even if they're not great."

Lou crossed his arms over his chest. "And how would I find these bands? How would I know if they're even any good?"

I crossed my arms too, showing him I wasn't messing around. "I could help you. We could put an add on Craig's List. I know a thing or two about music. I could help with the auditions. If they suck, we cut them loose. If they're good, we book them. It's not that hard."

Lou scratched his head. "Seems like a lot of work."

I turned my back on him and started to collect glasses off the bar. "Wow! I didn't peg you for the type, but if you're not interested in increasing business, that's fine. I just thought that you had higher goals. What do I know? I'm just a bartender."

Lou put his hand on my shoulder and turned me around. "You think we could pull this off?"

I placed the glasses in my hand on the bar. "I do. I even know someone who would be great as our first entertainer."

"You do?" he asked.

"I do. Let me work my magic and see what happens." I pulled out my phone and searched for Craig's List. I quickly wrote an ad and showed it to Lou. "We should have responses by the morning and then we can schedule auditions."

"I hope you know what you're doing. I don't want to end up with some hippie shit band preaching love and peace," he said disdainfully.

"Oh Lou, have you been scorned by love?" I teased. "I promise nothing before 80's hair bands. Although there was a lot of great music in the sixties and seventies."

He scratched at his goatee. "So true. I'm open to possibilities. Let's see what happens with the ad and go from there."

I reached up on my toes and planted a kiss on his cheek. "This is a good idea, Lou. I promise you won't be disappointed."

I left the bar feeling upbeat. When I met Zack on the sidewalk outside, I could hardly keep my smile contained. "You look like the cat that ate the canary."

I grabbed his belt loops and pulled him to me. "I just might have convinced Lou to start having live music."

"Oh yeah?" He pecked me on the lips.

"Yep. I placed an ad on Craig's List and I'm going to help him audition bands."

Zack held me by the shoulders. "Wait! You're going to audition other bands? Lou didn't want you to play?"

I aimlessly kicked at the ground beneath my feet. "No, that's not it."

He scowled at me. "Then explain."

I let out a breath of frustration. "I didn't tell him."

Zack groaned. "Sweetheart, how is he supposed to know if you don't tell him?"

I started walking. "I don't know. It feels weird. I never had to sell myself before. Things have changed, and I don't even know what I want anymore. That's why I didn't say anything."

Yes, I always wanted to make it big with my music. It was what my parents wanted for me. It was what Wes wanted for me. But, somewhere in the last twenty-four hours, reality had set in.

Why even start on a path I couldn't finish? My dreams were unrealistic. The faster I realized that, the easier it would be in the long run. I couldn't have a music career and a baby. Not by myself.

Zack tugged on my hand. "So, you don't want to sing anymore?"

I shrugged my shoulders. "It's complicated. Everything's changed. It was just a pipedream anyway. Stuff like that wasn't meant for people like me."

"I see," he said. We finished the rest of the walk in silence. When we returned to Forever Inked, Zack led me inside, but instead of stopping at the apartment he continued to the rooftop. We sat on the ledge that overlooked the city. He held my hand as we looked up at the stars. The moon was full tonight and it bathed us in a soft light. "Do you know when I first fell in love with you?" he asked.

"When you first had sex with me?" I guessed teasingly.

"That was amazing, but no. It started when you told off my father at the cemetery."

I nudged him with my shoulder. "Okay, that's creepy. Can you not tell people you fell in love with me at a grave?"

He laughed. "I didn't fall in love with you at the cemetery. It was the fire in you that attracted me. Then on the way home, I saw the soft vulnerable side of you and your determination to make the best out of a really shitty situation. But what sealed the deal... was when I heard you play the piano that night. Have you ever seen yourself when you sing?"

I shook my head.

"Well, you should. There's an unmistakable passion inside you. Everything is raw, pure, and nothing but beautiful. You positively glow when you're singing."

"Yeah, but..." I started.

"But nothing, Clarissa. You have a gift. Performing is what you were born to do. I don't want to see you give it up."

"So, what should I do? How do I make this work?" He didn't understand the full measure of what I was asking. How could he? My questions had far-reaching implications and much more complicated answers than he would be able to give me.

"You take your guitar and audition for Lou tomorrow. I'll even go with you." He winked at me.

"You'd do that for me?"

Zack took my face in his hands, "Don't you know? There isn't anything I wouldn't do for you."

And again, he was more than I deserved. It was going to crush me when this ended. I swallowed down the lump in my throat. "Thank you."

"You're more than welcome and if you really want to thank me, you can give me some of that dessert you promised," he said with a smirk.

♫♪♫♪

The next day, Zack and I walked over to The Locker between his appointments. My heart was beating wildly. I had never auditioned before. I got the job at The Hot Spot by chance, my other jobs had been because someone had seen me perform. But an actual audition? It was scary. I stopped dead in my tracks. "I don't think I can do this."

Zack quirked his eyebrow at me. "You're kidding, right?"

I shook my head and bit my lip. "No. I've never auditioned before."

He rubbed his hands down his face. "You're killing me. I watched you get on a stage at the fair and sing to a whole crowd and you sang for Bobby the other night in my studio."

"That was different," I defended.

"How so?" he questioned.

"That was me singing for me. I wasn't trying to get a job. It was for fun."

Zack took my guitar case from my hands and leaned it against a lamppost. Then he took both my hands in his. "Clarissa Lynne, you've sang in dozens of bars. This place isn't any different."

172

"But what if Lou hates my voice? I work there as a bartender, it'll be awkward."

Zack let out a frustrated sigh. "That's not even possible, but forget about Lou. When you start singing, focus on me. Think about how much your voice turns me on and how much I'm going to want to fuck you later."

I scrunched up my nose. "Really? It turns you on?"

"You have no idea." He groaned. "Take a deep breath, because you're doing this."

I started nodding like a bobblehead. "Right. I can do this." I pulled back my shoulders with determination. "Let's do this." I headed toward the bar before I could change my mind, walking faster than before.

"Uh, Clarissa," Zack called as I reached for the door handle, "you might need this." He thrust my guitar case into my hands.

"Oh, right." I grabbed the case from him and strode toward the bar where Lou was.

"Hey, Rissa. What are you doing here? Did you get some responses to our ad?" he asked.

"Yes and no," I answered.

He looked at me quizzically. "What the hell does that mean?"

I took a deep breath and focused on Zack's comforting presence behind me. "I didn't look yet, but I've scheduled our first audition."

"Okaaaay. Who is it and when are they coming?" Lou questioned.

I held up my guitar case. "It's me and it's right now." I tried to exude confidence, even if it was a lie.

Lou let out a little patronizing laugh. "Yeah, okay. Let's see what you've got. I'm not giving you special treatment because you work here, but knock yourself out."

That pissed me off and made me more determined. I glanced at Zack, and he gave me a slight nod. "I won't need special treatment, Lou. I'm damn good." I set my guitar case on the bar and pulled out my Gibson. I settled on a bar stool and set my prized possession in my lap. She was like an old friend that never let me down. She and I were a team, and I knew I could count on her.

I strummed a few random notes and then I was ready. I picked two songs to play for Lou and I started into the first one. My fingers danced over the strings and then I channeled my inner Stevie Nicks. The words to "Landslide" flowed from me. It was such a beautiful song that I quickly got lost in the lyrics. I closed my eyes and let my heart lead me.

When I finished, I looked towards Lou, but I couldn't read his expression. I started into my next song. This one was a little more upbeat and usually sung by a guy, but I loved it none the less.

After my second song, I set my guitar aside. "Well?"

Lou scowled at me. "I'm fucking pissed at you."

"What? Why? You didn't like it, did you?" I had embarrassed myself for no reason and now I had to work with Lou behind the bar. I started to put my guitar back into its case and tucked my tail between my legs.

"What the hell, Rissa?" Lou exclaimed. "I've had you working behind the bar when I could have had you packing this place with your music. I don't know shit about music, but I know talent when I see it. Girl, you've been given a gift and you're wasting it."

I could feel the blush creeping into my cheeks. "Does that mean I'm hired?"

"Tomorrow night. You need to be here to sing, not sling drinks."

I bit my lip, "Ummm.... I kind of have plans Friday night. How about Saturday?"

Lou shook his head. "I need you behind the bar on Saturday. How about this? Play tonight. It's Ladies' Night and we're going to be packed. Let's see how it goes."

I finally relaxed. It was short notice, but surely, I could put together a set list. I was going to play tonight and that was all that mattered. "Sounds good," I said casually. "What time should I be here?"

"You go on at seven. Does that work for you?" he asked.

"I'll make it work, but I was supposed to bartend tonight."

"I'll call Sonja. I want you singing. Let's see if we can keep the bar full tonight with you singing. My guess is that no one will be leaving early tonight. If this works, Rissa, we'll start auditioning other bands."

I kept my cool. "Thanks, Lou. I'll see you tonight." I grabbed my guitar and headed to the door with Zack hot on my tail.

When I got outside, I let out a squeal. "He liked it! I'm playing tonight!"

174

Zack wrapped his arms around me and swung me around. "Was there ever any doubt? You killed it, sweetheart!" He peppered me with kisses as we headed back to his shop.

"I have so much to do!" I exclaimed. "Oh, crap! I was supposed to work for you this afternoon. Is this going to be a problem? I can tell Lou that tonight doesn't work," I rambled.

"Are you kidding me?" Zack asked. "We'll survive. Do what you need to do. This is important and when I close tonight, I'll be there. I wouldn't miss your first night for anything."

Chapter 23
Zack

I looked at the appointment book and smiled. There was nothing that would go longer than seven-thirty. Clarissa locked herself away all afternoon. I checked on her a few times and she had been lost in some preshow ritual. I stayed out of her way and let her do her thing.

"Chase! Layla!" I yelled to them.

Both Chase and Layla scurried out from their studios. "What's up?" Chase asked.

"Good news and bad news," I said cryptically.

"Am I getting fired?" Layla asked. "Because that guy from earlier was a total dick. He was pissed because I wouldn't tattoo *"Love You Long Time"* on his cock. Seriously, the words wouldn't have even fit. There wasn't enough room, if you catch my drift," she said holding up her thumb and forefinger to make her point. "And I'm talking fully erect... which was disturbing."

I couldn't contain my laughter. "No one's getting fired," I assured them. "I'm giving you the night off... sort of."

"What does that mean?" Chase questioned, while crossing his arms.

"Listen. Rissa's playing tonight at The Locker. I thought it would be nice if we went to support her. Drinks are on me," I clarified.

Layla spoke up first. "So, you want us to take the night off to sit in a bar and drink. Is that what you're saying?"

I nodded my head. "That's exactly what I'm saying."

Chase rolled his eyes. "You're the worst boss ever. Do you know that? Can I bring Becca?"

"What the fuck, why not? The more the merrier." At this point, I would agree to anything.

"And you're paying?" he pushed. I loved the guy, but he was a pain in the ass.

I rolled my eyes. "Why the fuck not?" I repeated.

"I guess we can work that into our schedule. What do you think, Chase?" Layla busted my balls.

"Yeah. I guess that'll work," he said nonchalantly.

"It'll work or you'll both be fired," I threatened. It was an empty threat, and they knew it. It had taken me a long time to find two artists that were talented enough to work for me. I valued their talent and their friendship.

Shortly after seven, our last client left. I put a sign on the door, *Closed. Meet us at The Locker. My girl is singing tonight!* I was like a proud mama, and I didn't feel one bit of shame in it.

When we walked in, the place was packed. We were lucky enough to find a table in the back corner. The four of us ordered a round of drinks, all on my tab. Clarissa was on a makeshift stage Lou had devised. It was just her and her guitar. She was phenomenal, but something was missing.

I pulled out my phone and started searching the internet. Surely, she wasn't the only one to have this problem. I quickly found what I was looking for and read the customer reviews. This was perfect. I logged into my account and purchased it with one click. It should be here tomorrow, maybe the next day.

Then I did a few more searches and added to my order. Everything she needed would be here in a matter of days. I don't know why I hadn't thought of it before.

Chase nudged me, taking a sip of his second drink. "She's good. How come we didn't know about this?"

"She's not good," Layla interjected. "Girl Power!" she shouted. "She rocks!" Layla lifted her drink in salute to Clarissa.

"It wasn't my secret to tell," I answered Chase.

"I thought she was sexy before, but fuck, this kicks it up another notch." Chase stared at Clarissa.

Becca smacked him on the arm. "Hello! I'm sitting right here."

Layla smacked Chase in the head. "Don't be an asshole!"

I shook my head at the reaming Chase had inflicted upon himself. He was kind of a dumb fucker, but he was good with a tattoo gun and that was all I cared about. "You really don't have a clue, do you? She's way out of your league and more importantly, she's having sex with your boss. So, keep that shit locked down."

Chase looked between the three of us. "Jeez, can't a guy appreciate the merchandise? I think Layla's sexy too, but I don't want to sleep with her."

Layla smacked him in the head again. "And why the fuck not? What's wrong with me? I chew up boys like you for dinner and spit them out afterwards."

Chase pointed at Layla. "That's why. You're fucking scary as hell. You'd probably tie me to the bed and ball gag me." He pretended to let a shudder run down his back. "I stay away from the crazy chicks."

Layla glared at him. "Don't you forget it either. You couldn't handle a real woman."

"Again, I'm sitting right here," Becca interrupted, waving her hands in their faces.

"Sorry, sweetie. No offense intended." Layla half-apologized to the girl clinging to Chase's arm. But I knew Layla and she wasn't sorry at all. Layla was a hard-core bitch. It was what made her good at her job and why I loved the hell out of her. She had spunk and I admired it.

"Behave children," I scolded, "or this will be the last time I take you out."

"She started it," Chase defended.

"Oh, for Christ's sake, grow a set of balls, Chase." Layla admonished him while rolling her eyes.

Clarissa finished the song she was playing and announced that she was taking a quick break. She set her guitar down and headed our way. Thank God, she was going to save me from this torture I had inflicted upon myself by inviting Layla and Chase.

"Hey, guys," Clarissa greeted us as she approached the table.

I scooted my chair back and tapped my lap, inviting her to sit. Without hesitation, Clarissa sat down, and I wrapped my arms around her. "You sounded fantastic, sweetheart."

A slight blush crept up her cheeks. "Thanks. It feels good to perform again. I'm going to have to talk to Lou about getting a sound system though. I feel drowned out by the bar chatter."

I ran my nose along her neck and up to her ear, placing soft kisses on her skin. "Already handled," I told her.

"Really?" She pulled back in surprise.

"Um hmmm. Should be here in a couple of days."

"You didn't have to do that." She bit her lip.

"I don't have to do anything. Everything I do for you is because I want to, not because I have to," I assured her.

"Thank you, Zack." Clarissa pressed her lips to mine. Seeing her happy was all the thanks I needed.

"Break it up you two. You can make out later," Layla interrupted us. "Rissa, I had no idea. I mean, I knew you sang, but God girl, that voice. It's like smooth chocolate and silk all rolled into one."

"Yeah, it's sexy as hell," Chase chimed in.

Layla smacked him in the head again.

"Will you quit fucking hitting me?" he yelled at her.

"I will, when you quit being so clueless," Layla shot back.

"It's okay," Clarissa piped in. "I took it as a compliment."

Chase motioned to Clarissa. "See? She gets me."

"He's right though, Rissa. Your voice is pure sex. Trust me, this place is full of hard-ons tonight," Layla said crudely.

Clarissa shrugged. "Well, I guess there will be a lot of self-love tonight, because the only one I care about is the one I'm sitting on."

I pulled her back against my chest. "Damn right, woman."

Layla sighed. "That's so cute that you call it self-love. It sounds so much classier than whacking off."

"Oh, God!" Clarissa buried her head in my chest.

I rubbed the back of her head, feeling amusement at her embarrassment. Her innocence was a total turn on, but I knew the truth behind the façade she presented. Behind all that purity was a girl who would do whatever I wanted. She was dying to let go of her insecurities and let me take control. Tonight, I would give her another lesson in submission. My dick throbbed thinking about it.

The best part was knowing she would enjoy it as much as I did.

Clarissa headed back to the tiny stage, as the rest of us enjoyed another couple of rounds. I would have bought drinks for the entire bar if it meant they would stay and listen to my girl sing. But she was holding her own. No one was leaving early tonight. They were too entranced by her voice to go anywhere. It was amazing, the power she held over the crowd.

When the night ended, Chase and Becca left wrapped around each other. Fuck if I knew what Layla did when she left. I had my suspicions that she craved darker sex than me. I didn't know, and I wanted to keep it that way. Something told me she had a fucked up past I'd be better off not knowing. She was a mystery to me, and she worked hard to keep it that way.

The mystery I wanted to solve, was Clarissa Lynne Black. I didn't know what she'd done before, but I was willing to bet it was nothing that included blindfolds or handcuffs. I hardened more as I thought about all the possibilities with her. I looked down at the leather cuff on my wrist. And then I looked at the matching one on her wrist. All I could think about was a different set of leather cuffs I wanted to restrain her with. The ones that sat in my bottom dresser drawer and were calling her name.

Slow.

That was what I had promised her, and I planned on keeping that promise. Tonight, I would push her a little further. She would enjoy every minute of it and beg me for more.

As we left the bar, I wrapped my arm around her small frame and pulled her into my side. "Do you have any idea what you did to me tonight? And every other guy in that bar?"

"What do you mean? All I did was sing." Her naivety was endearing, but it wouldn't last long.

"You really have no idea the effect you have, do you?"

She shrugged. My little minx knew what she did but would never admit it. I grabbed her hand that was resting on my hip and rubbed it along my dick. "That's what you do?"

"To you," she answered.

"To every guy in that bar. Are you ready for a little more of that iceberg tonight?"

"I'll get more than the tip?" She looked at me with wide eyes.

"I'll always give you more than the tip." I smirked at her. "Is that what you want?" I asked.

"Yes. I want the whole iceberg."

180

She didn't have to ask me twice. I rushed her home and backed her against the door, kissing her hard and fast, bruising her delicate lips. "There's so much I want to do to you," I admitted. I pushed her towards the couch. "Strip."

"What?"

"You heard me. Strip. I want your tits and ass on display for me."

Clarissa slowly started to unbutton her blouse, but my patience was long gone. I grabbed the front of her blouse and ripped it open, the buttons scattering on the hardwood floor. The look on her face stilled me. "Are you afraid?"

She tried to exude confidence but failed miserably. "No," she whispered, looking away.

"Do you think I would hurt you?" I clasped her jaw in my hand, so she had to look at me.

"No," she whispered again.

She was scared. I saw it in her eyes. I relaxed my hold on her. "This is part of it. Control. But you have to know that I would never hurt you. Ever. Do you trust me?"

She nodded.

"Do you trust me?" I repeated.

"Yes." I barely heard the response that came from her swollen lips.

"Good, because it would kill me to know that you were afraid of me. I will push your limits, take you past your comfort zone, but I'll never hurt you. And if you don't want this, just tell me. It won't change anything between us. But if you do want this, I can promise you that you won't regret it.

"I'm trying. I want this with you. It's just…" She took a deep breath. "You're really intense when you get into the zone."

I ran my hand down her face, "Yeah, I am. I'll try to take it down a notch."

"I don't want to change you, Zack."

"Baby, don't you know? You've already changed me. I'm a better person when I'm with you." My edge was gone. I changed directions. "Let's try something else."

I laced her fingers with mine and led her to the bedroom. I stood her at the base of the bed and then pulled open my bottom dresser drawer. Pulling out a couple of long black scarves, I approached her. "Have you ever been blindfolded?"

Clarissa bit her lip and shook her head.

"This is all about trust and you said you trust me."

"I do," she said softly.

I placed one of the black scarves over her eyes and tied it behind her head. Her hands instinctively reached up to feel her face. I took her hands and gently pushed them down. "Nuh-uh. That stays in place until I say so. You won't be able to see me. I'm going to put in ear buds, so you won't be able to hear me. I want you to relax and feel. With everything else tuned out, you'll be focused on your pleasure. Nothing else will matter. Do you understand?"

Clarissa nodded. "I'm a little scared. What are you going to do to me?"

I placed a finger gently over her lips. "Nothing to be afraid of. I promise you. Are you ready?"

She let out a breathy, "Yes."

I grabbed my earbuds from my nightstand drawer and placed them in her ears. Then I hit play on my phone. The soundtrack from *Fifty Shades of Grey* started. I wasn't a huge fan of the movie, but the soundtrack was sexy and sinful. Exactly what I wanted to get Clarissa out of her head.

She leaned her head back and I saw her shoulders visibly relax. This was good. I wanted her in the zone with me.

I kneeled before her and unfastened the strap of one of her high heels. I gently slipped it off her foot and then took off the other. I stared at her dark red toenails as she wiggled her toes into the soft rug at the end of the bed. I was on my knees for her and there was nowhere else I wanted to be. She thought I had all the control, but that was just an illusion. Right now, she held all the power. This woman had complete control over me.

My hands skimmed up her calves and to her thighs. My fingers quickly worked to unfasten her pants and I slid them down her legs. Her hands reached out and found my shoulders, she held on as she lifted each leg for me to remove her pants.

My hands ghosted up the sides of her slender legs and to her waist. I placed soft kisses on her stomach and up between her breasts. I slid her opened blouse off her shoulders, and it fell to the floor. She stood before me, in her lacy purple panties and bra. She was exquisite. I ran my fingers over the cups of her bra and her nipples puckered as she let out a gasp. Exquisite.

Pulling down one cup, I sucked her nipple into my mouth. Clarissa let out a low groan, leaning her head back and rolling her neck. Her hands clasped the back of my head and pulled me in closer. I loved that she craved me as much as I craved her. I gently bit her nipple, and she hissed in pleasure. I moved to the other one and did the same, licking it to ease the sting. Her back arched, thrusting her tits into my face. With one quick flick, her bra was undone. I slowly slid the straps down her arms and threw it to the floor.

I reached down and placed one arm behind her knees, while the other supported her back. I gently lifted Clarissa, cradling her to my chest and set her in the middle of the bed. I stretched one of her arms above her head and brought the other to join it. Clasping both wrists in one hand, I wrapped the other silk scarf around her wrists. She tensed beneath me. Using my free hand, I removed one of her ear buds and leaned down next to her. "Don't be afraid. I'll never hurt you."

Clarissa took a deep breath and exhaled. "I'm not afraid. I trust you."

I almost believed her. I replaced the ear bud, then took the ends of the scarf and wrapped them through the bars on my headboard. It was no coincidence that my bed was perfect for this. It was a major consideration when I bought it. I tied it loose enough that she had some mobility, but not too much. Clarissa pulled at the binding, but she wasn't going anywhere.

I left her lying there, as I stripped off my own clothes. My cock was so hard for her, but that would have to wait. Tonight, was about the woman in the middle of my bed and gaining her trust.

I laid over the top of her, caging Clarissa in with my arms. Then I feasted on her beautiful tits. I massaged and licked and sucked and nipped. Her rosy tips formed into perfect points that I teased with my tongue.

I lifted her shoulders and ran my hands behind her back, gently lifting Clarissa to my mouth. I ran them down her back and she arched deliciously towards me. I savored every beautiful curve of her body. When my hands reached her ass, I gently squeezed her firm globes and lifted her pussy to my mouth. I licked her pussy through her soaked lace panties and then nipped at her clit. The texture of the lace against her sensitive nerves had her squirming, pulling against the silk restraints on her wrists.

I set her hips down and slipped her panties down her legs. I bent her knees and placed her feet flat on the mattress, spreading her legs wide with my shoulders. Her soft pink flesh glistened with her arousal. Nothing was fucking sexier than the woman laid out before me.

Innocent.

Trusting.

And totally at my mercy.

Chapter 24
Rissa

So far, this had been the most erotic night of my life. I'd be lying if I said my heart didn't ratchet up when he blindfolded me. Then he took away my sense of hearing too. The music that played in my ears was sensual and sexy. I got lost in the music and everything else faded away.

Zack had been nothing but gentle with me, but I'd be a fool to believe it would stay that way. I'd gotten a glimpse of what made him tick when we were in the shower. Hiding underneath all that sweetness was a darkness I'd never experienced.

I had tensed when he bound my wrists, but his deep, sexy voice was right there reassuring me. I relaxed and let him have me. All of me.

My panties were gone, and my legs were bent on the bed. I knew there was nothing he couldn't see. I could feel the wetness between my legs. I don't know that I had ever been so aroused.

I was dying to come.

For him to ease the ache inside me.

And I knew he would.

One thing I had learned about Zack was that he was as invested in pleasing me as he was in pleasing himself. I always came first.

His fingers ran through my arousal, running up and down my opening. He played with me. He slipped a finger inside. I bucked my hips, trying to increase the pressure. It wasn't nearly enough.

He quickly removed his finger and I moaned at the loss. He was teasing me. Building me up. "More," I pleaded. "Please don't stop."

His deep voice was in my ear again. "I'm not even close to stopping. Patience, sweetheart. You'll get everything you need and more." Then he was gone. I let the music fill my head. Let Beyoncé's sultry voice take me away, as "Crazy in Love" streamed into my ears. I imagined the look in Zack's eyes as he toyed with me.

My hips lifted, and I felt a soft pillow being shoved under them. Then his mouth was on me. He devoured every inch of me while he pinched my nipples and rolled them between his fingers. "Oh, fuck. Fuckfuckfuck," I hissed. "So good." My whole body was on fire. Every nerve lit like a flame.

His hand that was at my breasts, slid down to my stomach. It teased my clit, while his other fingers slipped inside me. More than one. More than two. At least three. They stretched me and filled me. They curled inside me and hit the spot that had me moaning and gasping for breath. His tongue replaced his fingers, and I bucked into his face. I had no control.

I was barely aware that his fingers were sliding lower. I was so blissfully distracted. His fingers slid toward a place that had never been touched and one slid inside me. I tensed at first, but it felt so good, I surrendered to the pleasure. I never thought I would like being touched there, but I couldn't deny that I enjoyed it. With everything his mouth and fingers were doing, I was going to come harder than ever before. It had been building and I couldn't hold on any longer. An intense orgasm ripped through me, the waves of pleasure better than anything I had ever experienced. "God, Zack. Fuck me! Fuck me please!"

Within seconds, Zack filled me in one quick thrust. He was buried deep inside me and all I could think was *moremoremore*. Nothing had ever felt this good before. He continued to thrust deep and hard, bruising me in the best way. His fingers dug into my hips, lifting and pulling me into every thrust.

Then he pulled out completely and I was left needy and wanting. Begging. "Don't stop! Don't stop!"

In a flash, I was flipped over onto my stomach, the air whooshing from my lungs. Zack pulled my legs up under me, forcing me to my knees. I rested on my elbows, with my ass high in the air. He pushed my legs apart and entered me from behind. Fuck, it was so good. So deliciously painful and mind numbing and everything he had promised.

I screamed as pleasure took over my body. His fingertips gripped me tightly, then one hand descended between my legs, teasing my clit. I was already so sensitive, and Zack was relentless as he pushed me toward my next orgasm. Within seconds, I shattered again.

Zack intensified his thrusts, leaning over my back and grabbing my shoulders for leverage. He slammed into me over and over, until I felt him still behind me. Then he finished with slow, lazy strokes. He leaned on my back, kissing the place between my shoulder blades and down my spine to my ass.

He slipped out of me, and I was left alone, still on my knees. He was only gone a minute, before he returned. The tension on my wrists released and I was being lifted like a child. He held me to his chest, carrying me somewhere. I was too tired to care where.

The next thing I knew I was lowered into warm water. Zack was behind me, holding me to his body as I sat between his legs. The ear buds were pulled from my ears, and I could hear the tub running. "You okay, sweetheart?"

I nodded, too tired for anything else.

He pulled the blindfold from my eyes, and I blinked a few times, adjusting to the harshness of the light. I let my head fall back against his hard chest.

"Did I hurt you?" Concern laced his voice.

I shook my head. "No. It was incredible. You're incredible. I want more next time." I wasn't ashamed to admit that I was addicted to Zack Kincaid.

He let out a low laugh. "Slow, sweetheart. We'll get there." He kissed my temple then took a washcloth and started to wipe down my body. "You're going to be sore in the morning," he warned.

"I don't care," I said dismissively.

"That's my girl. I knew you had it in you. It's only going to get better. I promise, you'll be begging for me to take you." His voice was soothing and confident.

"I already am," I admitted.

♫♪♫♪

Friday night, we hopped into the Chevelle and drove to Tori and Chris's house. Moving into September, the nights were becoming chilly. I wrapped my sweatshirt around me. "How long until it gets cold here?"

187

"It's similar to New York. The days will stay fairly warm for about another month, but the evenings will start getting cold. Do you need to buy a coat or anything?" he asked. "We can go shopping this weekend."

I shook my head for more reasons than one. First, I didn't want to add to the list of things I owed Zack. My debt was already out of control. He barely let me pay for anything. It was a blessing and a curse. I could save money, but one day I'd owe it all back to him. "I have a winter coat and boots," I assured him. All of it was still packed in boxes stacked in my room. I didn't see a need to unpack everything when I could have to move at a moment's notice.

Zack threaded his fingers with mine and lifted them to his lips. "Let me know if you need anything. All you have to do is say the word."

He was so protective of me. He reminded me so much of Wes. Wes never let me want for anything. He anticipated all my needs.

When I met Wes, I had been making it on my own for a year. I lived in a rough part of town, and I skimped on anything that could mildly be considered a luxury, but I was making it. I was proud of myself.

For the first month that Wes and I dated, I refused to let him see where I lived. I wasn't embarrassed, but I could tell that he had it more together than I did. I hadn't been to his apartment yet, but I suspected it was nicer than mine.

I remembered the night all of that changed. We had gone for coffee when I got off from bartending at The Hot Spot.

"Let me drive you home," he said.

I shook my head. "It's out of the way. I'll just catch the bus."

"You shouldn't be riding the bus this late at night," Wes said. "It's not safe."

I waved him off. "I've been taking the bus for a year. I have my pepper spray. No one has ever bothered me. I'll be fine." It wasn't the truth, but he didn't need to know that.

He kissed me outside the coffee shop. "Text me when you get home. I need to know you're safe."

"I will." I said good-bye and hopped onto the bus, relieved that he hadn't pushed the issue. The ten-minute drive took twice as long with all the

stops along the way. I popped in my ear buds and stared out the window, watching the busy downtown area slip away as the bus moved into a seedier part of town. It wasn't pretty, but I could afford the rent. That was all that mattered.

When the bus finally made it to my stop, I hopped off. I still had a couple of blocks to walk until I reached my apartment. My ear buds were out, and I was on high alert. Even though it was rare to be bothered, it didn't mean that I wasn't hyperaware of my surroundings. Don't make eye contact. That was the number one rule I followed. I passed a group of guys hanging out on the corner. The smell of marijuana filled my nose. It was just pot. That, I could handle. It was the drunks that usually gave me problems.

I walked a little quicker, anxious to get home. One hand was wrapped around my pepper spray, the other clutched my keys like a weapon. I sighed out a breath of relief when my building was in sight. I was just about to climb up the steps.

"Rissa?"

I stopped cold and turned to look over my shoulder. Wes stood across the street, calling to me. I spun around and looked both ways. "What are you doing here?"

"I followed you."

This was my dirty little secret. I didn't want him knowing where I lived. "Why?"

He strolled across the street and stood before me. "I was worried. I don't like you taking the bus." He looked up at the building behind me. "Is this where you live?"

I nodded and pushed my hair over my shoulder. "Home sweet home," I said nonchalantly.

"Let me walk you up."

"You don't have to," I said, as sirens blasted in the background.

"Yes. I do," he insisted.

"Really, you don't."

"Really, I do."

I relented and led him up the steps into my building. Half the lights in the hall were burnt out. I led him to the dim stairwell and began to climb

189

the five flights to my floor. As I opened the door to the fifth floor, I could hear loud arguing. I was used to it.

I stopped in front of my door. "Thank you for walking me up." I put the key in the door and undid the lock. "Good night." I pecked him on the cheek.

"Nuh-uh. I'm coming in," he said.

I stared at the stained carpet beneath my feet. "I don't think that's a good idea."

He put his hand on the door and pushed. "It's a perfect idea."

The door creaked open, and I flipped on the light. This was it. The moment when he would realize we didn't belong together. It was already done. I couldn't fight it, so I let him in. "This is where I live."

I dropped my keys on the small table by the door and he shut it behind us. I studied his face as he took in his surroundings. Shock would be a kind word. Disgust was more fitting.

A mattress sat on the floor at one end of the small room. Next to it, my make-up and curling iron sat on the floor by a small mirror. My clothes were folded neatly against the wall. The kitchen was nothing more than a mini-fridge and a microwave.

He looked around the small space and moved to the only other door. The bathroom. It was tiny to say the least. He came out of the bathroom and rubbed his hand over his face.

I swallowed down the lump in my throat. "Wes…"

"Get your shit. You're not staying here tonight or ever again."

I flopped down on the mattress. "My rent is paid through the end of the month."

"I don't give a fuck. No girl of mine is living in this shithole. Get what you need for the night. We'll get the rest tomorrow."

I buried my head in my hands and started to cry. "Just leave," I said. "I've been doing this on my own for a while now. I don't need you to save me."

He sat next to me and wrapped me in his arms. "I know you're proud, but I can't leave you here. You deserve so much better than this and I can give it to you. Let me take care of you."

"No! This is me. This is who I am."

190

"This isn't who you are. This…" he waved his arm around the small apartment, "doesn't define you."

I looked at him through tear-filled eyes. "I refuse to take advantage of you. I'm fine here."

He wiped the tears that ran down my cheeks. "I know you are. But I'm not fine with you being here. You're my princess and you deserve only the best. You deserve more."

We made love that night for the first time, right there on my mattress that sat on the floor. In the morning, Wes packed up all my things and moved them to his apartment. It was my first taste of luxury and money. I had no idea that he was rich. From that moment on, he doted on me and tended to my every need. I would never have to want for anything ever again.

"Where'd you go?" Zack's voice cut through my memory.

"Just thinking," I answered.

"About?"

"My life," I said vaguely, staring out the window. Wes was gone and so was that part of my life. I ran my hand over my stomach unconsciously. I still had him with me. Nobody could take that away from me. The longer I hid my secret the better.

"Hmmm. I just wanted to prepare you for the night. I've never hung out with these guys before. Kyla and I have been friends, but you seem to have made an impression on her. She wanted us to hang out and I couldn't say no. Their husbands are cool. I've only met them a handful of times and I don't know them that well. All I know is that Chris and Tori have been together forever. Tyler and Kyla dated in high school and college. Some major shit went down between them, but they're back together."

I remembered what Layla had said about Kyla. "Did you love her?"

"Who?"

"Kyla?"

Zack squirmed in his seat. "There were some feelings at one time, but that's the past. I never stood a chance. She's always belonged to Tyler."

I nodded. At least he didn't lie to me. "Is it going to make you uncomfortable hanging with them?" I asked.

191

"Fuck no! Like I said, it's the past. Tyler and Kyla were meant for each other. I'm happy that she's happy."

I had no right to be jealous, but part of me was. I stared out the window.

Zack squeezed my hand. "Hey. I'm with you and I couldn't be happier. Don't let the past ruin the future. Kyla's going to be pushing out twins in a few weeks. I've never seen anyone happier."

I couldn't resist. "What about you? Ever thought about having kids?"

Zack let out a low laugh. "Maybe one day. My life isn't exactly conducive to having kids. I like my freedom. I can do what I want, when I want."

My heart sank. Any hope that I had about him accepting this baby, vanished with his words. "You're right. Why complicate things?"

"Exactly."

We pulled up in front of a small house. It was cute. Maybe someday, I would live in a house like this. But right now, a tiny one-bedroom apartment seemed more likely. As we exited the car, Zack wrapped his arm around my shoulder. "I love you, Clarissa Lynne. Don't ever doubt that."

"I love you too," I said honestly.

I could hear music coming from the back yard. We walked through the side gate and approached the bonfire that was blazing.

"It's about fucking time!" Tori yelled.

"Nice mouth for a mom. You kiss your baby with that mouth?" A tall guy with dark hair and bright blue eyes scolded her.

"Shut the fuck up, Tyler. I'm a great mom."

So, this was Tyler. Kyla's husband. I couldn't blame her for being in love with him. He was gorgeous.

Another tall guy slid out through the slider, "Tor, Savannah just woke up. Do you want me to feed her?"

That was Tori's husband, Chris, I deduced. He was tall and very good looking. Italian through and through.

I was in the land of beautiful people. Both of these couples were gorgeous. And then there was Zack, another perfect specimen. I felt plain and out of place.

192

"I'll get her," Tori answered. "Can you make sure everyone has drinks?"

Chris kissed Tori as she headed into the house. Chris strode towards us and thrust out his hand to Zack. "Good to see you, man."

"You too," Zack said. He wrapped his arm around my shoulders. "This is my girl, Rissa."

Chris winked at me. "Tori already filled me in. It's nice to meet you, Rissa. What can I get you two to drink?"

"I'll just have water," I answered.

"Beer for me," Zack said.

"Coming right up." Chris disappeared into the house to get our drinks.

Zack and I wandered towards the bonfire that Tyler was tending. Zack clasped hands with him. "Congrats, man. How's playing for the Lions going?"

Tyler shook his head. "The practice schedule is intense, but it's all I ever wanted so I can't complain. I'm just glad to be playing for the home team. It would kill Kyla to move halfway across the country. I'm anxious to get on the field though. Sitting the bench is killing me."

Zack smiled at him. "Give it time. It'll happen. This is your first season."

Tyler ran a hand through his hair. "I know. But it's hard after being front and center at Michigan State."

"Tyler was the starting quarterback for Michigan State," Zack explained to me. As if realizing we hadn't been properly introduced, Zack looked at Tyler. "This is Rissa."

"Hi." I waved with my fingers.

Tyler shook his head. "If you're going to be part of this group, we hug." He leaned in and wrapped me in a warm embrace.

I tentatively hugged him back. That was unexpected. "Where's Kyla?" I asked.

"She'll be out shortly. She was getting some snacks. She should be sitting, but she refuses to relax. I'm afraid those babies are going to come early."

"She'll be fine," I said. "You have to trust her to know her limits. She doesn't strike me as the sit and wait kind of girl."

Tyler rolled his eyes. "You have no idea."

Just then Kyla emerged from the house, her arms full of snacks. Tyler rushed over to help her. "What's all this?" he asked.

"Supplies," she answered. "I want s'mores. You can't tell me no. Pregnant women can eat whatever they want."

She gave Zack and I each a hug. "I'm so glad you two came. This may be my last social gathering before I burst." Her hand ran over her stomach. "I don't know how much bigger I can possibly get."

"Sit," Tyler instructed. He kissed her on the forehead. "You get more beautiful every day."

I swooned inside. I wished I had a man who would support me like that. Instead, I felt alone. Zack would make a great dad one day, but not any day in the near future. He'd made that perfectly clear.

Chris and Tori joined us. Chris had our drinks in his hand and Tori cradled Savannah to her chest. "Looks like our little monkey didn't want to miss the party. She won't go back to sleep," Tori said.

I reached out my arms. "Do you want me to take her for a while? I don't mind."

"That would be great," Tori said. She placed Savannah in my arms, and I cradled her to my chest, rocking her gently.

"You're a natural," Tori said.

"She's so cute. How could I possibly resist?" I swung my hips instinctively. Savannah's eyes started to close. Her little lips puckered as she fell asleep. I looked down on the miracle in my arms. She was beautiful. In less than seven months I would be holding my own baby. I just wished I had someone to share it with.

After Kyla had made her s'mores and the guys were on their third round, Tori motioned for me to follow her. We went into the house, and she led me to Savannah's room. I handed the sweet girl to her mother and Tori placed her in the crib. Then she turned to me. "How far along are you?"

"Excuse me?" I asked, clearly not ready for that question.

Tori placed her hands on her hips. "Don't bullshit me."

"I'm not sure what you're implying." I started to walk away. She couldn't possibly know. No one knew.

"Then let me be more clear," she said to my back. I slowly turned and faced Tori. "I've been watching you all night. You haven't had even a sip of beer. As a matter of fact, Zack said he's never seen you drink. You've rubbed your stomach unconsciously more than a few times. And the longing in your eyes when you look at my daughter is unmistakable. You're pregnant. Does Zack know?"

I didn't deny it. "No. It's complicated."

"Isn't it always?" she asked.

I sat down in the rocker next to Savannah's crib and rested my arms on my legs. I didn't know Tori well at all, but I was dying to tell someone. I hoped that it would make me feel less lonely.

"You can't tell Zack," I insisted.

"What's going on?" she asked. "I know we're not exactly friends yet, but I'd like to be. You can trust me."

"It's really fucked up," I admitted.

"Go on," she encouraged.

I swallowed down my pride and spilled my guts. "It's not Zack's. The baby is his brother's."

Tori's eyes went wide. "That's a whole new level of fucked up."

"Yeah, I know."

Tori rolled her hand, encouraging me to elaborate.

I let out a sigh. "I was engaged to Zack's brother. And then he died."

"Fuck!" Tor said as she fell to her knees in front of me.

"Yeah, fuck doesn't even cover it," I continued. "Zack's brother, Wes, was the love of my life. After he died, their father stripped me of our bank account and kicked me out of the apartment. Zack took pity on me at the funeral and tried to help me. He reminded me so much of Wes. The night of the funeral, Zack and I slept together. I didn't mean for it to happen and neither did he. It just happened. We were both emotionally distraught."

"He doesn't know you're pregnant?" she asked.

I shook my head. "After we slept together, I couldn't tell him. I never expected anything to become of it. I thought we would go our separate ways and that would be it. An indiscretion I could forget about. But Zack had

195

other plans. I had nowhere to go, so he asked me to come home with him. It was supposed to be a new start for me. I should have never come because I fell in love with Zack." I looked at Tori with pleading eyes, "You have to believe that I really do love him."

"I see the way you look at each other. I believe it. He's over the moon for you."

A tear slipped down my face and I quickly wiped it away. "Zack doesn't want kids. How do I even tell him? I've known from day one that this was going to end badly. I'm so fucked. I'm in so deep that nothing will save me."

Tori wrapped me in her arms. "I won't tell your secret, but you won't be able to keep it for much longer."

"I know." I swallowed. "Time is running out. In the end, I'll be left alone again. I'm scared," I admitted.

"You're going to need a friend. Give me your phone." I willingly handed it over. "I added my number to your contacts. You can call me anytime," she said.

"Please don't tell Kyla," I begged. "She'll tell Zack and I need to be the one to do that."

"This is one fucked up mess. You'd be surprised though. Kyla might be more supportive than you think."

I raised an eyebrow at her.

"That's a story for another time. Just promise you'll call when this all falls apart."

I leaned forward and hugged Tori. "Thank you. You don't know how good it feels to tell someone. I've carried this around by myself for so long. No one, but Wes, even knew I was pregnant. I hate lying to Zack. He's going to hate me in the end and that kills me. I never wanted to hurt him."

"Where will you go when it ends?" she asked.

I shrugged. "I don't know, but I'll figure it out. I'm a survivor. It's the one thing I'm good at."

Chapter 25
Zack

I ran on the treadmill in the basement, trying to work out all my crazy thoughts. Running usually cleared my head, but the past was mixing with the future and I couldn't reconcile the two.

Watching Clarissa last night with the girls, confirmed that Kyla was right. Clarissa needed girlfriends. I saw a lightness in her that had been missing. She seemed carefree last night, laughing with Tori and Kyla like they were old friends.

But there was something else. Seeing her cradle Savannah, had stirred something in me. I'd had the fleeting thought that maybe someday she would be holding my baby.

And then reality set in. Number one, I had no business having a kid. What was I going to do? Raise a kid above a tattoo parlor? Number two, Clarissa was trying to start a music career. She didn't have time for kids. Number three, we had only been officially dating for a little over a week, even if it seemed longer.

I couldn't believe that I was actually thinking about this. I hadn't thought about having kids since Megan. When she told me she was pregnant, I was shocked. We'd been careful, but nothing was a hundred percent. I loved Megan and having a baby with her wasn't the worst thing that could have happened.

I bought her everything she could have possibly wanted or needed for a baby, from clothes and furniture to a stroller and car seat. I'd even bought an engagement ring. I'd wanted to surprise her, so I left work early, bought a dozen roses and headed to her apartment with a ring in my pocket.

Then Megan's ex-boyfriend answered the door with a towel wrapped around his waist. I barged through the door to find her naked, trying to cover her seven-month pregnant body. It didn't take long for her to admit the baby wasn't mine. She'd been messing around with her ex the entire time and the baby was his. All she had needed me for was to pay the bills. Megan had blown everything to shit with her admission.

I didn't date for a long time after that. Then I met Gina. We had both been screwed over. We became fast friends and soon realized we had off-the-charts sexual chemistry. We made an agreement that fulfilled both our needs with no strings attached. We cared about each other, but it wasn't love.

It wasn't what I felt for Clarissa. When I was with her, nothing else seemed to matter. Now, I was picturing a future for myself that I hadn't considered in years. Clarissa had dated Wes for almost two years before they got engaged. I didn't know if I could wait that long. Although we were together, I knew part of her heart was still healing.

"There you are," Clarissa's voice interrupted my thoughts.

I slowed the treadmill to a walk. "I needed to burn off some energy." I grabbed the towel that hung over the side rail of the machine and started wiping the sweat from my body.

Clarissa smirked at me and walked her fingers down my chest. "You should have let me know. I could have helped."

I grabbed her around the waist and pulled her close. "I'm sure you could have. Is that why you were looking for me?"

She crinkled her nose. "Actually, I have a favor to ask. Try to keep an open mind, okay?"

"Always."

"Can I borrow Betsy?" Clarissa took a step back and held up her hands. "I know she's your baby, but I'll be really careful. I promise." She clasped her hands together in a praying position.

The thought of her driving my car without me made my insides seize up. I placed my hands on my hips. "Where are you going?" It was a shit question that made me sound like I didn't trust her. I knew it as soon as the words left my mouth.

She let out a huff. "Forget it. I'll call for an Uber. It's not a big deal." She turned and started up the stairs.

I took two long strides and grabbed her arm. "I'll take you."

"You have appointments. It's fine. I understand," she said.

She continued up the stairs with me on her heels. "Where are you going?" I asked again.

"I need to go to a music store. One of the strings on my guitar is about to snap. I found one that looked close to here. How far is Rochester?"

"Fifteen or twenty minutes. I can have Layla take you," I suggested.

We reached the top of the stairs. "I don't want to inconvenience anyone. An Uber is fine. Maybe when I get back, I'll start looking at used cars. I've saved some money. I'm sure I can find something reasonable."

This whole conversation made me feel like shit. Clarissa never asked me for anything, and the one time she did, I acted like she asked for my left kidney. I strode to the front of the shop and picked up my appointment book. I didn't have anything until eleven. "Give me ten minutes to shower and we'll go."

"Zack," she protested.

"I have plenty of time," I said. I should have let her take my car, but instead I offered. "You can drive."

Her eyebrows shot up, "Really?"

"Yeah." I crossed my arms. "I just need some time to adjust to someone driving Betsy besides me."

"I promise I'll drive the speed limit and be really careful."

I kissed her on the head. "I know you will be. I shouldn't be such an ass, she's just a car."

"It's fine. You love her," Clarissa said.

"But I love you more."

Ten minutes later I was showered and dressed. I tossed the keys to Clarissa, and we headed out. She started my baby and eased out of the back lot, giving me her phone that had a map pulled up on it. "Can you tell me where I'm going?"

I looked at the map. I knew right where this place was and directed her through traffic. She drove cautiously, never making me even the tiniest bit nervous. This was totally different than when she drove on the expressway back from New York. She effortless parallel parked and grabbed her guitar from the back seat.

"I owe you an apology," I said, as we walked toward the store.

"What for?"

"I judged your driving ability on your craziness on the expressway. You're actually a really good driver."

Clarissa laughed. "That was just me having fun. I told you I knew how to drive. I can be responsible." She pointed at her chest. "Perfect score on my driver's test. My dad taught me when I fourteen." Then she winked at me. "But, if you ever need a getaway driver, I'm your girl. I can outdrive the cops with the best of them."

I wrapped my arm around her and kissed her temple. "Somehow, I believe you." I pulled the door open and motioned for her to enter.

Clarissa walked to the counter and laid her case on top.

The guy behind the counter was about my age. He was tall, obviously built, with blond hair tucked behind his ears that touched his shoulders. He smiled at my girl as he overtly checked her out. "How can I help you, darling?"

She opened the case and pulled out her guitar. "I need to get new strings for my Gibson." She rattled off the name and description of what she wanted.

He nodded and returned with the strings she had requested. "If you have a few minutes, I can change these while you look around."

Clarissa turned over her shoulder to me. "Do we have time? If not, I can do it myself."

We had time and I had noticed her scanning the store. "We have time," I assured her.

The guy behind the counter smiled at her. "This won't take long."

She smiled back. "Thank you."

He nodded, and Clarissa turned to look at the guitars on the wall. "God, Zack, this place is like a candy store. I could spend my whole paycheck in a matter of minutes."

"Do you want a new guitar?" I asked. She was right. This place had top of the line instruments. I wouldn't hesitate to buy her anything she wanted.

"God, no. I love my Gibson. It was a gift for my sixteenth birthday. My dad must have had to work major overtime to afford it."

I felt guilty for assuming Wes had bought her guitar. Knowing her dad bought it, I couldn't see her replacing it anytime soon. "I'm sorry. I didn't know."

"You can't be sorry. I never told you." She chuckled. Then Clarissa walked over to the corner where a baby grand piano sat. She ran her hand over the lacquered black finish. "This is beautiful." She sat down on the bench and ran her fingers aimlessly over the keys. And then she began to play. It was a song I didn't know, but it didn't matter. She was mesmerizing. It took me back to the only other time I had heard her play the piano. The night we first had sex.

Her hands flew over the keys effortlessly as her eyes closed. There were only a few customers in the store, but she had commanded their attention with her music. When she finished, she gave me a sly smile. "I've missed that."

"You look happy," I commented as I leaned on the piano. "Why don't you play another song."

She got a mischievous look in her eye. "How about something fun?"

"Whatever you want, sweetheart." I was curious what she had up her sleeve.

She stretched out her fingers and placed them on the keys. "I haven't played this in forever," she prefaced before standing. Then her fingers started pounding the keys at a frantic pace playing "Great Balls of Fire". She ran the back of her fingers along the length of the keys and continued pounding out the tune with precision.

I knew she was talented, but she never failed to amaze me. Her energy and love for music was captivating. When she finished the song, a round of applause from the lingering customers filled the store. The guy at the counter stuck his fingers in his mouth and let out a wolf whistle then clapped long and hard. Her cheeks turned pink, and she buried her head in my chest. "Oh, jeez."

I couldn't contain my laughter. I'd never seen someone so obviously born for entertaining, get embarrassed so easily. "You're going to have to get used to the attention," I told her.

"It's different when I'm on stage performing. I expect it there. Here, I'm just me."

"Well… just you, is phenomenal."

We went back to the counter and Clarissa paid the guy for her new strings, then tucked her guitar back into its case. I swiped one of the cards off the counter and stuck it in my pocket.

When we returned home, Clarissa took off to The Locker. She was going to help Lou audition bands before her shift tonight.

I was preparing for my first appointment when Layla came in holding a large, padded envelope in her hand. "Mail came. This one is addressed to you and Rissa."

I took it from her hands and flipped it over. I didn't recognize the return address. "Thanks. I have no idea what this is."

Layla stood in the doorway waiting for me to open it. "Well?"

I shook my head at her. "Nosey much."

"Whatever. Just open the damn envelope. My curiosity is killing me," she barked.

"Don't you have work to do?" I asked as I opened the envelope. "I doubt you're getting paid to watch me open the mail."

Layla waved her hand at me. "My boss is cool most of the time. He won't mind."

I quirked an eyebrow at her. "Most of the time?"

She shrugged her shoulders. "Sometimes he's a controlling ass, but I love him anyway."

"Yeah, well nobody's perfect," I said as I slid the contents of the envelope onto the counter. Two tickets, backstage passes, sheet music, a CD and a note fell out. I picked up the note and began to read. Then I reread. "You've got to be fucking kidding me!"

"What?" Layla asked. "Good news or bad news?"

I looked up at her with wide eyes. "Great news. Clarissa is going to flip!" I shoved the note at Layla, and she began to read.

"Our Rissa?" she asked in shock. "How did this even happen?"

I blew out a breath. "Confession time. He's one of my clients."

"You ass! How could you keep this from me? I want to meet him," Layla squealed.

I pointed at her. "That's why. He's private and doesn't like a lot of fanfare."

"Whatever! I would have been cool. I'm the queen of cool," she said squaring her shoulders.

"Yeah, okay," I laughed. "Anyways, he was here for a late-night appointment and asked Clarissa to play for him. He mentioned something about trying to help her out, but I thought he was just being nice. I never expected this."

"Wow! This could be huge for her. Are you going to call Rissa and tell her?" Layla asked.

My fingers tapped on the counter. "I should, but she's working. She'll be distracted all night. What do you think I should do?"

"Are you kidding me? Go! Tell her right now! I'll cover for you when your client gets here."

I scooped up the contents on the counter and stuffed them back into the envelope. Kissing Layla on the cheek, I rushed by her. "Thanks. I won't be gone long."

"Take your time," Layla shouted behind me. "I've got your back."

I walked quickly down the street and into The Locker. Clarissa and Lou sat on bar stools listening and whispering. The band playing was actually pretty good.

When they finished their song, Lou held up his hand. "Thanks. We like you. Let's talk business."

"Clarissa!" I yelled out.

"Zack? What are you doing here? I thought you had an appointment."

I held up the envelope. "I do, but this was more important."

We walked toward each other, and Clarissa took the envelope from my hand. "What's this?"

"Read it for yourself."

She dumped the contents on the bar and read the letter. "Oh. My. God. Is this for real? He wants me to perform a duet with him during his concert Friday night?"

"I think so. Do you want me to call him for you?"

She looked at me with wide eyes. "I don't think I can do this. It's too much. What if I screw it up? And the people. There will be thousands of people there."

203

I took her by the shoulders. "Look at me. Bobby wouldn't have asked you if he didn't think you were good enough. You can do this. It's just you and the music."

"And fifteen thousand people."

"Sweetheart, when you play nothing else exists. You need to do this. You deserve it."

She picked up the sheet music that had fallen out of the envelope and stared at it. "I know this song. Will you practice with me?"

"I'll do my best. Is that a yes?" I asked.

"It's a yes."

I picked up my girl and spun her around the bar. "You're going to be amazing. Should I call him?"

Clarissa nodded her head. "Yes. Tell Bobby thank you." She leaned in and pressed her lips to mine. "And thank you. This would have never been possible without you."

"I didn't do anything."

"You did everything," she insisted.

Chapter 26
Rissa

"You know, you really downplayed your talent." I stared at Zack. He had been practicing with me all week. He'd learned his part of the duet quickly. "You have a really nice voice."

Zack shrugged. "It was always a hobby for me. Drawing was more my thing. This was Wes's passion, not mine."

I swallowed down the lump in my throat. "I have a confession to make." My eyes filled with tears, and I looked away from him.

Zack held my chin and turned me back to him. "What's wrong, sweetheart?"

I removed his hand from my chin. "This song. It makes me think of Wes."

"Oh."

"Not the words. The song itself. We used to do this as a duet in the bar. The night he died, he was supposed to sing with me, but he never showed up. I called and called, and he never answered. I rushed home and found him on our couch. He was already gone. That was the night my life changed. I can't help but… miss him," I confessed.

Zack set his guitar to the side and wrapped me in his arms. "I'm sorry, baby."

I wiped at my eyes, "It doesn't mean that I love you any less. But he was an important part of my life for a long time. I can't erase that. This song just brings it all to the surface."

Zack took a deep breath and blew it out. "I understand. Think of it this way. He'll be with you when you sing in front of thousands of people. Wes would be proud of you. I'm proud of you."

"Do you think he'll be watching?" I asked.

"I know he will. So will your mom and dad."

I couldn't believe how supportive Zack was. I had just confessed to thinking about his brother, yet he was so sweet. I didn't know what I had done to deserve Zack, but I wasn't going to question it. "I want you on stage with me," I said.

"I don't think that was what Bobby had in mind, but I'll be there watching you."

"I want you to tattoo me before the show. Then I'll have a piece of you with me," I said.

Zack rubbed his hand over his scruffy chin. "Are you sure? I don't want you to make an impulsive decision."

"It's not impulsive," I insisted. "I've been thinking about it for a while. This opportunity has solidified my decision. I want you to do it."

"What did you have in mind?" he asked curiously.

"Nothing outrageous. I was thinking a treble clef with a heart."

Zack went to the kitchen and grabbed a pad of paper. "I have an idea." He quickly started sketching a treble clef. He took the bottom part of the music symbol and curved it into a heart. I watched in amazement as he shaded and added some scrolling. When he finished, he held it up for me to see. "What do you think?"

"I think you're amazing. I can't believe in all the time we've spent together that I never watched you draw before. It's beautiful."

"I aim to please," he said with a smile. "Where do you want it?"

I touched the space between my thumb and forefinger. "What about here?"

Zack picked up my hand and inspected the area. "That could work, but I'm afraid it would be too small, and the details would blur together over time." He turned my hand over. "I think the inside of your wrist would be better. But it's totally up to you."

"I'd be a fool to disagree with you. You're the professional, not me." I rubbed my wrist and tried to imagine what it would look like. "When do you think you'll have time?"

"You're sure about this? I mean, really sure?"

"Yes. I want you to mark me as yours," I assured him.

He got a smirk on his face. "Oh sweetheart, believe me, I've already marked you as mine." He pulled me into his lap and kissed me furiously, running his hands up and down my body.

My heart thumped out of my chest at his passion. His eagerness. His possessiveness. I was his. There was no denying it. I belonged to Zack.

When he released me, I took a second to catch my breath. "Tonight. Can you do it tonight?"

"Let's head downstairs. I can have it finished in an hour." He pulled me to my feet and pulled me toward the door.

"Wait! I need to get some money. How much will this cost?" I asked.

"Are you fucking with me right now? I'm not going to charge you. You're my girlfriend. Do you really think I'm that much of an asshole?" Zack sounded offended.

"Of course not. I didn't want to assume anything. This is your business. I wouldn't expect you to do it for free," I said.

"Oh sweetheart, nothing is for free. You'll be paying, but I won't take cash." He scanned my body up and down. "I have something much better in mind."

"I'm sure you do." I followed him down the stairs and into his studio.

"Sit," Zack directed me to the chair. I sat down, and he pulled out a form from the drawer next to his desk. "Here. Fill this out."

I looked at the form in front of me. It asked basic questions, like my name and phone number. I looked a little further down the form where the medical questions were. Number five read, *Are you pregnant?* I pushed the paper back at him. "Is this really necessary? You're my boyfriend. If I can't trust you, who can I trust?"

He took the form from me. "You're right. I don't know what I was thinking. Force of habit, I guess. Let me go make the transfer."

I had been in Zack's studio dozens of times, but this was the first time I was a client. I looked at the artwork on the walls. One picture caught my attention. I stood and walked over to the framed picture on the wall. I ran my fingers over it and gasped. It was like looking in a mirror.

Zack returned a few minutes later. "Is this me?" I asked. I knew the answer before he even spoke. It was a sketch of me sitting cross-legged with a guitar in my hands. There were angel wings protruding from my back.

"Do you like it?"

I nodded my head. "When did you do this?"

He blew out a breath. "The first night you played for me upstairs. I couldn't get you out of my head."

"I'm not an angel," I warned him.

"So you've said, but you're my angel. You're everything that is good and honest and pure. You make me want to corrupt you in the best way."

"You make me want to let you corrupt me," I answered.

"Let's get this started and then we'll talk about your payment. I have so many ideas." He placed the transfer on the inside of my wrist. "What do you think?

"I think it's going to be beautiful. Will it hurt?" My nerves kicked up a notch. I hated needles and now I was subjecting myself to them going in and out of my skin.

Zack kissed me on the cheek. "It'll sting a little, but nothing you can't handle. I promise."

Zack's promises meant everything to me. I trusted him implicitly. "Okay." Zack started his tattoo gun and touched it to my skin. I flinched at the contact.

"Easy, sweetheart. Just take a deep breath."

I did, and Zack continued. There was no turning back now. I watched as he did the outline of the treble clef. It was a continuous process of drawing and wiping the excess ink from my skin. There wasn't any blood that I could see. After a while I got used to the buzz on my wrist. I watched intently as his vision came to life. Zack was in a zone. He hardly talked at all as he created beautiful artwork on my skin.

When he finished, he cleaned the area and rubbed some salve on it. "You're all done. What do you think?"

I inspected the finished product. "I think that every time I look at it, I'll think of you. It's better than I ever expected."

Zack put a hand over his heart. "You wound me, sweetheart. Did you think I'd give you anything but the best?"

I wrapped my arms around his neck and pulled him down on top of me in the chair. "You never do. I love you, Zack. Thank you." I kissed him and ran my hands through the short strands of his hair. "Take me to bed."

"Your wish is my command. Let me bandage this first." Zack took my arm and covered my new tattoo, taping the bandage in place. "In five minutes, this is the only thing you'll be wearing."

We went upstairs, and I went directly to his room, dragging him behind me. "I want you to take me a little further tonight," I whispered.

He caressed my face. "What do you want?"

"I don't know," I admitted.

He picked up my wrist. "I want to wait until this is healed before I cuff you."

I swallowed down my fear. "You want to handcuff me?"

"Yeah. I do. Are you afraid?"

"No." I was sure he could see through my lie. "You won't hurt me." I don't know who I was trying to convince, him or myself. All I knew was that I wanted to be whatever he wanted me to be.

"I couldn't. I wouldn't." He went to his dresser and pulled out a long velvet box. "I bought you a present." He handed it to me. "I want you to wear this when we're together."

I scrunched up my face, "Zack, you shouldn't buy me anything. Everything you've done for me is more than enough." I tried to hand the box back to him.

"Open it Clarissa Lynne."

I opened the box and gasped. "Are those...?"

"Diamonds? Yes. You can only wear this when I fuck you." He pulled out the piece of jewelry— if that's what you wanted to call it— and fastened it around my neck.

I went to the mirror and looked. It was more like a collar. The black leather band was about a half-inch wide that buckled in the back. The surface of it was covered in the largest, most beautiful diamonds I had ever seen. I ran my hand over my throat. "I'm not a dog," I whispered.

He stood behind me and kissed my neck. "That's not what I was implying. But when you're wearing this, you are mine. You belong to me. You're mine to do with as I like."

"I'm already yours. I don't need this."

"You don't like it." Disappointment filled his voice and I immediately felt bad. He began to unbuckle it from my neck.

My hand went up to stop him. "It's beautiful. I am yours. But this goes both ways. If I wear this, then that means that you are mine."

I looked in the mirror and his green eyes stared back at me. "Was that ever a question? I've been yours since you came into my life. I wouldn't have asked you to move here if I wasn't committed to you. I'll always take care of you and protect you. I never knew what my life was missing until you came into it. This isn't a game to me. You are my life."

Guilt washed over me. Zack was laying his heart on the line, and I was lying to him. He'd been understanding when I told him the song made me think of his brother. Maybe we could make this work. I had to hold onto the hope that he would still love me when he found out I was carrying his nephew or niece. There was so much wrong with this situation, but it couldn't all be bad. There had to be some good. This baby was going to need a father. Who could love this baby more than his or her uncle? If Zack accepted us, as a package deal, no one would ever need to know. We could be happy.

"I want to wear this," I said. "I am yours and you are mine."

"That's all I need tonight," Zack said, as he kissed my neck again. His lips moved to my collar bone and to the swell of my breast. I nearly melted at his touch. "I want you to wear this, and only this," he touched the collar, "as I worship your body."

I couldn't protest. There was no use anyway. I was his. He slowly undressed me and carried me to the bed. He placed me gently into the middle and did exactly what he promised. He kissed and licked and savored every inch of my skin.

Zack lit me on fire.

♫♪♫♪

We had gotten to the arena early. Zack and I showed our passes and were led down a maze of hallways to Bobby's dressing room. I was dressed in a pair of hip-hugging jeans, that were a little tighter than they should have been, a black sequined tank top and sky-high heels. My hair fell in loose curls down my shoulders and my make-up was a little darker than normal.

Zack could see the nerves that were threatening to take over my body. "Just breathe." He raised his hand and knocked on the closed door. Zack had no reason to be nervous. He and Bobby had known each other a while. I, on the other hand, was a mess.

The door creaked open. A huge guy blocked our view into the room. "I'm Rissa. Bobby is expecting me," I croaked.

The door swung open, and Bobby sat on the couch with a joint hanging from his lips. He looked like the quintessential rock star. "Come on in," he said. Bobby grabbed his drink off the table and took a sip. "What can I get you?"

"I'll have the same as you. Jim Beam, right?" Zack said lightly.

"You know it, man." Bobby rose from the couch and wrapped Zack in a one-armed hug. "Rissa. Pleasure to see ya, darling. Are you ready for tonight?"

I placed my guitar case on the floor and shook out my arms. "Honestly? I'm nervous as fuck."

Bobby laughed at my response. "God, I love her, Zack. Where did you find her?"

Zack laughed. "New York, sitting on a bench." Bobby had no idea what our history was, and I couldn't have cared less. That was between Zack and me. It wasn't anyone else's business.

A beefy guy handed Zack his drink. "What would you like, Rissa?"

"Water will be fine," I said.

Bobby looked at me skeptically. "You don't want a drink to loosen up?" He extended his joint to me. "Maybe a little hash?"

I held up my hand. "I'm good." I took the offered water and gulped down half of it, trying to ease my nerves.

Zack took the joint and brought it to his lips, inhaling deeply. I desperately wanted something to take the edge off, but what kind of mother would that make me? No matter what life dealt me, I was determined to do the right thing for my baby.

I watched as Zack and Bobby shared the joint and indulged in a few drinks. I didn't know Zack smoked weed, but it didn't altogether surprise me.

I should have known that being in the Marines, he had smoked pot. I'm sure he saw a ton of awful shit and had done anything he could to erase the memories. I was equally sure that his propensity for unconventional sex stemmed from the same experiences.

After a few minutes of silent awkwardness on my part, Bobby stared at me as he stubbed out the joint. "Are you ready to do this?" I got the feeling he might be second guessing his invitation for me to sing. If I wasn't what he was expecting, there was no doubt he had a back-up plan.

"As ready as I'll ever be." I nervously wiped my hands on my jeans, picked up my guitar case and took out my Gibson.

"Let's hear it." He picked up his own guitar. I sat in the chair opposite him. He began strumming and I joined in. He sang the first verse and chorus. I closed my eyes and focused on the words. Then it was my turn. I sang the second verse and the chorus. Our voices blended together for the last verse. It was an easy back and forth as we finished the song together. It was pure magic.

It was silent when we finished. I wiped the tear that had run down my face on my shoulder. Bobby's bodyguard spoke first. "Wow."

Bobby spoke up next. "That's a fucking understatement. I knew it would be good, but that was…" He wiped a hand over his face.

"Exceptional," Zack provided.

"Way better than the original," Bobby confirmed.

A little smile worked its way onto my lips. I'd been too nervous to smile before, but now I couldn't stop it.

Bobby eyed me intently. "You know you're beautiful when you smile? You should do that more."

I dipped my head in embarrassment. "I'll take that under advisement. Are we going to do a sound check or anything? I'd really like to do it again on the stage."

He clapped his hands and rubbed them together. "No better time than the present. I'm stoked, Rissa. This is going to be amazing."

"I'm excited too," I admitted.

Bobby led us through the maze of hallways and out to the stage. Zack wrapped his arm around my shoulders and kissed the side of my head. "I'm so proud of you. How are your nerves?"

212

"Better. I can do this."

"Yes, you can."

We approached the stage and I looked at it from behind the curtain. It was so big. Thousands of empty seats stared back at me. I could already feel the heat from the lights and sweat dotted my forehead. Fear consumed every part of me. I took one step forward, then quickly turned around and crashed into Zack's chest. "I can't do this," I mumbled.

Zack took my face in his hands and stared into my eyes. "Yes. You can." He gripped my shoulders and turned me around, giving me a little push.

I stumbled onto the stage and walked toward the two bar stools placed in the center. I sat down as my heart beat so hard I was sure it was going to burst through my chest. I gave Bobby a worried look.

"I know what you're feeling," he assured me. "Forget about the lights. Forget about the crowd. Forget about everything but the music. It's what people like us live for. I have confidence in you. I would never have suggested this if I didn't think you could do it. Your voice is truly beautiful. You're going to blow them away. People will be talking about you for days. Trust me. I know what I'm talking about."

"How do you know all of this?" I asked. "I'm just me. There's nothing special about who I am."

Bobby tilted his head. "Is that what you really think?" I nodded. "Let me assure you, darling, nothing could be further from the truth. Tonight, is your night. All I want you to do is shine."

Bobby's words gave me the confidence I needed. I made it through the sound check and was astonished at the sound of our voices as they echoed through the empty arena. Never had my voice sounded so strong, so sure and so foreign to my own ears. I blinked when I was done, unsure that the voice I heard was mine.

Bobby kissed me on the cheek. "You're ready."

I wasn't sure if he was right or not, but I agreed anyway. If Bobby had confidence in me, I needed to have confidence in myself.

As it got closer to the time for the concert to start, the area backstage got crazy. Equipment was being moved. People ran around, scurrying to attend to last minute details. The opening band milled around, getting amped up for the show. The energy was electric. All of it should have made me excited, but it just made me more nervous.

We sat backstage in Bobby's dressing room, waiting for his concert to start. I drank down a ton of water and played around with my guitar, if for no other reason than to have something to do. I started to feel lightheaded, and my stomach began to feel queasy.

Not wanting to bring attention to myself, I snuck into the bathroom. I didn't even have time to lock the door before I lost the contents of my stomach into the toilet. I broke out into a cold sweat as I kneeled on the floor. I rested my arm on the rim of the toilet and let the tears flow. I was a mess. I couldn't hear anything but the sound of blood whooshing in my ears.

I don't know how long I kneeled there before the door opened behind me. "Sweetheart?"

I couldn't lift my head. Couldn't look at him. Embarrassment consumed me. "Go away," I whispered.

"Not a chance." Zack rubbed my back. "Are you okay?"

I didn't have time to answer before my stomach clenched again and spilled into the toilet. Nothing about this felt good. Not only was I letting myself down, but Bobby too. I wiped at my eyes. "I'll be okay."

Zack pulled me to my feet and wrapped me in his arms. I couldn't say anything. I buried my head in his chest and drew my strength from him. I took a couple of calming breathes. "Can you get me my purse?"

"Of course."

He returned with my bag. I set it on the counter and pulled out the makeup I kept there. Staring at myself in the mirror, I begged, "Please don't tell anyone."

"I won't."

"Thank you," I sighed. Using toilet paper, I wiped the black smudges from beneath my eyes. "I can't believe I'm this weak." I smoothed concealer under my eyes and began to reapply my eyeliner.

Zack leaned against the closed door watching me. "Think about Wes," he said.

My head snapped in his direction. "What?"

"Forget about everything else. Picture yourself with Wes, sitting in a bar."

"Why would I do that?" I stuttered. His suggestion was completely unexpected. I didn't know how else to respond.

"Because this song meant something to the two of you. I think it might help. I think you feel guilty singing it without him. So, just pretend he's with you."

I thought about what Zack said. His words couldn't have been any closer to the truth if he tried. And yet, they held no sense of betrayal or jealously. Just concern for me. My heart beat faster. "I can't do that to you. I love you too much."

"Do it *for* me. You don't have to choose between us. I'm not naïve enough to think that he doesn't still mean something to you. I can't compete with a ghost. Tonight, you need him more than me," he said solemnly.

♫♪♫♪

I stood waiting in the wings, Zack standing solidly behind me. I listened as Bobby gave me my cue. "Here singing with me tonight is a young lady whose is as sweet as she is beautiful and talented. Please welcome Miss Rissa Black!"

Zack kissed my wrist where he had marked me and gave me a little push. I strolled onto the stage like I owned it, as the crowd erupted with applause for me. Somewhere in the last hour I'd found my confidence. I gave the crowd a wave as I approached Bobby. He took my hand, and I sat down on the stool opposite him. I stared at my wrist and found the strength I was searching for.

Bobby strummed the opening chords to the song, and I imagined it was Wes singing and we were sitting together on the stage at The Hot Spot, playing this song together like we had so many times. The lights faded away. The crowd no longer existed. It was just the two of us. Wes and me.

I sat across from him, one foot on the ground the other resting on the rung of the barstool. Wes's stance mirrored mine. I stared into his green eyes as he began to play. Strands of blond hair fell into his eyes. He'd used gel on it before we left the apartment, but the strands were now messy and loose from running his hands through it. He looked so sexy and sweet.

215

I thanked God every day that we had found each other. That he had chosen me from the thousands of women in Brooklyn. That he had been sitting at the bar that fateful night we met.

His voice was deep and husky, with more than a hint of sexiness that pulled me and every other woman in. But yet, he had chosen me. He had taken a poor girl from Oklahoma and made her feel like the only woman in the room. His eyes focused on me with softness and love.

I returned the sentiment, letting him know he was the only one who held my heart. My voice softened with a sexy undertone only he could coax from me. When I sang with Wes, the rest of the world melted away. It was just the two of us and the words that poured from our hearts. There was no denying the love between us.

When we got to the third verse our voices melded together in perfect harmony. We weren't just singing; we were baring our souls to each other. Making promises of forever. Knowing that nothing could ever pull us apart. Making love on the stage without ever touching.

When we finished singing, Wes rested his forehead on mine. "I love you, baby. Now and forever. Don't ever forget that."

I opened my eyes and stared at Zack who stood just out of sight at the side of the stage. He pressed both hands to his lips and blew me a kiss. I mouthed the words *thank you.* He nodded in understanding, although I don't know that he could truly understand what he had done for me tonight.

The crowd was quiet and then the applause started low. It began to grow, and people were on their feet screaming my name. My face broke out in a huge smile that overtook me. I bowed my head and blushed. Bobby grabbed my hand and held it up high. "Ladies and gentleman, Miss Rissa Black! Give her another round of applause!"

Chapter 27
Zack

I watched Clarissa sitting on the stage. I saw the moment she disappeared. She was sitting next to Bobby, but she wasn't really there. She was with Wes.

There was something in her voice I hadn't heard before. It was a soft sexiness, as if each word came directly from her heart. The audience had no choice to be captured by it and sucked in.

I felt it. My chest ached as I listened to her sing. I felt the tears welling in my eyes, but I refused to let them fall.

Wes had given her something tonight that I couldn't. He'd been here with her, his spirit overshadowing me, even though I was standing right here.

And it hurt.

Knowing that as hard as I tried, I couldn't give her this… killed me. The sense of peace and happiness that emanated from her. A sense of closure she'd never been given the opportunity to find. He was all she needed tonight.

And I was pissed at my brother for leaving her alone. For choosing cocaine over the sweet, beautiful woman singing on the stage. For hurting her so deeply.

But at the same time, I thank him. Without my brother I would have never found the woman who had so wholly captured my heart. She was a gift he never intended to give me. But greedily I took her and made her mine.

As I watched her, I knew she would never stop loving Wes. I prayed she could love me just as much. I prayed she had enough room in her heart for both of us.

When she finished the song, she lifted her head, her eyes finding mine. I brought my hands to my lips and blew her a kiss. She bit her lip and mouthed *thank you*. And in that moment, I knew I had done the right thing tonight, no matter how much it hurt.

♫♪♫♪

We spent the rest of the concert watching from behind the curtain where we were just out of sight. I'd seen Bobby on television but seeing him perform live was different. There was an energy that emanated from him that couldn't be appreciated watching on a screen.

Clarissa jumped and danced around, singing along with him. I held her hips as she swayed to the music, my body moving with hers. She leaned back into my chest and wrapped her arms around my neck. She tilted her head back, staring at me with her bright blue eyes. "I love you, Zack."

"I love you too, sweetheart."

We rocked together a little longer before a guy in a suit approached us. "Rissa Black?"

Clarissa scrunched up her eyes. "Yes?"

He reached his hand out for Clarissa to take. "I'm Daniel McClain. I'm Bobby's agent."

She shook his hand. "It's nice to meet you Mr. McClain."

He released her hand. "It's Daniel and I assure you the pleasure is all mine. You put on quite a show tonight." His hands sunk deep into his pants pockets.

Clarissa pushed her hair over her shoulder. "Thanks. It was just one song though."

He nodded. "One song that everyone will be talking about." He pulled out his phone and showed her the screen. "It's already been posted on YouTube."

Clarissa took his phone and stared at herself on the screen as I looked over her shoulder. It had been posted twenty minutes ago and already had over a hundred thousand hits. "Scroll down," I said.

Clarissa's finger moved over the screen, making the comments come into view. There were hundreds.

Who is this girl?

Amazing!

218

Wow! I think my heart just broke.

Why don't we know her?

When is her album coming out? I want it!

Pure magic!!!!!!

Clarissa put her hand to her lips and looked up at me. "They're talking about me," she whispered.

"Yeah, they are," I confirmed.

Daniel took his phone back from her hands. "This is going to go viral. By tomorrow you're going to be a hot commodity. Nothing would make me happier than to represent you." Daniel took a card out from his suit pocket and handed it to Clarissa.

Her face paled as she held the shiny, black card in her hand. "I don't think I'm ready for that. It was one song."

"Trust me, I know the business. You're ready. Call me this week and we'll talk."

"Thank you, Mr. McClain... umm Daniel. I'll be in touch." I could see everything she was holding in, her excitement that was simmering right below the surface.

"Be sure you are. Talk to you soon." And with that he walked away.

Clarissa gripped the card tight in her hand. "Am I dreaming?"

I held her face between my hands. "No, this is very real. I'm so proud of you."

She let out a squeal of delight and danced around in a circle, shaking her sexy little ass. She launched herself at me and wrapped her arms around my neck. "This is all because of you, Zack. I don't know how to thank you."

"I didn't do anything. You're the one with all the talent."

When the show ended, we went back to Bobby's dressing room where a celebration was already starting. "Are you two gonna hang around for the afterparty?" he asked.

I was ready to leave but I left it up to Clarissa. This was her night, and I wouldn't take that away from her. "I think we're going to head back to the hotel," she said. She reached out her arms for a hug and he stepped towards her. They clung to each other for no more than a few seconds and I could already feel the jealousy creeping up inside me. She released him.

"This was one of the most amazing nights of my life. I'll never forget it. Thank you for taking a chance on me."

He smiled at her. "I knew the moment I heard you sing, it was a chance worth taking. I'll keep it touch. Maybe we can do it again sometime."

"I'd like that," she said.

Bobby pulled an envelope from his pocket and thrust it into her hands. "Good luck" He winked at her.

Clarissa peeked into the envelope and thrust it back at him. "I can't take this."

"You earned it."

Refusing to take the envelope back, she said, "Singing tonight was enough."

Bobby looked at me. "Where did you find her again?"

I laughed. "New York. Go find your own."

"I might just do that."

We said our final goodbyes and started the short walk to the Atheneum Hotel. It was only a few short blocks. I booked us a suite for the night, not knowing what we would be doing after the concert. I didn't want to worry about driving home if we were having fun.

I swung our hands between us as we strolled along the crowded Detroit sidewalk. "We could have stayed," I said.

"It's not really my scene. I'd rather just spend the night with you. We don't get to do this very often. One of the two of us is usually working."

She was right. Between her bar schedule and my late-night appointments, it was rarely before two in the morning when we got to spend time together. The envelope Bobby had tried to give her stroked my curiosity. "What was in the envelope?"

"Money," she said nonchalantly.

I stopped and turned her toward me. "How much money?"

She pulled on my hand to keep me walking. "A thousand dollars."

She could have really used that money. I knew she wanted to buy a car and she wasn't willing to let me help her. "Why didn't you take it?"

"It didn't feel right. I sang one song that took all of five minutes. A thousand dollars seemed a little outrageous."

"What about your car?" I asked.

220

"I'll get there. I didn't sing for the money. I sang for me. To prove to myself that I could do it. And if it hadn't been for you, I probably would have chickened out. It meant a lot that you believed in me. Thank you."

I pulled our joined hands to my mouth and placed a soft kiss on the back of her fingers. "Anytime." We passed a bar and dance music streamed through the outside speakers. "Wanna go in?"

Her hips were already wiggling to the music, and it was so damn cute. "Sure."

We approached the bar, and she hopped up on a stool. I leaned next to her. I ordered a beer while Clarissa got a Sprite with lemon. "You really don't drink do you? I thought we were celebrating."

She squeezed the lemon into her drink and took a sip. "I'm on a natural high. I don't need alcohol to make me feel good. I want to remember every moment of tonight. I want to remember every moment with you."

"Are you going to call that guy this week?" I asked her.

"Maybe." She shrugged. "I'm sure by next week, no one will even remember who I am."

"I think people will remember you," I assured her. "You should call and at least hear what he has to say."

"I will," she promised.

A group of girls about Clarissa's age stood nearby. They kept glancing at us and whispering. Clarissa ran her hand over her head. "Is my hair sticking up or something?"

I pulled her hand down. "Your hair is perfect. You look beautiful."

Her eyes glanced to the group of girls and then back to me. "Then why are they staring at us?"

I shrugged. "I don't know. Just ignore them."

One of the girls broke from the pack and strode toward us, her dark hair swinging behind her. She invaded our space and spoke to Clarissa. "Are you that girl that sang tonight? With Bobby?" she clarified.

Clarissa looked at me and then back at the brunette. "Yeah, that was me."

The girl hopped up and down and clapped her hands excitedly. "I knew it. You were great!" Her hands went to her chest dramatically. "I couldn't stop crying."

"I'm glad you liked it," Clarissa said shyly.

The girl reached behind us and grabbed a napkin off the bar. "Can I have your autograph?"

Clarissa laughed. "What for? I'm not anyone famous."

"Maybe not now, but you will be. Please…" she begged.

"Okay, but I'm pretty sure this will never be worth anything." Rissa grabbed a pen off the bar and scribbled her name on it in big bold letters, *Rissa Black,* dotting the i with a little heart.

The girl snatched up the napkin and held it her chest. "Thank you!" She walked away, waving the napkin in the air at her friends. "It's her!" she yelled.

Clarissa clutched her stomach and let out a hysterical laugh. "That was the most ridiculous thing that's ever happened to me. Don't you think?"

"Hey, people know a star when they see one. It could happen, you never know," I answered.

She waved me off. "You're ridiculous too." Then she hopped off her stool and grabbed my hand. "Dance with me."

I drained my beer and left the bottle on the bar, following her as she led us to the dance floor. We pushed through the throng of people moving to the music and found a spot we could squeeze into. I hadn't been dancing in forever. When I lived in New York, my weekends had been spent in bars hanging out and dancing until closing time. Most nights I'd take a pretty girl home to share my bed.

When I moved here, I didn't have much time for fun. I'd been too focused on starting my business. And after Megan, having random one-night stands lost their appeal to me. I didn't trust easily, and the thought of being scammed again had kept my dick in my pants. That was why what Gina and I had worked. Zero expectations.

But with Clarissa I felt free. Free to give myself to her. Free to trust her. Free to love her.

Her arms raised high above her head and swayed as she moved her hips to the beat of the music. My hands grabbed her hips and pulled her close to me. Her legs straddled one of mine, her center pushed into me, and her hands came up to rest on my shoulders.

Her smile broke free and she laughed as one of my hands snaked around to palm her ass, pulling her in tighter. She turned in my arms, resting her back against my chest. She wiggled her way down my body, rubbing her sweet, round ass up and down on me. My hands skimmed up the sides of her beautiful body, lightly grazing her breast. I wouldn't be able to hold out much longer. She'd already made my dick hard and wasn't playing fair. I leaned down and whispered in her ear. "You're teasing me."

She shook her head, her curls bouncing back and forth. "I'm, not teasing you. It's foreplay. I have every intention of following through."

"How long?" I breathed in her ear. "How long do I have to wait?"

She flashed me her smile. "A few more songs. I love dancing with you." She extended my arm out and twirled underneath it, laughing and smiling so brightly I couldn't say no.

We continued that way until the fast-beat songs slowed. She wrapped her arms around my shoulders and ran her fingers through the hair at the base of my neck. Her blue eyes looked up at me as I pulled her close. "I love you, Zack. I'm thankful every day that you came into my life. I don't care how it happened or why it happened, I'm just so happy when I'm with you. You've become everything to me. Everything I never knew I needed."

I ran a hand up her back and through her long blond curls. "I feel the same way. You have no idea what you do to me."

She rubbed her body up against mine, "I think I have an idea. I can feel it against my stomach."

I dipped my forehead against hers. "I can't help it. You make me crazy."

She stretched up on her tiptoes and I leaned down to meet her lips. They brushed together gently. I ran my tongue along her bottom lip, tasting her sweetness. She opened just enough to let me in, and our tongues tangled together in a dance of their own. We stood in the middle of the dance floor, kissing as if nothing else existed. Easing back before I took her right there in the bar, I whispered in her ear, "I'm done waiting."

"Take me to bed," she begged.

There was nothing else to say. I wrapped her hand in mine and led her out of the bar towards our hotel room. We didn't need to say a word, we both knew where we were headed. I rushed her through the lobby and over to

223

the bank of elevators. The doors opened and I all but pushed her in. I couldn't wait any longer. I needed her. Something about tonight made me want her even more than normal. I trapped her against the wall with the weight of my body, holding her wrists above her head. I pressed my lips to her neck and buried my head in the crook of her shoulder. "I need you, Clarissa."

She let out a little moan just before the ding of the elevator alerted us to our stop. It took only moments for us to reach our room. We were a mess of hands and tongues and teeth, stripping down to only our underwear in a matter of seconds.

I ran my hands down the sides of her body. The first night I was with Clarissa, she'd been beautiful, but so thin. The weight of losing Wes had taken its toll on her. In the last few weeks, she began to look healthier. Her hips had filled out a little bit. She'd become curvier. Fuller. Sexier. I couldn't keep my hands off her.

"Wait just a minute." I went to my duffle and pulled out the long black box. I removed the diamonds within and fastened them around her neck. I ran my fingers over them. "You are mine."

"I am yours. Are you going to fuck me now?" she gasped.

"No," I shook my head. "Not tonight. Tonight, I'm going to make love to you. I don't think you have any idea how much I love you, Clarissa Lynne."

Her face softened from lust to something entirely different. The air shifted between us. Something deeper was taking ahold of us. A connection that pulled us together and threatened to never let us go. I couldn't define it, because I'd never felt it before. But tonight, standing here with her in this hotel room, I felt it. And I didn't ever want to lose this feeling.

I pulled the straps of her bra down over her shoulders, pulled the cups of her black lacy bra down to expose her perfect tits. I took her in my mouth, my tongue running over the hard tips. She let out a little whimper and dropped her head back. I flicked the clasp and let the material fall from her body. "You are perfect."

She took two steps back until her knees hit the bed. Her arms wrapped around my shoulders as she fell back into the soft mattress, taking me with her. She started to giggle as I fell on top of her. I pulled up on my

224

elbows and pushed the hair from her face. "Tell me you're real. Tell me this isn't a dream."

"It's not a dream."

Her nails ran down the length of my back and beneath the elastic of my boxer briefs. Her nails scraped over my ass and her hands pushed at the fabric. I lifted my hips and let her push it down.

I ached to be inside her, to live in her warmth. She was my girl and I wanted nothing more than to take care of her, to protect her, to keep her with me forever. I kissed down her neck, between her breasts, over her stomach. Her panties were black lace and satin with pink bows at the hips. I ran my fingers over the bows. "I love these."

"So much, you don't want to take them off?" she teased.

"Oh, no. They're coming off, sweetheart. As much as I love them, I love what's underneath even more." I pulled them over her hips and down her legs, throwing them to the side. My hands ran up her legs and under her ass, lifting her to my face. My tongue made slow, lazy licks over her clit and through her wet pussy. She was soaked for me, and I loved that about her.

"Oh, God," she whimpered softly. "Make me come, Zack. Please...please." One hand fisted the sheets while the other pushed on the back of my head. She bucked and squirmed beneath me. "It's so good, baby. Oh my...oh my..." Her back arched high off the mattress. "Oh fuck." It came out breathless, as she sucked in a deep breath.

I crawled up her body and pushed into her in one long, deep stroke. She was so tight, so wet, she felt like heaven wrapped around my dick. I stilled inside her. "You all right, sweetheart?"

She held my face between her hands. "More than all right. Make love to me."

I kissed her forehead, then pulled back and gently pushed in again. I wasn't a making love type of guy. I usually liked it hard and fast. A little on the rough side. I liked the control. I liked the power. I liked her screaming my name. I liked to fuck, plain and simple.

But with Clarissa it was different. This was the third time I'd made love to her, and I found that I enjoyed it as much as I liked fucking her. Don't get me wrong, I loved having total control over her body and having her at my mercy as I slammed into her. But, pushing into her slowly made me feel emotionally connected. Closer. More intimate. More in love.

Maybe that was the difference. I had never been truly in love before. I had thought I was, but I had been wrong. Since I'd been with Clarissa it was clear that everything I felt before was just a prelude to this.

I pulled her leg up around my hip and pushed in deeper. I felt I couldn't get deep enough inside her. I wanted to consume her, let her know that no one would ever love her like I did.

Her back arched and she grabbed onto my shoulders, her nails digging into the skin. I loved the pain and the pleasure rolled together. I continued to pump into her slowly. I wanted to come so bad, but this sweet torture was so good.

I ran my hands under her shoulders and lifted her from the mattress and onto my lap. Her hands wrapped around my head as I buried it between her breasts. She rode me slowly as I pushed up into her. She tilted my head back and peered down into my eyes. It was the connection I was longing for. "I love you, Zack. So, so much."

We rocked together in a rhythm all our own. There was no hurry. We wanted to make this last as long as possible. There was no her. There was no me. There was only us.

"Come for me, Clarissa. Let go with me." As if on demand, her pussy clenched my dick, squeezing me so tight that I let go too. We came together and basked in the love that we shared. I held her tight to my chest, wrapping her in my arms. I never wanted this to end.

I reluctantly laid her back on the bed and pulled out. Grabbing a towel from the bathroom I wiped us both down and we crawled under the covers. We laid face to face, her fingers tracing the line of my jaw. "Where was my demanding man, tonight?"

"Oh, he's still here." I twined my fingers with hers, kissing the back of each one. "I needed you like this tonight. I don't want you to think that when I blindfold you or handcuff you or get a little rough, it means anything less than when I'm soft and gentle with you. I don't know what you're doing to me, but you've embedded yourself right here." I took her hand and placed it on my heart.

"You're right here too." She moved our hands to her chest.

226

I copped a little feel, giving her breast a squeeze and running my thumb over her nipple. "I like being here."

She fell on her back laughing. "Oh, jeez."

I climbed over her, cupping both tits in my hands. "What? You don't like that?"

She shook her head back and forth on the pillow. "Nope. Not at all. It does nothing for me," she tried to say with a straight face.

"Who's the little liar now?" I leaned downed and took one nipple in my mouth, running my tongue over her hard peak. She let out an unintentional moan. "You don't like that at all?"

"Nope. Absolutely nothing," she moaned.

I reached down between her legs and pushed two fingers inside her. "Liar, liar, pants on fire," I teased.

"I'm not wearing any pants," she whispered.

"No. You're definitely not." I curled my fingers deep inside her, pumping her slowly.

"God, Zack, do you have any idea what you do to me?"

"What we do to each other," I corrected.

"Can we keep doing this to each other all night?"

"Yes, we absolutely can."

Chapter 28
Rissa

After a lazy morning in bed and room service for breakfast, we got home around noon. I was exhausted and had to work tonight and sing at The Locker the next night. We trudged in the back door. "I'm going to go up and lay down for a while. I didn't get much sleep last night." I winked at him. "Not that I'm complaining, I'd spend every night like that if we could."

Zack grabbed me around the waist and placed a kiss on my lips. "Oh, we can."

"But then I'd be a walking zombie every day."

He smacked me on the ass. "Go on. Get some sleep. I'm going to do a little paperwork."

"Again, with the spanking," I teased as I climbed up the stairs. I was so tired, every step felt like a huge effort.

I unlocked the door and headed towards my room, picking up Priss on the way. "Hey, sweet girl, did you miss us?" She purred as I stroked her long, black fur. I snuggled my face into her softness and loved on her, something I would have never imagined myself doing a month ago. I dropped my bag outside my door and headed to the kitchen. "I bet you're hungry." Grabbing some food from the cupboard, I scooped some into her dish and refilled her water bowl. Priss eagerly started eating, while purring contentedly.

I headed back toward my room and stopped dead in my tracks. "Holy shit," I whispered. *What had he done?* I walked in shock to the corner where there now stood something that wasn't there yesterday. I ran my fingers over the black lacquered finish and sat down on the bench. This was the exact same piano I had seen at the music store. *He shouldn't have.*

My eyes welled with tears as I started to play some random notes. I hadn't realized how much I missed having my own piano until this moment.

No longer tired, I rushed from the apartment and down the stairs. "Zack! Zack! Where are you?"

He poked his head out of his studio. "What's up?"

"Why would you do that?" I tried not to sound irritated, but I couldn't help it.

Zack frowned. "You don't like it?"

I buried my face in my hands. I should have felt appreciative, but I couldn't. All I saw was one more debt. "It's beautiful and I love it, but I can't afford it, Zack. I don't know how I'll ever pay you back."

He stepped forward and held my face in his hands. "Here's the thing about a gift, you don't have to pay anything back. I wanted to get you something nice to celebrate last night. I watched you in the music store and I remembered what it was like to listen to you play that first night. The guitar is great, but you've been missing this. I know you have."

The tears streamed down my face. "I have, but…"

Zack held his finger to my lips. "But nothing. I don't expect you to pay a dime for it. All I want you to do is enjoy it. Make music and sing until your heart is content.

"I don't know what to say."

"Just say… thank you, Zack. I love it and I'll play it every day."

I wrapped my arms around his neck. "Thank you, Zack. I love it. I really do, and I'll play it every day."

He pressed his forehead against mine. "Now, was that so hard?"

"No," I lied. This was hard. It was hard because I knew that soon he would hate me and then I would feel even guiltier. Time was running out.

I had to find a way to tell him about the baby. There never seemed to be a right time. Was there even such a thing? There was no handbook for telling your boyfriend that you were pregnant with his brother's baby.

I had a couple of weeks. Maybe. Pretty soon I would start showing and I wouldn't be able to hide it. My stomach had popped just a tad, but nothing that was too noticeable. I needed to make it to my next doctor's appointment and then I would tell him, I promised myself. It was getting harder and harder with each day that went by. The guilt was heavier. And then he had to go and buy me a piano. Paying for that, would completely wipeout my savings.

But I couldn't dwell on the money right now. Making him return the piano would crush Zack. I wanted to hold off on crushing him as long as possible. For now, I would enjoy the gift.

I went upstairs and sat down on the bench of the beautiful instrument in front of me. My fingers danced over the keys, playing songs that just couldn't be done on the guitar. I sang and let my voice fill the silence of our apartment.

Our apartment. Funny how something that didn't belong to me felt like home. I loved that stupid cat that I refused to touch the first few weeks. I loved the brick walls and the hardwood floors. I loved that Zack had given up his art studio to make a bedroom for me. I loved wiping Zack's whiskers down the sink every other morning. I loved doing his laundry, folding it, and placing it on his bed. I loved Zack. Zack was my home.

♫♪♫♪

The next week flew by. Singing and bartending had taken up most of my time. I called Daniel McClain to see what he had to offer. He asked about original songs I had written. I had a couple. They weren't great, but they were something. He gave me a month to come up with some new songs. After I came up with something, he wanted to meet to hear what I had. No pressure.

Yeah, right!

Pressure was something I had become increasingly familiar with. I needed to straighten out my personal life and be a creative genius. I scribbled lyrics in my notebook when thoughts hit me, but nothing I had written so far had that "wow" factor. The only thing inspirational in my life was Zack. Writing about my relationship with him was complicated at best.

His birthday was right around the corner, and I wanted to do something special for him. I enlisted Layla and Chase to help me. It wasn't anything spectacular, but I thought a night out with his friends would be nice. Zack was always working and barely made time to enjoy himself.

Chase and Layla assured me that they would contact his friends, so we could all have a bar night. A little drinking, a little dancing, and hopefully a lot of fun.

230

Kyla and Tyler were out. She delivered those babies in an ambulance the day after I sang with Bobby. She'd had two beautiful boys. My heart did an extra pitter-patter when I saw the picture on Facebook. They looked so happy.

I hoped that Tori and Chris would come. I needed a friend and Tori was the closest thing I had. She knew my secret and was surprisingly unjudgmental. I needed her. Desperately!

Chase, Layla, Tori, and Chris. That was the extent of Zack's friends that I knew. It was sad when I thought about it. How could I know so much, but so little about Zack? Thankfully, I had enlisted some help.

The night of his birthday, I convinced Zack to leave early by asking him out on an official date. We walked out to his Chevelle hand in hand. "Where are we going?" he asked.

"First stop is Outback Steakhouse. Then we're going bowling," I answered.

"Bowling? Seriously?" he scoffed.

"Yes, bowling. When is the last time you've gone bowling?" I asked.

"Honestly? It's been a while," he admitted. He didn't sound too enthused.

"Don't be such a party pooper," I scolded him. "Maybe I'll actually find something that I'm better at than you."

Zack side-eyed me. "Dream on, sweetheart. I may have not bowled in a while, but that doesn't mean that I suck. I am a force to be reckoned with." He flexed his arm to emphasize his point.

I laughed. "Are you seriously getting competitive about bowling?"

"I'm always competitive. I don't like to lose."

"Well, hold that thought until after dinner. Tonight, is all on me, so don't even think about pulling out your fancy credit card. Sit back and enjoy someone treating you for a change," I insisted.

"Fuck that!" he said.

"No. I'm serious, Zack. Let me do something for you for once."

His mouth twitched. "I don't like it."

"Too bad for you. It's your birthday." I ran my hand along his smooth jaw. "Let me spoil you tonight for a change."

"Fine, but I'm doing it under protest. It's my job to take care of you, not the other way around."

"That sounds a little chauvinistic, but I'm willing to overlook it because it's your birthday. How old are you today? Like forty?"

"Are you saying that I can't keep up with you? Because I can guarantee that won't be a problem. I'm twenty-eight, sweetheart. I'm in my prime. Don't you forget it."

"Yeah, okay." I laughed. "Just park the car or we'll be late for our reservation."

Zack parked, and we exited the car hand in hand. We were seated almost immediately. Zack and I both ordered steaks. It was a luxury I hadn't had in a while, not that Zack ever deprived me, but steak hadn't been on the menu. I savored every bite of my steak and my loaded baked potato. For dessert, I had the waitress bring him the Chocolate Thunder, a warm brownie covered in ice cream and chocolate. It was huge and came with two spoons.

"Are you going to eat that whole thing by yourself?" I asked.

"I could. But I can think of about a thousand things I'd like to do with all this chocolate. I'd like to smear it all over your body and then lick..."

I slapped my hand over his mouth. "Behave yourself. You're not getting anything until after bowling." I grabbed one of the spoons and dug into his dessert. "Oh, this is sooo good." I moaned while licking the spoon and savoring the chocolate.

"Keep doing that, and there won't be any bowling. The only place we'll go is back to my bed where I'll fuck you long and hard," he said in a low growl.

I loved this side of him. The side that couldn't get enough of me and wanted to fuck me senseless. But this was his birthday and I needed to remember my mission. Bowling was my way to extend our evening until his friends got to the bar. That was the plan I had concocted with Layla and Chase. As much as I wanted to follow through with his plan of going back to the apartment, that wasn't going to happen.

I stuck the spoon back into the chocolate heaven in front of us. "Okay, it wasn't that good. Finish up so I can beat you in bowling."

"You're saying no to sex?" he frowned.

232

"I'll never say no," I assured him. "I'm just saying later."

"You should be nicer to me on my birthday. I should get to choose what we do," he argued.

"Are you pouting?" I teased him.

"I don't pout, Clarissa," he said, pouting even more.

"Yeah, you do." I tapped the side of his face. "Let me run to the bathroom and then we'll get out of here." I excused myself and intercepted our waitress on the way. I took the bill from her and fished some money from my purse. I handed her the cash, giving her a generous tip.

After using the bathroom, which seemed to be more frequent lately, I grabbed my jacket and wrapped it around me. "Let's get out of here."

"We didn't pay yet, sweetheart."

"I'm pretty sure we did," I winked.

"Clarissa Lynne," he scolded.

I shrugged. "What's done is done. Let's go." I held out my hand for him to take and we headed out to the car.

The night had gotten cold, but Zack warmed me up by wrapping me in his arms. "So, why bowling?"

"Why not? I haven't bowled in a long time and it's fun. You're not afraid I'll beat you, are you?"

"Hardly," he scoffed.

He drove us to the bowling alley and paid for our bowling and rental shoes. He wasn't taking the chance I would sneak one by him again.

By the third frame we had a fierce competition going. Neither one of us was great, but we didn't suck either. I had just gotten a strike and was going for a double. I released the ball and knew right away it was going to be bad. The ball bounced on the alley, rolled halfway down and then plopped into the gutter. "Crap," I muttered with disappointment.

"It's okay, baby. You're on a strike, you still have another ball," Zack encouraged.

I waited for my ball to return, then tried again. This time it went right down the center, knocking down nine pins. I did a fist pump, turned, and walked back to Zack. I sat sideways on his lap and wrapped my arms around his neck. "Tell me you're not having fun."

He pushed my hair over my shoulder and kissed me softly. "I am having fun. It doesn't really matter what we do. I always enjoy my time with you."

"Me too. So much, Zack." I rested my head on his shoulder.

He tapped my bottom. "My turn. I can't let you beat me, especially on my birthday."

I scooted off his lap to let him up. He grabbed his ball and approached the lane. I couldn't help but stare at his ass. It looked so good, wrapped in tight denim, the material hugging his hips. As he bent over to release the ball, I decided I definitely liked bowling with Zack. I loved watching him from behind and admiring everything that made him a devastatingly, gorgeous man.

After our second game, both of which Zack had won, I sneaked a glance at my phone. Everyone should have been to the bar by now. I slipped it back into my pocket. "Are you ready to get out of here?" I asked.

He ran his hands from my hips all the way up my curves. "So ready. Thank you for taking me out tonight. We should get out and do things more often. We both work too much. I don't want to ever have regrets with you. I don't ever want to say that I wish we had taken more time to appreciate each other."

I leaned up on my toes and gave him a kiss. "I totally agree. We have one more stop and then we can go home. We need to stop by The Locker. Lou said he was going to mess around with the schedule, and I want to check it."

"Quick in and out? I like the sound of that. I'm so ready to get you in bed," he groaned.

I hoped he wasn't going to be disappointed I planned a get together at the bar. We would definitely make it to bed, but he had a party to attend first.

Zack pulled up to the curb. "Do you want to just run in real quick?"

I squeezed his hand, "Come in with me. I don't want you to have to wait in the car if Lou is busy." I had texted Layla to tell her we were on our way in.

"Okay." Zack parked the car and came around to my side. He wrapped his arm around my waist as we walked in through the door.

"SURPRISE! Happy Birthday, Zack!" A couple dozen people shouted as we walked in the door.

His face went from shock to a huge smile. He leaned down to my ear. "Was this you?"

I shrugged my shoulders. "I have no idea what you're talking about."

"I love you, sweetheart. Thank you. No one has ever thrown me a surprise party before."

"Well, I'm glad I could be the first, but I couldn't have done it without Layla and Chase. I wouldn't have known who to call," I admitted. "Be sure to thank them too."

"Will do. What do you want to drink?"

"Just water for me," I answered.

He scrunched up his nose. "Really? On my birthday?"

"Someone has to drive home," I rationalized.

"We could walk home, Clarissa. I can get it in the morning."

"You're kidding, right? We can't leave Betsy on the street all night." I mock gasped in horror, grabbing at my chest. "Don't worry about me. You know I don't really drink. This is your party. Go have fun," I encouraged.

"I think I will." Zack tapped me on the nose and made his way to the bar. He was stopped along the way by friends I had never met. Some faces looked familiar... maybe clients of his.

I looked around for someone I actually knew. Tori and Chris were hanging by the bar. I walked over to them. "Thanks for coming guys. I don't know anyone here, except you two, Layla, and Chase."

Tori leaned in and gave me a big hug. "Thanks for inviting us. We were due for a night out."

Chris rubbed his hands together. "Savannah is with grandma for the night. So, a little drinking, a little dancing, and a lot of uninterrupted sex when we get home." He leaned down and kissed Tori on the temple. "I'm going to get us some drinks. Be back in a minute."

Chris left Tori and I alone. "So, how are you doing?" she asked. "I'm assuming you haven't told Zack yet."

I shook my head. "No, but soon. I can't wait much longer. I'm starting to show a little. Zack hasn't noticed yet, but I'm out of time."

Tori nodded. "Good luck. I hope it goes better than you expect. He might surprise you. He's obviously in love with you, but if you need anything, call me. Even if it's just a shoulder to cry on. Anything. I'm serious."

I hugged Tori again. "Thank you. You don't know how much it means to have someone I can talk to. I've felt very alone. Did you tell Kyla?"

She shook her head. "No. She's been a little busy getting adjusted to having twin boys. But I have no doubt that she would help you. She's gone through her own issues. Trust me, she'd understand."

Just then, Chris came back with drinks in hand. "I should go find Layla and Chase to thank them for their help in arranging all this." I motioned around the bar with my hand.

"Go on. We'll catch up later," Tori insisted.

I saw Layla and Chase in the corner having a heated discussion. I crept a little closer, wondering what the problem was. Layla smacked Chase in the head. "Why would you have invited her?" she demanded.

Chase pushed her hand away. "What's your problem? They're friends. Have been friends for a long time. Why wouldn't I have invited her?"

Layla rolled her eyes. "You're an idiot. They're not friends. They were fuck buddies. She shouldn't be at a party that Rissa planned."

I scanned the room to see who they could be talking about. Not that I would know anybody, but maybe I could figure it out. I found Zack leaning against the bar talking to… Oh My God!

It couldn't be!

What were the chances?

This was bad. Really bad!

What the fuck was I going to do?

Was she Zack's fuck buddy before he met me?

Crap! Fuck! Shit! Double fuck!

I watched her lean into Zack and whisper in his ear. Zack threw his head back and laughed at whatever she had said. What the hell? Obviously, they had some sort of connection. I approached Layla and Chase. "Hey, guys."

Chase and Layla straightened up as if they hadn't just been having a secret argument. "Hey, Rissa. This was a great idea. Zack was really surprised," Layla said with a smile.

"Well, I couldn't have done it without you two. Thanks for all the help. I wouldn't have had a clue who to invite. I don't know any of Zack's friends," I said, trying to keep things casual.

"No problem, darling. We were happy to help," Chase answered.

I looked toward Zack. "Who's that girl Zack's talking to?"

"That's Gina," Layla offered vaguely. "They're old friends."

"Oh," I said, trying to seem unaffected.

"They used to hang out a lot before you moved here," Chase added. "They were pretty close at one time."

I saw Layla jab Chase with her elbow. "That was before he fell in love with you, Rissa. She's nothing to worry about."

I was sure Layla was trying to make me feel better, but it wasn't working. I wasn't afraid that Zack would cheat on me, but Gina knew my secret and that scared the shit out of me. I felt the walls closing in and my chest started to hurt. I think I was starting to have a panic attack. "I'm going to find the ladies' room. I'll talk to you two later." I excused myself.

"Nice job, asshole." I heard Layla scold Chase.

"What'd I do?" Chase's voice faded away as I walked with purpose towards the bathroom. I was having a hard time breathing and I was starting to sweat. Everything started to go fuzzy. Just a little bit further and then I could lock myself in a stall.

"Clarissa!" I heard Zack yell. I pretended not to hear, but he called my name again. "Clarissa!"

I stopped and took a deep breath. I turned toward him with a fake smile on my face and pointed to the bathroom.

He waved me over, not realizing I needed to get away. "Come here. I want you to meet someone."

Fucking hell! I straightened my shoulders and headed towards the bar. This was it. The moment everything could fall apart. I approached Zack, ignoring Gina, and placed a kiss on his lips.

Zack kissed me back, then placed a hand on my head. "Are you feeling all right? You look flushed and you're all clammy," he said with concern.

I smiled at him. "I'm fine. It's just hot in here," I lied.

He scrunched up his eyebrows. "Are you sure?"

"I'm sure." I nodded.

"I want you to meet my friend." He motioned to Gina.

I knew she recognized me, but she gave nothing away. She reached out her hand for me to shake. "I'm Gina. I wanted to meet the girl who's stolen Zack's heart."

I eyed her suspiciously, wondering how she was going to play this. I shook her hand. "Nice to meet you. I'm Rissa."

"Oh, I know who you are." She quirked an eyebrow at me. "Zack hasn't stopped talking about you. So, how long have you two known each other?" She was fishing for details I wasn't going to provide.

"A couple of months," Zack answered when I hesitated. "We met in New York and have been inseparable ever since."

Gina tapped her long fingernails on the bar. "Interesting. Never thought I'd see the day Zack settled down. He's always been a bit wild and untamed. We had a lot of fun together."

I knew what she was getting at from what I had heard Layla and Chase discussing. Gina and Zack had had sex together. Multiple times. And from what Gina was implying, it was wild and untamed. I tried not to let the images fill my head, but I couldn't help it. I'd bet money she'd played into all his little fantasies. Now that I saw her out of her scrubs, she had a phenomenal body. Tall. Long legs. Big boobs. Round ass.

"He's a handful, for sure." I winked at her. "But I can handle him."

"More than a handful." She smirked. "Soooo… what do you do, Rissa?"

Zack squeezed me tight, sensing the tension between Gina and me. "Rissa works here as a bartender and sings a couple of nights a week. She's super talented, with the voice of an angel."

"A bartender, huh?" she said condescendingly, totally ignoring the fact that I sang. "Well, that's way more exciting than being a receptionist for

238

Doc Peterson. Although… sometimes interesting things pop up. You never know what or who's going to walk in the door. It can get very interesting."

I let out a fake laugh. "I'd ask for details, but I'm sure you're sworn to secrecy. You know, patient confidentiality and all? I wouldn't want you to risk your job."

She cackled like I was ridiculous. "I doubt that would happen. I've worked for Doc Peterson forever, besides secrets have a way of coming out all on their own. Some secrets are impossible to keep, all it takes is time."

I gave her a stern glare. "Well, it was a pleasure meeting you. Gina, right?" I pretended that she wasn't worth remembering. "If you'll excuse me, I was on my way to the ladies' room."

"The pleasure was all mine. I'm sure I'll see you around. Soon," Gina countered.

I made my escape, barely keeping it together. I wasn't sure what her problem was. Was she upset that I had moved in on her relationship with Zack or was it about the secret I was keeping? Either way, she had the upper hand.

Time wasn't running out. Time was up!

I made it to the bathroom and leaned on the counter, staring at myself in the mirror. How had things gotten this far? This out of control? This fucked up?

I should have told Zack from the very beginning, but then I slept with him and I couldn't. The longer I let it go, the more tangled the web got. Now it was just one big mess. It wasn't even about the pregnancy anymore. It was the fact that I had been lying to him. That was the part that was going to destroy us.

A tear rolled down my cheek and I wiped it away with my shoulder. The door to the bathroom opened and in walked Gina.

She leaned against the wall with her arms crossed, staring at me with an unreadable expression. "He doesn't know, does he?"

I glared at her through the mirror.

"Is it even his?" she continued.

I ignored her questions and posed my own. "Why do you even care?"

"Why do I care? I've known Zack for years. We fucked… a lot. He wanted to keep it no strings attached. No complications. He wanted down

239

and dirty fucking. That man has a dark side he keeps buried deep. I let him unleash it on me. I let him release his anger and frustration by using my body. It was more than pleasing, but I wanted more. I was hoping he would come around to wanting a relationship. Then you waltzed into the picture and suddenly I'm out. He's giving you everything I wanted, and you don't deserve it. So, why do I care? Because I've loved him for a long time. You're going to hurt him."

"It was never my intention to hurt Zack."

"But yet, you haven't told him. He deserves to know." She stepped forward and leaned her back against the counter, getting into my personal space. "If this is a ploy to get ahold of Zack's money, it'll never work. When he finds out you lied to him, he'll throw you out like yesterday's trash."

I glared at her. "It's not what you think. You have no idea what you're talking about."

"So, the baby is his?"

She took my silence as my answer.

"That's what I thought." She headed to the door, then faced me to get in her last dig. "I should be thanking you. When this all falls apart, who do you think he's going to run to?" Then she gave me a little wave. "See you in a few days for your appointment."

As soon as the door shut, I ran into a stall, barely making it before I puked into the toilet. Not once, but three times. And then the dry heaving started, making my stomach ache and my throat burn. When I was sure there was nothing left, I wiped my mouth with the back of my hand. I rinsed my mouth and spit into the sink, silent tears falling down my face.

This was not what I had planned tonight to be. It was supposed to be about Zack. We were supposed to be having a good time and here I was hiding in the bathroom, feeling worse than I had during my entire pregnancy.

Why? Why of all the girls Zack could have dated, did it have to be Gina?

The bathroom door opened again, and I quickly wiped at my eyes. "There you are. I was wondering…" Tori stopped mid-sentence. I looked away, not wanting to meet her eyes. "Rissa? What's wrong? Why are you crying?"

I snuffed. "I'm not crying." I continued to wipe at my eyes.

240

She hugged me, and I clung to her like she was my only friend, which only made me cry harder. "God, you're a terrible liar," Tori said as she rubbed my back.

I let out a sarcastic laugh. "That's funny, considering I've managed to lie to Zack for almost two months and I've gotten away with it." I released Tori. "Come out back with me? I need some air."

"Of course."

I led her to the back door and out to the alley. Leaning against the wall, I stared up at the starry sky. "God, I wish I wasn't pregnant. I could really go for a smoke or a drink or something."

"What happened?" Tori asked. "An hour ago, you were fine."

I nodded. "I was... until I met Zack's ex. She wants him back."

Tori scrunched up her nose. "I didn't know Zack had a girlfriend?"

I put my hand to my chest. "Oh, did I say girlfriend? I meant fuck buddy and she's totally in love with Zack."

"And he's totally in love with you, so what's the problem?"

"Aaah, here's where it gets interesting... she's the receptionist at Doc Peterson's office. When she saw me, she put two and two together. She's basically threatened to tell Zack I'm pregnant. Thinks he'll dump me and run back to her. And you know what? She's probably right."

Tori bit her thumb. "Shit. Does she know about Wes?" I shook my head. "So, she only knows half the story."

"It's enough. I have to tell him myself. It's got to be tonight."

"On his birthday?" she questioned.

"I don't have a choice. Better he hears it from me than her. I don't trust Gina. She's chomping at the bit." I ran my hands through my hair. "It was going to suck no matter what, it's just gonna suck a little bit more doing it tonight."

Tori let out a breath. "Call me and let me know how it goes. Whatever you need, I'll be there."

I nodded. "Thanks. We better go back in before someone realizes we're missing."

Tori and I headed back into the bar. The music was blaring, and the dance floor was packed. I scanned the crowd and saw Zack talking to some guys I recognized from Forever Inked. Gina was nowhere in sight. Zack was

241

laughing, so that was a good sign. I tentatively approached him and wrapped my arms around his waist.

"Where'd you go?" he asked, looking down at me. His eyes were glassy, and I could tell he had a good buzz going.

"I just needed some air, but I'm better now." I smiled up at him. "Dance with me?"

Zack took my hand and led me to the dance floor. He held my hips tight as we swayed together to the music. A few songs in, he pulled me tight against his chest. "Let's get out of here."

"We can't leave yet, it's your birthday party," I insisted.

He ran his hands through my hair. "And I've enjoyed every minute of it, but I'm ready to take you home and unwrap my present." He leaned down close to my ear and whispered, "I want to fuck you all night long."

I swallowed down the lump in my throat. Despite knowing what I had to do tonight, my panties got wet thinking about everything Zack would do to me. "Then let's go."

We said our good-byes and he tossed me his keys. I drove us the short distance and parked Betsy safely in the garage.

Zack and I barely made it to the door before he started undressing me. "I'm not holding back tonight, Clarissa," he said, slurring his words slightly. He was drunker than I initially thought. "I want you so fucking bad."

My panties weren't just wet, they were soaked. One thing about being pregnant, was it sent my sex drive way past anything I'd ever experienced. I was horny all the time, but Zack satisfied my every need. I would *do* anything he wanted me to do. "Take me," I offered myself to him.

He stripped my shirt and jeans off in record time, then ripped his own shirt over his head. "I'm gonna fuck you so hard tonight. It won't be soft, and it won't be gentle." He bent down, untied his boots, and slipped them off along with his socks. He carelessly kicked everything to the side.

And there he was again, standing in only his jeans with bare feet. I don't know what it was about him in jeans and nothing else that turned me on, but it just did. His muscled body was a work of art, ink covering his chest and arms. In the dim light of his bedroom, he was darkness personified. He was so damn sexy standing there eyeing me in only my bra and panties.

"What are you thinking?" I asked.

He scanned me from head to toe. "I was thinking about how long I've waited to do this to you." He fastened the diamond collar around my neck, and I knew what that meant. He was claiming me as his. Then he reached into his bottom drawer and pulled out a box. He set it on the bed and took off the top. "Give me your hands," he demanded.

I hesitantly pulled my hands in front of me, holding them in fists, face up. I thought he was going to handcuff me. But what he had weren't basic handcuffs, they were wide leather bands connected by a long chain. He took one hand and wrapped the cuff around it and fastened the buckle. "Get on the bed, Clarissa."

I sat on the edge and scooted myself back towards the middle, the cuff hanging from my wrist like a shackle. Zack crawled over the top of me and kissed me hard, pushing me down into the mattress. He grabbed my cuffed wrist and yanked it above my head. He threaded the chain through the bars on the headboard then pulled my other wrist to meet it, fastening the other cuff around me. I pulled on the restraints. I wasn't going anywhere. This was different than the soft scarf he had tied me with before. It felt more possessive. This was for him, not for me. I'd be lying to say it didn't scare me a little. He moved off me, leaving me chained to the bed in my underwear. I watched him carefully. He returned with a blindfold and snapped it over my head. I felt my bra and panties being ripped from my body, then my legs being spread wide apart. I laid there helplessly, naked and vulnerable.

"Fucking beautiful," he growled. "Big, full tits and a dripping pussy. I can't wait to play with you."

I felt another gush of wetness between my legs, thinking about what he would do to me. "Zack, I..."

"Don't talk, Clarissa. Don't say a fucking word. I need this tonight."

I shut my mouth and swallowed hard. Why tonight?

The answer hit me like an anvil over the head.

Gina. This was the kind of shit he had done with her. She had practically thrown it in my face.

He wasn't fucking me tonight. He was fucking her.

I could have stopped it. All I had to say was NO. But I couldn't. After everything he had given me, I would give him this. I had practically begged for it. I wouldn't chicken out. I could take it. I would be whatever he needed tonight.

He trailed his fingers along my body from my neck, over my breasts and then down my stomach, until he reached the ache between my legs. He gave my clit a pinch and then ran his fingers through my arousal, lingering around the edges but never pushing in. "Do you want to come, Clarissa?" His voice was deep and low, filled with seduction.

"Yes."

"Do you want me to play with your pussy? Lick you? Finger you? Suck on your clit?"

"Yes."

"How bad do you want it?"

"So bad." I did. I wanted this with him. I knew this might be the last time and I wanted to enjoy every minute of it.

He continued to run his fingers around my opening, teasing me. "Are you sure?"

"Yes, Zack. Please… please make me come. Touch me the way only you can."

He slipped a finger inside me. It was hardly enough. "More… please."

He sank another finger into me. "Like this?"

He was still playing with me. He knew what I wanted but was holding back on purpose. I writhed under his touch, seeking more. Trying to please myself. "More."

"You're so needy, Clarissa. Never satisfied." He pulled his fingers from inside me and began an assault with his mouth. It was lips and tongue and teeth. I arched my back and pulled on my wrists. I wanted to sink my hands into his hair and push his head down into me, but I was left helpless. He was in total control.

He ate at me savagely. He couldn't get enough, and neither could I. He would bring me to the edge and then back away, leaving me wanting more and more. It was cruel. "Let me come, Zack. Stop teasing me."

"It doesn't feel so good, does it? What do you think you did to me for a month, Clarissa? You made me want you but kept me at arm's length. Walking around this apartment in your little tank tops with no bra. Your tits bouncing. Your nipples poking through. Do you know how many times I jerked off in the shower thinking about you? Do you know how bad I wanted you? You're the tease, Clarissa."

"I'm sorry," I cried. "I didn't mean to hurt you." The words poured out of me. Tears pooled in my eyes trapped behind the blindfold. I apologized for the past, for my current acts of deception, and for the future hurt I was going to inflict. "I'm sorry, Zack." The words caught in my throat. "So sorry."

His finger covered my lips. "Shhh. You're with me now. That's all that matters." He kissed me harder than he ever had before. It was forceful and demanding. "I'm going to take care of you."

He descended upon my pussy with a tenacity I'd never felt before. Zack always gave great orgasms, but this was different. He was on a mission. Every thought left my head as the pleasure seeped in. It was all consuming. He brought me to the brink over and over again, and then I felt the thin thread holding me together snap. I screamed. A gut-wrenching scream that came from deep inside me. It was foreign to my own ears, but yet I was sure it was mine.

Pleasure tore through my body from head to toe. Every nerve was electrified. My body was on fire. I wasn't sure I would survive it. I writhed and pulled and tried to escape the sensory overload. It was no use. I let it flow through my body, gave into the pleasure and the pain. The two so close, I could barely tell the difference. Zack never relented, and another orgasm ripped through me. He continued to torture me with ecstasy. I didn't even know such a thing existed until this moment.

My head was swimming in endorphins. I had slipped away into a world I never knew existed, still conscience but barely hanging on. I could hear the blood rushing in my ears, but that was all I heard. A white noise that blocked out everything, nothing else mattered. I felt the darkness closing in and I let it take over. And then there was nothing. My body went limp.

I woke to a tap on the side of my face, not quite a slap, but hard enough to bring me back. "Where'd you go? We're not even close to being done, Clarissa. Now it's my turn. You got yours and I'll get mine." There was a darkness in his voice I hadn't heard before. It sent a chill down my spine.

I was disoriented at best. I had to focus, pull it together. Zack moved my wrists up the headboard and wrapped my fingers around the top from underneath. "Hold on and don't let go." Then he moved me to a sitting position, with my back against the headboard.

His fingers pulled on my bottom lip. I flicked out my tongue to lick them and tasted myself. It felt so wrong and yet so right that it turned me on. I licked my lips and then I felt the head of his cock pushing between them. "Open up, baby. You're going to suck me off. I want to feel those luscious lips wrapped around my dick. I want you to take me deep."

I opened willingly and ran my tongue along the soft skin that surrounded his hardness. I suctioned my lips around him and hollowed out my cheeks, trying to give him what he wanted. His hands wrapped in my hair, moving my head back and forth to please him. I took him deep and then he pushed harder, thrusting his hips up into my face. Tears started to run down my cheeks. He moved faster and faster, thrusting harder and harder, my throat barely keeping up with the pace he was setting. "Fuck, Clarissa," he grunted. Then he pulled my head away and shot his cum all over my breasts. I felt it running down the front of me, helpless to wipe it away. He spread it all over me, marking me as his. "I love seeing you covered in my cum. You are mine."

"I am yours," I repeated. I'd never seen this side of him before. I'd seen glimpses of it, but never the full force. He wielded sex like a weapon, and I was his willing victim.

He grabbed ahold of my ankles and pulled me flat onto the mattress. I gasped, the suddenness leaving me breathless. The cuffs bit into my wrists at his forcefulness. Then he placed a hand behind each knee and pushed my legs to my chest. "I'm going to fuck you now, Clarissa. Do you want my cock inside you?"

"Yes." I wanted it so bad. I wanted to feel him pounding in and out of me. I wanted to grab ahold of his biceps and hold on tight, but there was nothing I could do while chained to the bed.

He impaled me on the first thrust. There was no gentleness, none of the tenderness that I'd come to expect from Zack. This was something else entirely. It wasn't bad, just different. He released my legs and rested them on his shoulders. He grabbed my hips and lifted me up, thrusting into me over and over. "You're so sexy like this... so fucking wet, dripping for me. You feel so good wrapped around my cock. Warm and wet and perfect, but I need more."

What more could he possibly want? He was already buried balls deep inside of me. Every stroke in and out rubbed against my sensitive clit. I felt my orgasm building again and then... he was gone.

My legs fell to the bed with a thud. His words repeated in my head, *I need more.* All I could think about was Gina and the dirty things she implied they had done. How she said he would run back to her. I couldn't get her out of my head. Still blind and unable to feel him anymore, I pleaded, "Zack, don't leave me. Please! Come back. Come back to me... please!" It was a pathetic, desperate cry for him. I couldn't stop the tears from coming. He was going to leave me here naked and alone, chained to his bed. The sobs caught in my throat, and I couldn't stop the ugly cry that escaped me. "I'm sorry, Zack... please. I'm so sorry." I was in a state of complete and utter distress. "Don't leave me like this!" Every insecurity and vulnerability poured out of me.

The blindfold was ripped from my eyes and Zack cupped my face, "I'm right here, sweetheart. I'm not going anywhere." Concern and confusion were etched in his face.

My arms were still restrained above my head, and my chest heaved in agony. I couldn't catch my breath. I felt the tears falling down my face into the pillow. "You left me," I choked out.

"I didn't leave you." He reached above my head and unbuckled my wrists. "I thought you were ready. I'm sorry I pushed you too far." He pulled me to his chest and cradled me. I hung onto him for dear life and cried into his shoulder. I couldn't pull it together. "Hey, it's okay. I'm here, Clarissa. I'm right here." He smoothed my hair down the back of my head and held me.

"I'm sorry," I cried. "I'm sorry I can't be what you need. I'll try harder." I hated myself for being so weak.

247

"Oh, babe." He sighed. "You're everything I need and want." He rocked me gently and held me tight.

"But you said…" My breath came in short gasps. I couldn't get the words out. "You said you needed more," I whispered.

"Clarissa." He sighed again. "I was getting ready to give you more. For you. For me. For both of us. You have to trust me."

"I do."

He rocked me some more and rubbed my back. My tears subsided, and I unburied my head from his chest. I kissed him softly. Our lips parted, and the kiss became hungry, our tongues thrashing together. He held my face tightly. "Do you want to finish this?"

I crawled off his lap, laid back on the bed and lifted my arms above my head. "Yes. I trust you." The last thing I wanted to do was ruin our night together. I wanted to salvage what I could. And honestly, I wanted whatever it was he wanted to give me. "Can we skip the blindfold? I need to see you."

He nodded. "Are you sure you want this? Are you going to freak out on me again?" he asked.

"I won't freak out. I promise. I want to do this with you. I want to give you what you want," I insisted.

Zack leaned over me and refastened my wrists in the leather cuffs. "Oh, sweetheart, this isn't just for me. Keep an open mind and I guarantee you'll enjoy it. Trust me to push your boundaries and create new ones."

I pulled on the restraints. "I will."

Zack ran his fingers feather-light over my body from my neck to my pussy. "Now, where were we?" He thrust his fingers inside me, curling them to hit my G-spot. And just like that, we were back to where we started.

"Oh, God!" I moaned. "That feels so good…fuck!" I pulled on my arms but kept Zack in my line of sight as I writhed on the bed.

"I love seeing you like this. You want my cock inside you, Clarissa?" His thumb stroked my clit, and I could feel the stirrings of an orgasm.

"Yes. I want your cock inside me. I want you to fuck me hard. I want everything you want to give me."

He grabbed me by the hips and flipped me onto my stomach. I heard the chain between my wrists clink together and twist. He slipped an arm

248

under me and pulled me to my knees, as I braced myself on my elbows. I stared at him over my shoulder.

Zack rubbed his hands over my ass, massaging my cheeks. "You are perfect like this. Ass in the air," he pushed my legs apart, "pussy glistening, ready for me."

Then without any warning his hand came up and smacked my ass. "Ouch!" I flinched, dropping my head between my arms. It hurt but felt oddly arousing. His hand rubbed over the sting, then he smacked me again. Harder. Then again. And again. I felt my pussy clench. I couldn't believe I was turned on by this. I swallowed my instinct to scream out and took the pain with the pleasure.

His hand ran between my legs and ran his fingers through my arousal. "Dripping wet." Zack grabbed my hips and slowly pushed his cock inside me. "Fucking perfect." It was slow and deep. I turned my head and watch him fuck me. He moved his hips in a slow circle, grinding in deep and making me clench him tighter. "That's right, Clarissa, squeeze my dick with your pussy." His dirty talk made me want him more.

Although he had already given me several killer orgasms, I wanted more. I wiggled my ass, trying to get him to go even deeper. I wished my hands weren't bound so I could touch myself. "Please touch me, Zack. Make me come again," I begged.

He tapped my ass, gently this time. "So fucking greedy. Haven't I already pleased you? Several times?" His tone was low and seductive.

"Yes, but I can't stop wanting you. I love the way you touch me. I need it."

His fingers ran along my spine. "I can't say no to you, Clarissa. I'm addicted to your pussy." His hand snaked under my belly and found my clit. He circled his fingers over my sensitive bundle of nerves. I moaned in pleasure. "Like this?" he teased.

"Yes! God...yes!" I was ready to explode.

"Not yet, sweetheart. I'm going to make you come harder than you ever have," he promised.

"Please... do it. Make me come, Zack."

"I will." I felt something wet drip between my ass cheeks, then Zack rubbed it all over me, pushing in with his finger. He'd done this to me before, so I wasn't totally taken aback. I had learned that I liked when he fingered my ass. Zack had already pushed past so many of my boundaries.

A soft buzzing sound filled the silence. I whipped my head up to see what he was going to do. He ran his hand over my ass. "Relax. It'll feel good. I promise." I took a deep breath and watched as he held up a small vibrator. It was bigger than his finger, but not too big. I had promised I would try. I took another deep breath and felt him push the vibrator into my ass. He eased it in gently until it was seated inside me. It felt obtrusive, but its vibrations awakened every nerve inside me. It started to feel good, and I thought I might come simply from the vibrator alone. "Don't come yet, Clarissa. I'm gonna fuck you with that in your ass."

Oh. OH! I was already mentally on another plane, my head swimming with pleasure. Zack slid inside me and groaned. He started slow, pushing in deeply. It felt tighter, better, more pleasing than anything I had ever felt before. He leaned over my back and reached one hand around me, rubbing my breasts and pinching my nipples. It sent a shot of arousal right to my core. Then he began to rub my clit again. With so much stimulation, my orgasm came fast and hard. I let out a loud scream. "Zack! Oh my...fuck!" It went on and on and when it started to subside, a second orgasm ripped through me. Zack grabbed my hips hard and thrust in with a speed and force I'd never experienced. Harder and harder. Faster and faster. He was a man possessed. I could barely hold myself up.

Zack roared with his own release, punishing me with his thrusts. He collapsed on top of me, pushing me flat to the bed. He was breathing hard, the sweat of his body slicking my skin. He rolled to the side and pulled the vibrator from inside me. I snuck a peek at him, watching his chest heave up and down. His arm was thrown over his face as he tried to recover.

"Zack," I whispered.

"Give me a minute."

I laid there quietly on my stomach; wrists still cuffed to the bed. I gave him several minutes. Afraid he might have fallen asleep, I tried to unbuckle my wrists with my fingers. The buckles were tight, and you really needed two hands to unfasten them. "Zack," I said a little louder. He was out cold. *Shit!* I scooted forward and grabbed the loose end with my teeth, pulling it backward, then used my fingers to finish the job. I finally got both

250

wrists free and rubbed my red skin. I was sore and tired, but I was also covered in cum, both inside and out.

I quietly snuck from the bed and into the shower. I let the hot water rush over me and wash everything away. Tonight, had been a roller coaster of emotions and I wasn't just physically exhausted, but mentally as well. I slid down the tile and sat on the floor, with my elbows on my knees and my head in my hands. Silent tears ran down my face. I was a ball of emotions that I couldn't unravel or make sense of. Tonight, had started out so well. Zack and I had a nice dinner and had fun bowling. I thought the party would be a good idea, and then Gina showed up, twisting me inside. She'd messed with my mind and caused me to have a breakdown in the middle of sex. How would I ever explain to him what had happened? I wasn't even sure I understood it myself. She had brought out all my insecurities. She made me doubt myself and Zack's commitment to me, and with good reason. If I was being honest with myself, it was my guilt that was eating at me the most.

Tomorrow. I would tell him tomorrow that I was pregnant with his brother's baby. Maybe he would accept us both. It wasn't like I had cheated on Zack. I was pregnant when we started this. Nothing had changed, except everything he thought he knew about me was a lie.

Chapter 29
Zack

I woke in the middle of the night, a little confused and a lot hungover. I was lying naked on one side of the bed, Clarissa was curled up in a tight ball on the other, as far apart as physically possible while sharing the same bed. She was dressed in her sleep shorts and a tank top, and her hair was wet, clinging to her skin. She must have taken a shower. I didn't remember that. I didn't even remember falling asleep.

Visions of last night flitted through my head. I remembered cuffing her to the bed. I remembered my dick being buried in her pussy. I remembered her freaking out and saying she was sorry. I remembered her crying and me holding her, then fucking her again.

She'd had a breakdown last night and I fucked her anyways. I pounded my fist against my forehead, *What the fuck was wrong with me?*

Sometimes when I went dark, I barely remembered anything. It was as if someone else took over and I was just a bystander, watching but helpless to stop it. It scared the hell out of me.

I had a feeling I had done that to Clarissa last night, unleashed my demons on her. I mean, I'd done it with Gina, but she'd accepted me for who I was. She'd take anything I gave her without complaint or question. But Clarissa was different. She made me a better man and I tried to be as sweet as possible with her, to put her needs first. Last night, I put myself first and I was rough with her. I felt shitty about it.

I remembered fucking her from behind and then collapsing on top of her. What I didn't remember was uncuffing her. I must have though, no way would she have been able to uncuff herself. I looked for the cuffs and saw them still threaded through the iron bars of the headboard.

Usually when Clarissa and I had sex, she curled up into me afterwards. She liked to cuddle, but not tonight. Tonight, she was far away from me. I felt the distance, not only physically but emotionally. Something had changed. I felt like she was pulling away.

I got up and placed a kiss on her forehead, then went to shower.

Tomorrow. Tomorrow I would apologize to her and make things right.

♪♫♪♫

The early October sun cut through the blinds and caught me in the eye. I squeezed my eyes shut tighter and rolled over. The bed next to me was empty. My bedroom door was shut, and I could hear the soft sound of the piano. It was a haunting and foreboding song that didn't help the unease inside me.

I rolled out of bed, threw on some jeans and a black t-shirt. I crept from my room and into the kitchen where Clarissa had a pot of coffee waiting for me. I poured myself a cup, grabbed my phone and headed toward her. I set my phone on the top of the piano next to hers, then scooted onto the bench. She continued to play, glancing at me.

"That sounds like a sad song," I said.

She stopped playing and then angled herself away from me. "We need to talk, Zack."

I dropped my head. "I know. I know why you're upset."

Her eyes went wide. "You know?"

"Yeah." I took her hands in mine. "We can get through this. It doesn't change anything. It doesn't change the way I feel about you. Last night… I don't know what happened… I just lost it." What I had done was selfish and uncaring. I promised I would always take care of her and I didn't. I needed to assure her that we were okay, that I still wanted her if she'd have me.

She bit her lip and shook her head. "You had a right to be upset. What I did was unforgivable. I'm so sorry."

I cupped her face. "You have nothing to be sorry for. Shit happens. We deal with it and move on. The way I reacted was worse. I want you to be able to trust me and I damaged that last night. I took it too far." I couldn't be upset with her for being scared. I knew this was all new to her.

She leaned into me and rested her head on my shoulder. "This isn't the way I thought this would go. I thought you would be more upset. I thought you would leave me, and I'd be all alone again."

I wrapped my arms around her. "It's going to take more than that for me to leave you." I ran my hands through her hair. "I love you, Clarissa. I don't care that you had a freak out. It was my fault for pushing you when you weren't ready. I shouldn't have kept going. I should have been gentler with you. I should have taken care of you."

Clarissa braced her hands on my chest and pushed back on the bench. "Wait. What?" She hopped off the bench and started pacing, biting the side of her thumb.

I reached over and pulled her thumb from her mouth. "What's wrong?"

She let out a long breath, dropped her head back and stared at the ceiling. "So many things." She started pacing again. "Okay, I was upset last night, but not about the sex. I mean, it was about the sex, but not really."

I furrowed my eyebrows. "Then why were you upset?"

She bit her thumb again. "Honestly? I thought you were punishing me. Getting in one good last fuck before you left me. And then you left me chained to the bed."

I was so confused about everything she said. None of it made sense to me. "So much of what you just said confused the fuck out of me," I admitted. "First of all, I left you chained to the bed?"

She nodded. "Like I said, I thought you were punishing me. I tried to wake you, but you didn't move. I pulled on the straps with my teeth to free myself. It took some time, but I managed."

"Jesus Christ," I groaned, rubbing my hands over my face. I was more out of it last night than I had thought. It was a miracle she was still here at all. "I'm so sorry. I wasn't punishing you. Why would you think that?"

"You really don't know?" she asked, looking more nervous than I had ever seen her.

I shook my head. I wished she would just spit it out because I didn't like the feeling I was getting. What could she have done that I would punish her for?

"Zack," she took a deep breath, "you need to know that it was never my intention to hurt you. Everything just got so out of control so fast and then I didn't know how to tell you."

I was starting to lose patience. She was dancing around whatever this was. "Fucking say it, Clarissa. Tell me," I said harsher than intended. I wasn't into games and felt like that was exactly what she was doing. Playing a game with me. Now I was on my feet, pacing back and forth. One of our phones buzzed on top of the piano. I reached over to silence it. The last thing we needed right now was a distraction.

I grabbed Clarissa's buzzing phone. I went to turn it off, and then I read the message that had popped up on the screen. *Appointment reminder: Doctor Peterson, ultrasound at 10:00 tomorrow.* I looked at it again and then looked at her. A warm feeling filled my chest. Clarissa was pregnant. We were having a baby.

It had to have happened that first night. Anything else would be too soon to be getting an ultrasound. She'd told me she was on birth control, but it must have failed. We were the one percent.

"What?" she asked.

I held up a finger to silence her as I processed. Clarissa was having my baby. A feeling I couldn't identify overtook me. I wanted this with her so bad. She was going to look so beautiful, big and round with my baby inside her. There was a little piece of us growing in Clarissa. No wonder she had been so nervous. She probably thought I was going to freak out, but the opposite was happening. I was so fucking happy, I could barely contain it.

"Zack? You're acting weird. What is it?" she asked.

I turned the phone, so she could see the screen. "You're pregnant?" I asked.

She took two steps back against the window and nodded.

"We're having a baby?"

She closed her eyes and swallowed. "I'm having a baby."

I set the phone down on the piano and squinted my eyes at her. "What does that mean? The baby is mine, right?" It was a shitty question, but one I needed to ask. If I had learned anything from the past, it was to get confirmation. I'd been burned before, and I wasn't taking any chances.

Clarissa looked like a deer in headlights. She stayed silent. Now I was starting to freak out.

I tentatively stepped toward her. "Sweetheart, it's okay. Just tell me it's mine, that you're having my baby." I cupped her face and tried to set her at ease.

She turned away from my hand and stepped to the side, putting space between us. "It's not yours."

I was burned. I took a sharp step back, "Excuse me?"

She backed herself into a corner and held her hands up. "It's not what you think. Let me explain…"

Fuck that! I didn't need to hear explanations, I'd heard enough. Something inside me exploded and all I could see was red. "Fuck you, Clarissa! I don't need to hear your lame excuses. You fucking cheated!" It wasn't a question, but a declaration.

She sank to the floor and wrapped her arms around herself. Good! I wanted her to hurt as much as I was hurting. I couldn't believe this was happening again. Everything with Megan flashed through my mind like a reoccurring nightmare I couldn't wake up from.

"You don't understand…" she started.

But I couldn't, I wouldn't listen to her bullshit. Nothing she could say would change the fact that she was a fucking, lying whore. "What don't I understand?" I screamed at her.

"I didn't cheat," she croaked out.

She couldn't be serious. "What? Just because we weren't officially together, that gave you a right to fuck anyone you wanted? Screw you! My father was so right about you. You're nothing but a money grubbing whore. You used Wes and now you're using me. The Kincaid gravy train is over." I was on a roll and wasn't stopping anytime soon. I was so furious I could barely see straight. "Who was it? One of those assholes that passed you his number over the bar? Did you fuck him in the back alley? You lived in *my* apartment, spent *my* money! Were you ever going to tell me? I can't even stand to look at you right now! You make me sick."

I stormed away from her and to my room. I opened my top dresser drawer and pulled out a wad of cash. Then I returned to her. She was crouched in the corner, crying because she'd been caught.

I threw the money at her. "You want to act like a whore then I'll treat you like one! Consider that your payment! I want you the fuck out of my apartment today! I don't care where you fucking go, just leave!" I started to walk away and turned back to her. "And by the way, you're fucking fired! Get the hell out! I never want to see you again!"

I threw my shoes on, grabbed my coat off the hook and stormed down the stairs, slamming the door behind me. Layla and Chase were chatting by the front counter. I strode toward them. "You two... cancel all appointments for the day and reschedule."

Layla quirked her eyebrow at me. "Somebody woke up on the wrong side of the bed. What's up your ass?"

"Not now, Layla," I growled. "Chase, get Rissa's shit out of my apartment. I don't give a fuck where you take her or her stuff. I just want you to take the garbage out. Text me when she's gone, until then I'll be AWOL."

Layla looked shell-shocked. Well, she could join the fucking club. "Zack?"

"You wanna know? You can fucking ask her. Just get it done. There'll be a bonus for both of you if she's gone by tonight."

"Where am I supposed to take her?" Chase asked hesitantly.

"Like I said, I don't give a fuck! I left her money. She can go to a hotel or hop a plane back to New York for all I care." I was done discussing. I all but ran out the back door toward my Harley.

I grabbed my helmet and backed out of the garage. Where I was going, I had no idea. I just needed to drive. I headed out west on M-59. Fifteen minutes later I took the exit ramp and headed north on I-75. How could she do this to me? I thought it was real. I was so fucking in love with her, and I thought she loved me. My heart seized in my chest. At least she didn't lie to me when I asked if it was mine. I had to give her credit for that. I destroyed her with my words, but how else could she have expected me to respond? I couldn't stay there another minute and listen to what she had to say.

Nothing could make this better.

257

♪♪♪♪

Zack and Rissa's story continues in *Tattooed Souls.* You won't want to miss what happens in the conclusion of their journey.

If you have a few moments, I'd love to hear what you thought of *Tattooed Hearts*, by leaving a review. I am so grateful for your support and that of the thousands of books available, you chose to read mine.

Want to read more about the Forever Inked crew?
Check out the rest of the Forever Inked Novels.
Books 1~ Tattooed Hearts: Tattooed Duet #1 (Zack & Rissa)
Book 2~ Tattooed Souls: Tattooed Duet #2 (Zack & Rissa)
Book 3~ Smoke and Mirrors (Draven & Layla)
Book 4~ Regret and Redemption (Chase & Maggie)
Book 5~ Sin and Salvation (Eli & Roxy)

Song List on Spotify

Tattooed Hearts.

Stairway to Heaven~ Led Zeppelin
My Immortal~ Evanescence
Titanium~ Sia
I'm Not an Angel~ Halestorm
Gunpowder and Lead~ Miranda Lambert
Broken~ Seether
Wicked Game~ Chris Isaak
Landslide~ Fleetwood Mac
Crazy in Love~ Beyoncé
Great Balls of Fire~ Jerry Lee Lewis

Listen and Enjoy!

Acknowledgments

Thank you choosing to read *Tattooed Hearts*. After writing the "Hearts Series", all I heard from readers was that they loved Zack. I mean, who wouldn't love to have a man like him. I loved Zack too and knew that he needed his own story.

My husband and I joke that right now, I'm making less than ten cents an hour writing. The funny thing is, I couldn't be happier. I enjoy what I'm doing and the creative outlet it provides me. Writing romance novels has been one of the most fulfilling experiences of my life. My dream is to walk into a bookstore and actually see one of my novels on the shelf. One day...

To my husband~ I could have never done this without your love and support. Thank you for putting up with my endless hours of writing, all the take-out dinners, and my hounding of you to read and offer input. I know I've made you crazy, but you were a trooper through it all! Thank you for believing in me!

To Denise, Kristy, Ari, and Amy~ You girls are the best beta readers anyone could ask for! You supported my journey and spent endless hours reading and rereading. Your suggestions, critiques, and encouragement helped me in ways you'll never understand. Thank you for listening to my obsession day after day!

To Linda~ Thank you for the endless hours you spent proofreading. After reading the book several times myself, I still missed errors. Your expertise and constructive criticism helped me to make this book so much better. I could never thank you enough for all your help!

To Jill~ You've been a great friend! I wasn't very specific about what I wanted for this cover, just that I wanted it to look like a tattoo. I know it was somewhat challenging and out of your norm, but between our two creative brains we came up with something amazing. Thank you for the beautiful cover of *Tattooed Hearts*... I absolutely love it!

To my readers~ Thank you for supporting me in this journey. Please spread the word and leave a quick review on Amazon, if you have enjoyed this book. Without you, writing would still be a dream.

About the Author

Sabrina Wagner lives in Sterling Heights, Michigan. She writes sweet, sassy, sexy romance novels featuring alpha males and the strong women who challenge them.

Sabrina believes that true friends should be treasured, a woman's strength is forged by the fire of affliction, and everyone deserves a happy ending. She enjoys spending time with her family, walking on the beach, cuddling her kittens, and great books. Sabrina is a hopeless romantic and knows all too well that life is full of twists and turns, but the bumpy road is what leads to our true destination.

**Want to be the first to learn book news, updates and more?
Sign up for my Newsletter.**

https://www.subscribepage.com/sabrinawagnernewsletter

**Want to know about my new releases and upcoming sales?
Stay connected on:**

Facebook~Instagram~Twitter~TikTok
Goodreads~BookBub~Amazon

**I'd love to hear from you.
Visit my website to connect with me.**

www.sabrinawagnerauthor.com

Made in the USA
Middletown, DE
05 June 2024

55305694R00150